CHILDREN OF STEEL

SHORT FICTION FROM OUR HISTORIC STEEL MILL TOWNS

Gloria Ptacek McMillan
Editor

ANAPHORA LITERARY PRESS

QUANAH, TEXAS

Anaphora Literary Press
1108 W 3rd Street
Quanah, TX 79252
https://anaphoraliterary.com

Book design by Anna Faktorovich, Ph.D.

Copyright © 2023 by Gloria Ptacek McMillan

All rights reserved. No part of this book may be reproduced in any form or by any electronic or mechanical means, including information storage and retrieval systems, without permission in writing from Gloria Ptacek McMillan. Writers are welcome to quote brief passages in their critical studies, as American copyright law dictates.

Printed in the United States of America, United Kingdom and in Australia on acid-free paper.

Cover Image: "Main Street from the Intersection with Broadway Street, at the Downtown Business Area of East Chicago, Indiana", *The William Brubaker Digital Image Collection*, Special Collections and University Archives, University of Illinois at Chicago.

Published in 2023 by Anaphora Literary Press

Children of Steel: Short Fiction from Our Historic Steel Mill Towns
Gloria Ptacek McMillan—1st edition.

Library of Congress Control Number: 2023921865

Library Cataloging Information
McMillan, Gloria Ptacek, 1948-, author.
    Children of steel : Short fiction from our historic steel mill towns / Gloria Ptacek McMillan
    228 p. ; 9 in.
    ISBN 978-1-68114-605-8 (softcover : alk. paper)
    ISBN 978-1-68114-606-5 (hardcover : alk. paper)
    Kindle (e-book)
1. Books—Literature & Fiction—Short Stories & Anthologies—Short Stories
2. Books—Literature & Fiction—Historical Fiction—Short Stories & Anthologies—Short Stories. 3. Books—Politics & Social Sciences—Social Sciences—Poverty.
PN3311-3503: Literature: Prose fiction
813: American fiction in English

CONTENTS

Gloria Ptacek McMillan	Introduction	7
Jeff Manes	Monarchs	10
Joan Paylo	Blue Collar Land	12
Kathy Bashaar	The Girl from Bethel Park	37
Karen Banks Pearson	Granny's Traveling Trunk	52
Patrick Michael Finn	Smokestack Polka	64
Sharon Hale Hotko	Toe Picks and Hoar Frost	85
Curtis Mazzaferri	The Other Side of the Fence	89
Barbara Dubos	Consumed	103
Joseph S. Pete	Lo, the Steel They Forged on That Boundless Lake	113
Kurt Samano	Clockwork	119
John Szostek	Time Hangs a Louie	121
Hardarshan Sing Valia	Volcanoes of NW Indiana	128
Connie Wachala	Holy Cross	130
Alice Whittenburg	What the Dogs Knew	136
Stacy Alderman	Steel Valley	138
Robert McKean	Man Down	159
Phyllis Woods	The Next Big Thing	177
Bianca Roman	Homebodies	202
Jane Ammeson	An Indiana Harbor Christmas	211
Gloria Ptacek McMillan	Sprightly Aphrodite	214
	Contributing Writer Biographies	221

Dedication

We dedicate *Children of Steel* to everybody in that industrial "village" (however big or small) who worked so hard to help us make it into adulthood, so that we could write these stories.

Introduction

The idea for this collection came in Tillie Warnock's "Community Literacy" seminar because not being able to represent ourselves in culture leaves a void to be filled by others who would define us as they wish or ignore us. And this can affect mental health. In the University of Arizona Ph.D. program, we had mentors who helped us to recover from past abuse. These people included Tillie and John Warnock, Carol Nowotny-Young, classmate M.J. Braun, Tom Miller, Ed White, and the late Theresa Enos, my dissertation director. They showed that the most priceless possession we have is our health and how writing can preserve sanity, not only for individuals but for whole communities. Our collection of short fiction, *Children of Steel,* is an act of faith in our collective healing. Part of our mental and emotional health is feeling part of a community that respects its various parts. I feel fortunate to have grown up in East Chicago, Indiana, a steel mill town and home of historic Inland Steel. When we went on Chicago Avenue or Main Street on "The Harbor" side of our town, we knew people. We had bakers, butchers, green grocers who later became the supermarkets.

In the steel mill town where I grew up, there were all manner of parks, churches, synagogues, and—of course—bars. We girls had our groups of friends and so did the boys. In all of these urban places we had vivid lives in varied settings. We had streets of apartments and tree-lined streets of duplexes and houses. Our schools were integrated racially and mostly integrated in terms of housing by the 1960s. But integration *was a slow process*, even in East Chicago, as Karen Banks Pearson's story "Granny's Traveling Trunk" shows. And things could have been better on the issue of gays in my town as in others back then when I was in high school just before 1970. Each person I would meet and get to know in East Chicago had a point-of-view and no two were alike. That feeling of community made up for other things such as the polluted air we breathed. Thankfully, the EPA has now regulated the output of steel mills and some places are really cleaning up their air. Air quality seems better in East Chicago. I know what I am saying is not unique to our town.

Our Town... because we were a steel mill town and a company town, I always knew that the plays and other literature I read in high school and in college were not about us but about other, more rustic villages and towns. Certainly, a confident sense of being "normal" and "in the norm" pervaded Grover's Corners, New Hampshire, the setting of the play *Our Town* in a way that never pervaded our town. Our teachers and drama coach never overtly instructed us to ignore the differences between East Chicago and the all-American Grover's Corners. However, we inferred that we needed to identify because this was and is the norm. Our invisibility was a basic theme of our lives and we had just better get used to that. It was just that there were plenty of fiction-worthy and dramatic theatre-worthy things going on around us, as well, and wouldn't anybody like to see them performed or read about them? In this collection, we have stories about towns that are unlike Grover's Corners in some ways, but very like that iconic town in other ways, leaving it to the reader to guess which is which.

Were we wrong to try to become writers? As some of us moved to great cities and lived over thousands of miles from our steel mill towns, what did we say when we met people and they asked where we were from? By adulthood, we switched verbal register and spoke trying to match those we were meeting. We might answer, "Oh, Chicago. I am from Chicago." Or we might say, "I'm from a suburb of Chicago," keeping it good and vague. I watched this on one occasion at arts events in my Arizona city when another person was introduced to me as being from my steel mill hometown of East Chicago—the shame, the humiliation. The embarrassed party-goer continued apologetically, her chin tucked down in her neck, mumbling that "Of course, my parents moved us to 'Upscale Town,' Indiana, before I knew what was what." The embarrassed woman blurted her explanation to a room of people holding cocktails, as if to say that her move at so early an age took that "steel mill town" stain off her and she wanted people to know that she was "normal." Wink. I am okay to know. Ironically, we were so far away from Chicago that the stratification back home meant little.

Some of us moved to suburbs and attempted to fit into a preexisting plan of static homogeneity. The prize was comfort, more landscaping, and peace of mind—we thought. Robert Beuka's 2004 cultural geographical study *Suburbianation* is finally theorizing what the explosive growth of the suburbs meant in terms of the whole social fabric via the lens of literary texts. In order for the suburbs to have positive values, the suburban life had to play off something to disparage and enact daily as negative: the city. In geographer David Harvey's 1996 text *Justice, Nature, and the Geography of Difference,* he stipulates that "Place, in whatever guise, is like space and time, a social construct... The only interesting question that can then be asked is: by what social processes is place constructed?" Do these stories answer this question? Readers must decide.

Looking at places via Pierre Bourdieu's notion of the "habitus" in which we live mentally, our "internal disposition" creates what we think and do in our everyday surroundings. That is, two neighborhoods in a great city may be only blocks apart but function as "island universes," separated by invisible walls.

Cultural geographer Martyn Lee has extended Bourdieu's notion of the habitus to the realm of place studies, speculating that what he calls a "habitus of location" generates place-specific actions and cultural predispositions, contributing to the "cultural character" of specific places. In short, some places have the rhetorical power to make their positive self-references stick and to erase evidence to the contrary, regardless of any costs to the landscape that bulldozing animal habitats and forests may have, for example.

Mental health. When we visit the creative writing college classrooms in places such as Northwest Indiana, the greater Youngstown, Ohio, the Allegheny and Monongahela River valleys of Pennsylvania, among other industrial regions, we encounter students who feel confused by such conflicted urban and suburban spatial arrangements. In frustration, writers (student or otherwise) tend to ignore the giant steel mills that are still in full operation in some steel towns, though robotized and downsized. Our historic steel mill town writers have an additional layer of problem that nobody from proto-suburban Grover's Corners has had to deal with in the play *Our Town.* They hail from a cast-off community. Some rhetoric of the ecology movement has allowed the worthy goals and urgency of cleaning up and going green to permit their feeling of disgust with pollution to color the attitudes toward fellow human beings to the extent that, like the woman at the party above, many student writers cannot situate themselves in a *place.*

Long gone are *the media's positive attitudes* that reigned up to about the 1960s praising industrial plants being some of the country's vital industries. People relate to the physical conditions around them in cognitively different ways, but the tendency in our current rhetoric that turns people who work in "dirty industry" or near industrial towns into social "untouchables" or monsters does not help to clean the environment. But tarring industrial workers and their communities is tremendously effective at creating self-censorship for people of any age to write about where they are from. The labor involved in not self-censoring is heroic and mostly never heard because the resulting texts go unpublished, are considered unpublishable, and sit in drawers unperformed, if drama.

More than most editors, perhaps, I want to cheer every person who wrote a draft of any length and who tried to get into our collection of stories. I wish them all luck. These ones who were selected hope to amuse, entertain, and move their readers. We need to relate to each other, to build bridges and not walls or gates between the urban and suburban lives we lead. This collection places before readers the voices of those who are seldom heard, given that our writers also face the task of making their stories "universal" enough (a term sometimes misused in practice) to interest others from backgrounds different from their own. I wish them all well and promise readers of this collection an interesting journey of discovery.

Gloria Ptacek McMillan, Editor

October 10, 2023

Monarchs[1]

Jeff Manes

My long underwear was drenched. It was a sweltering day in August. January was sweltering on top of the coke battery. Having just finished welding on the gas main, I was pretty much spent.

While cooling down, I shot the shit with Fly and Weasel. They worked a production job called patcher—a poor man's bricklayer at #2 Coke Plant. The three of us worked on the battery top. Unlike most departments within the steel mill, there was no roof to that chunk of smoldering refractory and rust. The monolithic prick was just out there—like Devil's Island.

We were all about the same age and about the same size too, not an ounce of body fat on us; the battery made sure of that. Fly and Weasel used to fuck with me, saying I could take the heat better than any white guy they had ever met. Blacks accounted for ninety percent of the production jobs on the battery, always did, until the day she shut down. Just the way of it, I suppose.

Fly hailed from the South Side of Chicago, 87th and Cottage Grove. In fact, he grew up in the same area my father spent his early years, before the family lost the house during The Great Depression. The neighborhood was all Italian and Irish back then. Not anymore. Just the way of it, I suppose. Weasel, the raspy-voiced one, stayed in Gary. I think his real name was Wade. I was never sure if that was his first name or surname. And for that I am ashamed.

Fly had been a great miler in high school, and I'd done some long distance running myself. The three of us could have been talking about going the distance when something caught my eye. In all my years in the coke plant I had never seen a butterfly anywhere near the

---

1 "Monarchs" story courtesy of Jeff Manes, Matt Werner Web, 11 July 2019. Accessed: 20 October 2023. https://matthewawerner.com/monarchs-jeff-manes.

battery top. Usually, Nature's creations veer away from environments not conducive to their survival, if possible. The coke battery, belching white clouds, black smoke, and orange fireballs was no place for a butterfly. We stood mesmerized as the delicate wisp of silk fluttered, miraculously dodging the flames yearning to make ash of it.

Finally, either exhausted or gassed, the interloper settled upon a section of track that guided the Lary Car; a steely behemoth that had severed the limbs and crushed the life out of steelworkers in the past. But how would a butterfly know such a thing? Besides, he was dying.

Weasel took off his hot mill glove and allowed the butterfly to attach itself to his finger. He walked over to the edge of the battery setting the creature on the hand railing forty feet above ground level. It did not move. Fly, always the more hyper of the two patchers, removed the fragile vagabond from the safety rail. Weary wings opened and closed in Fly's cupped hands. Tenderly, he tossed it into the air. Black, white, orange.

"Sink or swim, baby," is all he whispered. The confused butterfly struggled and then flew off.

Weasel Wade died of cancer a few years later. He was about forty years old. Haven't seen Fly in years. They fired him. Rumor has it he left the United States—in a hurry. Headed down Mexico way.

Seems me and Fly been tormented by similar demons, another parallel between us. Thirty years in the big mill may be the ultimate marathon. Some hit the wall.

Sink or swim, baby.

BlueCollarLand

Joan Paylo

Leslie Lujak dreaded having to sit on Santa's lap at the Slovak Club Christmas party, held each year on the Saturday after Thanksgiving. She had just turned ten, so 1957 would be the last time she would have to endure the mayhem in the huge, but humble ballroom with its beige stucco walls and polished wooden floor, the scene of many a union meeting and wedding.

Squealing toddlers smeared red and green icing on their chins and everything thing else they touched. Rambunctious boys with tiny bow ties and red and green plaid suspenders chased and pushed each other around the overly ornamented Christmas tree that quivered in the middle of the room. They tumbled on the dance floor under the patent-leather maryjanes of little girls with big hair bows, who swirled and sang to the polka that the mayor's teenage son played on the accordion.

Oh, how Leslie loved the music! One-two-three, one-two-three, one-two-three, hop. *Hey*! Her white felt poodle skirt with its puppy and candy cane appliqués swirled to the rhythm, as she spun round and round with her friend Myra Chapreky until both were dizzy.

Leslie was the one that other parents pointed to and said, "I wish you were well-behaved, like Leslie." The kids who were compared to her would point out that they saw Leslie wipe her nose on her sleeve or that Leslie took a candy cane from an elf and they didn't hear her say "thank you."

Leslie's father was on the City Council, a lawyer with bigger ambitions, so he insisted that she and her mother show up to "be among the people." She knew he had affection for these men—the grandfathers who had immigrated to the smog-covered southern tip of Lake Michigan to work in the mills and refineries, and their progeny—her uncles, neighbors, policemen, shopkeepers, judges and priests. With few exceptions, they were veterans of the European or

Pacific theaters, and the laborers were union men. Having shed their flannel shirts and work boots for long-sleeved dress shirts and ties for the celebration, they surrounded the well-stocked bar in a large, dark alcove at the end of the room. Their eyes were fixed on the Notre Dame game on the 17-inch black and white TV perched between rows of liquor bottles. Her father, suave, well-groomed, almost movie idol handsome, stood out in the crowd. Leslie's mother Lizzie and Aunt Nadia were slightly overdressed as always, wearing taffeta and brocade, a bit aloof from the other women.

Leslie hated Santa's lap because she was shy. Furthermore, she didn't need more presents. She was an only child, unlike most of the other kids in Peacepipe, Indiana. She already had her own chemistry set with a microscope, a paint-by-numbers set with a real easel and a Shirley Temple doll with an extensive wardrobe of frills.

Waiting in line, she studied Santa. The man in the red suit and white nylon beard looked and sounded very much like Myra's jolly, red-cheeked father who oversaw the city's garbage trucks and dog pound. When she climbed politely onto his lap, she asked only for a new, long blue nightgown. She had outgrown last year's. She didn't tell Mr. Chapreky that it was the last year she would be young enough to maybe fly away with Peter Pan and she always kept a properly fitting Wendy-blue nightgown on standby, just in case.

"Ho, Ho, Ho, little Leslie, is that all you want?" Strands of his Santa beard caught in his teeth. "There must be some secret thing, something you have wanted for a very long time. Santa knows that every little girl wants something exciting—a Schwinn bike? A puppy? We have two new litters in the pound."

Maybe it was his warm laugh. Maybe he had a way with kids since he had six sons and a daughter.

"What is it, Leslie, that you want most of all?"

Caught off guard and wanting to please him so she could go back to dancing, Leslie thought hard. *The nuns said to always tell the truth, even though it's not always easy.* She took a deep breath. "Mr. Chapreky," she announced with all confidence. The mothers and children gasped. His name was "Santa." How disrespectful! The Slovak ballroom stood still; the men looked up and stepped away from the bar. Leslie was unaware of all this, because she had finally worked up enough nerve to express her strongest wish.

She blurted it out.

"For Christmas, Mr. Chapreky, I want my Daddy to stop drinking so much!"

Her mother, with face twice as red as Mr. Chapreky's, swooped across the room in her three-inch heels, yanked Leslie up by the arm, dangled her in the air above Santa's lap and scratchy fake hair for one terrifying moment and dragged her out of the Christmas celebration. Lizzie Lujak said not a word until they reached home, three blocks away.

She slammed the door behind them. "How stupid, stupid, stupid can you be?" Her raging face reminded Leslie of a thunderstorm blowing in over Lake Michigan.

"But Momma, I'll bet most of the kids want the same thing, besides dolls and Lionel trains. And so do you, Momma."

"Haven't I ever told you about keeping family secrets?" Momma hissed.

Daddy staggered in after midnight.

"Grow up, Lujak!" She heard Momma holler at Daddy through the thin wall between their bedrooms.

***

Time and again—birthdays, Christmas, First Communion—Leslie's wish had been the same. She prayed to her guardian angel and to his guardian angel that Daddy would stop drinking. So that Momma would stop crying and begging and yelling at him. And that they could be a happy family, just like they had been when she was very young.

And so it was this year, as Christmas approached.

But now, for the first time, she told herself she was getting too old to meet the imaginary boy who would never grow up.

For years, she had imagined that her green leaf-clad hero would brave the gusty winds over Lake Michigan, choking on the noxious clouds that billowed from the miles of smokestacks and sulfurous pits of industry that lined the south shore. She had imagined that somehow, Peter, his unruly shadow singed after grazing one of the flaming exhaust towers in the oil tank farm up Rockefeller Road, would find her window and tap on it, and she would pull on her blue nightgown and ballet slippers and take off into the sky with him and Tinkerbell.

The nuns said that we all have our own cross to bear, so Leslie resigned herself to the belief that her cross, her mission, was to be so kind and good and well-behaved—not in Neverland, but at home in Peacepipe—that if she hoped and prayed and cajoled, she could convince Daddy to stop drinking, or at least to come home sober once in a while.

***

Winter barged in early that year, with darkened skies and daily rains. No snow yet, just the whole known world suspended in chill and bleakness.

At 7 a.m. on December 13, Leslie began her Saturday routine. Momma was asleep on the couch in her bouffant foam rollers, curled up with a pillow and a blanket. Her parents' bedroom door was shut. Daddy was probably sleeping off a hangover. Leslie pulled on her red plaid wool coat, over-the-knee socks and the white wool ear warmer that she had knit last summer and shut the front door quietly. Light was just breaking, but it was a short trip across the street and down the block to Penny's little grocery shop, where five people were already in line to pick up a warm loaf of fresh-baked rye bread. She hoped there would still be a loaf with caraway seeds and there was. What a great start to the day! She thanked her guardian angel. After she paid her quarter, she held the waxed white paper bag close to her chest and shared her muffler with it on the way home. Maybe some bread and sweet butter could even soothe a hangover.

She could tell it would be another day in a string of raw December days. Like most kids who grew up in Peacepipe, she had learned early on that she didn't need a weathervane to tell which way the wind was blowing. Her nose knew each point on the compass. Dead fish? Anticipate a damp wind out of the east, with enough snow to cancel school in the winter. Smoke and sulfur? Orangish, stagnant air from the refineries and steel mills to the southeast, maybe microscopic droplets of oil in the murk. Daddy called it "flog," which made Leslie giggle. Could she taste grit on her tongue? That came from the south, when dry air currents wafted the dust into the neighborhoods, from the slag heaps that bordered the tank farms. West and southwesterly breezes provided brief relief on a hot summer day, until lightning-laced storms rolled in from beyond the towering steeple of St. Benedict's. After the rain, gusting cold fronts clogged local throats with the heavy taste of corn slurry from the corn milling plant. Northwesterly breezes swept in the tickling smell of soap flakes from the largest soap factory in the country, making the whole town smell like it had just come out of the washing machine and was hung out to dry. Everyone went around sneezing until the wind shifted slightly to send some fresh northerly air off the lake, until the weather cycle spun round again. But Daddy said that industry provided jobs. The whining of the stills and the atonal grinding and coupling of the freight trains that ran along the lakefront night after night provided a secure and cozy lullaby for the people of Peacepipe, just east of the Southeast Side of Chicago.

And it was home.

After watching the Saturday morning cartoons and finishing another Nancy Drew mystery, it was time to do chores. Momma and Daddy didn't actually *give* her chores, but Leslie learned from reading books and watching television that children were supposed to do chores. So, she stood washing dishes in the shabby kitchen, where the hot water wasn't always hot and the sink drained in slow motion, because the roots of that scraggly oak in the yard had invaded the sewer pipes. The steamed-up kitchen windows clouded her usual view of the Dominion Oil refinery, three blocks away, beyond the railroad tracks. Water droplets slid down the windowpane, like paratroops of angels, sent to answer her prayers for peace between Momma and Daddy.

Leslie sighed a deep sigh, imitating Snow White wishing in a Disney movie. As she did, she drew in the sweet perfume of promise: *kapusta*. That's Slovak for "cabbage." All five, tiny rooms of the Lujak's rented house on Elm Avenue were warm and steamy, filled with anticipation. A feast of *halupki*—stuffed cabbage—was simmering in the pot.

Its bubbles called to Leslie, as one by one, they burst in the heavy broth. Each soft pop drew her deeper in, to the sweet-sounding, cozy cauldron of hope on the stove.

Some say that boiling cabbage stinks; that it's mere peasant sustenance. But *kapusta*, and the sweet, rich *halupki* that it makes, was Proust's madeleine to Leslie. The all-encompassing scent of green and yellow leaves of cabbage wrapped around a filling of ground pork and veal, bacon, rice and onion filling, then tucked tight together in peppery, thick tomato broth, lifted her to happy reverie.

Momma, ivory-skinned, with her Susan Hayward hairdo, had little patience for the kitchen, yet she addressed *halupki*-making like an ancient priestess in her temple, preparing a ritual offering to the gods.

Leslie loved to watch as Momma gathered the ingredients and mixed the filling, as if it were her birthright, carefully peeling parboiled leaves from the cabbage head, then gently rolling each precious bundle and piercing it with a wooden toothpick to hold it together. She'd layer them with sauerkraut in the tall pot and set the flame low. Perhaps savoring this food together would set everything right. *Maybe, even, Daddy would come straight home tonight, instead of stopping at the bar.*

"He's so funny when he isn't drinking," Momma would say.

It was late when his two-tone mint and forest green Ford Fairlane pulled into the driveway. Leslie heard his staggering gait on the porch. As he stepped through the kitchen door, "*Kapusta!*" he boomed, like Jackie Gleason hollering for Alice. "Why the hell, Lizzie, are you stinking up the house like that?"

But the pungent balm of *halupki* beckoned to his bourbon-soaked tastebuds. Bacon, tomato sauce and sauerkraut vied for his attention. Momma and Leslie carried their plates to the small dining table where the bills were stacked. They watched him take off his suit jacket and tie and hang them neatly over the back of his chair at the head of the table. He piled his bowl high, slathered a thick slice of rye bread with fresh, unsalted butter, then sat on the couch in front of the TV and gobbled his food with a shot and a beer, surrendering to the crunchy cabbage and its chewy filling.

And so it happened every time. After a second round of food and drink, Daddy would doze off in a contented, sloppy snore, while Momma sipped a Pepsi and talked on the phone with her baby sister. Suddenly, her husband's inevitable, *kapusta*-induced, ripping pass of gas would jolt him awake and interrupt her conversation.

"Tommy!" Momma would exclaim.

"Damned *kapusta*," he'd mumble.

"He really loves my cooking," she would whisper to Aunt Nadia.

And Leslie would fall asleep to the music of her mother's nightly plaint, with ambrosial *halupki* gurgling in her tummy.

***

That Christmas Eve, Leslie was still too young to go to Midnight Mass at St. Benedict's with her friends, like the eighth graders did. Around sunset, Tommy drove mother and daughter out of their working-class neighborhood where picture windows, lawns and rooftops blinked with holiday lights. He bounced along the poorly-lit potholed roads that served as shortcuts for those who worked in the mills and refineries.

"Jesus, Tommy," Momma moaned. "You're hauling us into the middle of nowhere. I hope your tires hold up." Leslie loved how Daddy always knew the back roads.

He made a sharp left and slammed on his brakes. "We've found the line, Lizzie," he announced.

Sure enough, slowly snaking along in front of them were several hundred sedans and station wagons, their red taillights blinking on and off as they started and stopped again and again, adding to the festival of lights that they had come to see. They were headed for the competing Christmas displays erected in front of the administration buildings of Hoosier Sheet and Milling and its neighbor, the Midwest Steel Plant. After half an hour, the Lujaks got their chance to stop for a few minutes in front of a 40-foot pine behemoth. Its branches, laden with colored bulbs the size of basketballs and silver strands of tinsel that might be polished steel, bobbed in the wind.

"You know that's not one tree." Daddy said the same thing every year. "It's actually 200 trees from northern Michigan all strapped together."

The windows fogged up, so Leslie cranked down her back-seat window. It smelled like snow. Clouds of exhaust from scores of tailpipes caught the moist air, all but obscuring the manger off to the side and Santa and his reindeer on the roof. Little white pellets of ice began hitting the windshield.

"Sleet," said Daddy. "We're only seeing one tree this year."

"Can we come back tomorrow, Daddy? After Momma and me go to church?"

"We'll see."

"If he doesn't get boozed up tonight," Momma muttered.

The weather eased up just a few blocks from the lake, so it was on to dinner at Grandma's. Her large kitchen window sat fifteen feet from rows of train tracks that separated her from the tank farm of one of the largest refineries in the nation. Leslie and her cousins waved to the trainmen on the red cabooses and felt sorry for them because they weren't home on Christmas Eve. "Triple overtime," Daddy said.

The sweet scent of Grandma's eight-foot-tall Christmas pine, tickling the ceiling with bubbling lights, mingled with the aroma of her traditional meatless Christmas Eve dinner. The stove was piled with pots—a thick brown soup of dried wild mushrooms, picked on an October dawn in the dunes state forest by Grandma and her sons; pierogi filled with plum butter, cheese or butter-drenched sauerkraut; fried fish, surrounded by thinly sliced potatoes and onions. Grandpa, sons and sons-in-law poured endlessly from the gallon of Seagram's 7 Crown that Grandma would lock up tomorrow, in hopes it would last through New Year's.

***

During the half-mile drive home from Grandma's house that frigid Christmas Eve, Daddy skidded into a snowbank. Through chattering teeth, Momma announced she would learn to drive.

"Never again will I get in the car when you're soused, Tommy," she vowed.

"So how will you go anywhere?" He lit a Winston. Leslie prayed his breath wouldn't catch fire.

On December 26th, with Daddy sober and the three of them singing "Purple People Eater" to the car radio, they drove to the Chevy dealership. It was the year of the batwing tailfins. Momma plunked down cash, from her executive stenographer's job at the smelting factory, for a brand-new red-and-white Impala that enhanced her lustrous black hair, Revlon red lips and creamy skin. She chose the deluxe package—power steering, automatic transmission, whitewall tires.

Daddy strode over to his Ford. "Drive your car home, Lizzie," he called to her. "Hop in, Leslie." He winked. "They'll bring her home after she signs the papers."

Leslie wondered whether Momma would sign using Elzibetka, the name given her by her immigrant parents; or Betty, the name she adopted in high school; but probably not Lizette, the French-sounding alias she claimed during the War, when she worked in the Loop and flirted with GIs in the bars before hopping the train back to Peacepipe. No matter, a bold, sparkling Chevy graced their driveway that afternoon.

***

Daddy pulled strings; Momma got her license without a test. Leslie was relieved, considering Auntie Nadia's first driving lesson. Momma and Nadia often talked as if Leslie weren't in the room, which is how the fifth grader learned so much.

The three "girls" had been sitting at Nadia's kitchen table with its sunshine yellow plastic tablecloth, eating crunchy, half-defrosted Sara Lee cheesecake.

Aunt Nadia swirled strawberry sauce around the aqua Melmac dessert plate that matched her eyes. "Betka, you know Joe? From the flower shop?" She caught her own reflection in the mirror of her glass-doored knick-knack cabinet. Her face appeared between a Hummel Alpine hiker and a statuette of St. Christopher carrying the Christ Child. "What do you think?" She pulled back her platinum curls. "Should I try a French twist like Debbie Reynolds?"

"You were talking about Joe, Nadia," Lizzie snapped.

"Well… you remember he gave me bowling lessons?"

"I went to school with Joe. He isn't very bright."

"But he's fun, Betka. He makes me laugh! He's not grumpy like my Jerry."

"Be careful, Nadia. He has six kids. And his wife is probably holding out on him if she knows what's good for her."

"My ladies' team won the trophy, didn't we?" Nadia's voice was sweetly musical, seeking the affirmation she craved from her older sister. "Anyway, last week, Joe offered to help me perfect my hook ball. But when I showed up at the lanes, he offered to teach me to drive. He remembered I wanted to learn! He listens, not like my Jerry."

"Your husband built you a house, Nadia," her older sister scolded.

Leslie took another sliver of cake and smashed the graham cracker crust with her fork.

Aunt Nadia lowered her voice. "Well, I sat in Joe's station wagon in the parking lot behind the bowling alley—in the driver's seat, Betka. I was fumbling around for the ignition and boom! He leaned over and kissed me! I slapped him, pitched his keys into the weeds and stomped home! Men are all the same. Like my last boss. Remember? I told him 'No,' and a new girl was sitting at my desk when I showed up the next morning!"

Aunt Nadia enrolled in driving school. Momma taught herself with her daughter at her side. She got into the habit of practicing her new skills on Friday evenings after work by driving around the quiet neighborhoods of Peacepipe after dark.

Momma and her devoted passenger would rattle across the railroad tracks into Peacepipe Park. She'd turn into the gravel lot, up to the barrier of boulders that the WPA had piled along the Lake Michigan shoreline long before Leslie was born. The two would sit in silence, listening to the lapping waves, taking in the Chicago skyline to the left and Dominion Oil's belching smokestacks and flaring exhaust torches to the right. For Leslie, it was reassuring, like that world map with the arrow in the Museum of Science and Industry: "You Are Here."

***

Momma jerked the gear shift into reverse. "Let's see if your father's still at the club."

"We know he is, Momma."

But she was the captain of her four-wheeled ship, just as her husband was the Commander of the VFW. The red and white Impala bumped across the tracks back to the black-tarred alley that ran behind Peacepipe's main street. She passed the VFW's one-story yellow brick building and sure enough: Daddy's two-tone green Fairlane was among the dozen cars in the parking lot. Why Momma had to do this every week, Leslie wasn't sure. Did it provide some sort of twisted reassurance that the situation was, indeed, as awful as she thought? Did it stoke the anger in her blood and fire up the independent streak manifested in her dream of driving a car—her own car, paid for with her own money in her own name? Or maybe she just wanted to be close to him.

That ritual complete, they'd drive the mile to the newer part of town where the people who were doctors, engineers, chemists and factory executives lived. A well-forested recreational park ran along one side of the neighborhood, protecting it from Coyote Lake that marked the state line between Indiana and Illinois. On another side of the prosperous, well-manicured blocks, were the soap factory (where they also made margarine) and the corn mill.

"This was all marsh when I was a kid, Leslie," Momma kept her eyes on the road. "And they still have the mosquito swarms to prove it. Larger lots, more expensive homes, more bugs."

Thus, Momma opined on life at twenty miles per hour. As she followed the limiting grid of the dimly lit streets from behind the red, man-sized steering wheel, her VO-5 hairspray cast a hypnotic spell. The contours of her face—high cheekbones, long lashes, narrow nose with only the suggestion of a hook—glowed eerily in the blinking reds, greens and yellows of the dashboard lights.

Leslie liked being so close to Momma, feeling important beside her in the front seat, hearing the voice she had known before birth, keeping company to her mother's lonely misery, going nowhere. Momma would share her own brand of working-class feminism, the iconoclastic world according to Elzibetka, punctuated regularly by her faithful and obedient use of the directional signal every time she made a turn on the empty streets.

"Those priests never lived with a woman, and all they do is imagine what it would be like." Momma's harangue began as their aimless pilgrimage swung down the street that ran between the school and the church: "More than that, priests are all men. Who says they can understand what a woman goes through with her husband? Women who go to a priest to ask for marriage advice are crazy. Noody-nods, who can't think for themselves."

Leslie cringed. She could have recited Momma's sermon along with her by rote, just like the schoolkids chanted the trancelike "*Ora pro nobis*" in the endless litanies they sang as they marched slowly up and down St. Benedict's aisles in the annual May procession with bright wreaths of fresh flowers on their heads.

"What does a priest know? Father Dave says that the Church condemns rubbers. He says it's like washing your hands with your gloves on. Did *he* ever have to get pregnant and put up with another snotty nose to feed? He better think twice before he vacations in Florida and takes off his collar again. Mrs. Kakchachky saw him down there without his collar, you know?"

"Yes, Momma. You told me that before." (It happened when Leslie was three.) "Maybe it was just hot down there."

"Until the church lets women become priests, I've got no use for it."

Being an only child and having no brothers, Leslie couldn't imagine what a rubber did. She only knew that it was birth control—a sin, according to the nuns—used to prevent the possibility of making more children, always a disgusting burden, according to Momma.

Momma pulled into the Jewel Foods parking lot, grabbed a cart and set off through the glaringly bright store. As she pushed the cart down the aisle, its whomping wheels were accompanied by the sharp clicks of her black patent spike heels. Leslie watched the glint of the fluorescent lights on the tiled floor as they went. They stopped at the pristine white butcher counter.

"Look," Momma said. "That steak costs 69-cents a pound whether you're a man or a woman. A woman doesn't get paid as much as a man, but she has to pay the same for steak. So really, a woman pays *twice* what a man pays for a simple slab of meat. What do priests know? The church feeds them from our collection money."

Leslie braced herself.

"Your father almost became a priest. He should've stayed in the seminary. He always expects someone else to feed him."

Leslie inhaled.

"Just like you, kid."

As usual, Momma had drawn her daughter into her confidence, then dangled her up for the punch. Leslie couldn't stop Daddy from drinking. She hadn't asked Momma to sacrifice and work so hard just so that she could pay twice as much for their hamburger patties. She wanted Momma's companionship yet felt her Daddy's shame.

As they waited with their cart at the checkout counter, right above the rack of Wrigley's chewing gum, Leslie saw the National Enquirer. "Secret Talks: UFOs Ask Ike for Airport."

***

The new year brought a big change to St. Benedict's. The church had long begun training fifth grade boys to be altar boys, to serve at the Mass that all the kids attended every day before starting classes. The girls had to learn the Latin Mass, too, but could only recite it from the pews. They didn't dare grumble that even though they knew the Latin, why weren't they allowed to be altar boys?

Finally, the principal, Sister Bridget Patrick, appealed to the priests to let the girls keep the vigil light shrines tidy. They would, she said, be called "The Lightkeepers."

St. Benedict's was a magnificent, cavernous church, even larger than the cathedral in Stilltown, the county seat. Benedict's nave was so large that there were four more aisles of seats on either side of the wide pews on the main aisle. There were statues of all the saints, from Jesus, Mary and Joseph on down the hierarchy. Each statue stood in its own alcove, surrounded by plenty of cherubs and angels, and beneath each alcove was a multi-tiered rack with small ruby red glasses holding small candles. Worshippers would choose the saint of their devotion—St Anthony for things lost, St. Joseph to sell their house, The Virgin Mary for expectant mothers, St. Francis for sick pets and so on.

Every St. Benedict's child remembered the thrill of being lifted up and allowed to light a vigil light for the first time. There was a ritual to it. They would solemnly slip a quarter into a slot labeled "poor box," locate a glass with an unlit candle, carefully dip the tip of a long toothpick into the flame of a lit candle, slowly light the wick of the new candle with their flaming stick, blow out the stick like a birthday candle and say a prayer. Leslie wondered whether the saints competed against each other, counting the number of lights that glimmered below their feet, or whether Mr. Zamarsky, the church custodian, went around before 6 a.m. Mass every day and redistributed the lit candles so that every saint would look down on St. Benedict's with favor.

Leslie, who was usually the first pupil chosen for any new class project, was not selected to be a Lightkeeper. Those honorary assignments went to the children of active Rosary Society and Knights of Columbus officers.

"You have better things to do than collect ashes and matchsticks," said her mother. "Besides, you ought to be an altar boy, um, altar girl. Don't settle for second place."

***

In mid-January, Leslie's class took a field trip to the Loop to see "The Ten Commandments" with Charlton Heston. Still enthralled with the enormity of the plagues and the parting of the sea, she could not settle down when she rolled into bed. Listening to the whining stills and grinding train wheels on the rail tracks, she remembered the scenes of the enslaved Israelites, lugging mammoth stones through the blazing Egyptian desert to build the pyramids. She wondered if the Israelites could work at night by torchlight because it might have been cooler. When she drifted off, the images morphed into a pre-dawn rush hour on Rockefeller Boulevard, when the daddies getting off work at the plants and the daddies who were driving to the day shift slowed traffic to a halt both ways for a full ten minutes. In her dream, the cars on Rockefeller Boulevard towed long steel beams and giant lead pipes to build a pyramid.

The cast iron frying pan clunked down on the stove and jolted Leslie awake. The kitchen was right outside her closed bedroom door.

"Tommy, put that paper down and listen to me!" Momma commanded.

Her parents hardly ever sat down to breakfast together. Something must be up, and Leslie dared not interfere. She lay in bed and listened.

"Tommy, all those headlines of troopers just 30 miles from here. Away from all the mills and smokestacks. South of Valpo, at the bottom of Potawatomie County? By the cornfields..." Lizzie Lujak's usually belligerent morning voice was instead the matter-of-fact tone she reserved for talking with the phone company or ordering groceries. "Tommy, do you believe they're really seeing flying saucers like the paper says? Down in Vincennes, motorists reported that car radios went dead, when a formation of silver lights hovered over a golf course!"

"Why not?" Daddy slurped his percolated coffee. Its strong aroma swirled under the bedroom door. "You don't think we're alone in the universe," he said. "But what if those saucers are sent by the Russkies and they're reconnoitering? Just one of those spaceships kamikaze-ing into the middle of Dominion Oil would make Pearl Harbor look like a weenie roast."

"Tommy!" her mom cried, half serious, half laughing. "I believe this is bigger than the Russians."

There was silence for a time and Leslie smelled bacon sizzling. It was hard not to skip into the kitchen.

"Tommy. Tommy?" Leslie heard coffee sloshing into a cup. "Is... saw... a... flying saucer last night."

"Uh-huh," Daddy said. "You and everyone else who believes in fairy tales." The newspaper pages rustled.

"Tommy, I tell you. It wasn't those red and green lights the troopers reported. It was right here, drifting over the garage, a silent, glowing ivory globe. Maybe 50 feet off the ground."

"You always wanted to be a writer, Lizzie."

"Seriously, Tommy. I couldn't sleep and I was just looking out the back window, thinking how unusually quiet it was. There were no trucks thumping up the boulevard. You couldn't hear the trains whistle or the refinery groan. Very unusual."

"It was probably a blimp heading toward Midway."

"At 3 a.m., Tommy? I've seen blimps. Blimps whir. This craft had no windows or markings. And it moved so slowly. Smoothly. Silently."

"If this *craft* was so great, why didn't you come get me then?" Leslie could almost hear Daddy smirk.

"I was mesmerized. I felt that I was chosen," Momma said dreamily. "Just me and that round ship from somewhere else in the Universe."

"If I told a story like that, they'd say I'd been drinking, but you don't drink, Lizzie. You must've been dreaming. What did you eat last night?"

"Tommy, I tell you, it was real."

"You've told me your family hears your mother's ghost drag her wooden leg across the attic floor, but this beats 'em all."

"I wasn't imagining this, Tommy."

"Yeah, your crazy family. I shoulda known something was up when you cooked bacon on a weekday. Well, I'm glad you didn't wake me up and you shouldn't tell anyone else, either."

"Oh, but I did."

"Did what?"

"I told someone. I called the Peacepipe Police."

"You did *what?*" Daddy slammed his fist on the table. The dishes rattled, as did the tiny trapeze and the jingle bells in the wrought iron parakeet cage beside the table. The cage was empty, since the bird won at the church fair in August was found lifeless atop the newspapers at the bottom of the cage in October. "I want to be mayor, and you called the police about some sacred vision you've imagined?"

"I did."

"What the hell did they say?"

"Sgt. Hahn said, 'Well, Lizzie, it's almost 3 o'clock in the morning. I know that you don't drink.' And he took down my information. All of it."

"Goddammit, Lizzie! I'm going down to the station right now to have them tear up those records. Will the goddamned bacon still be good at dinnertime?"

"Oh, like you'll be home on time," Momma hollered. "Take the bacon with you and shove it up your ass!"

Leslie waited until her swearing father slammed the door and stormed down the back stairs. She opened her bedroom door, feigned sleepiness and acted ignorant of the conversation, which allowed her mother to eagerly re-tell her story. Knowing how Momma's family saw ghosts, Leslie found the saucer tale plausible, but was thankful that Momma had let her sleep through it.

The abandoned bacon was a little crisp, just the way she liked it.

The afternoon edition of the Peacepipe Press buried Elzbietka Lujak's story on the one page that everyone in town read religiously: the obituary page. Momma bought five copies of the paper and carried a Saran-wrapped clipping in her purse. She flaunted it to friends when her husband wasn't around.

***

On Tuesday, Sister Agatha Stanislaus gave a homework assignment: choose an interesting newspaper article and talk about it in front of the class.

"Daddy, I found this great article that Elvis Presley's Army basic training is going well! Leslie and her father sat at the kitchen table late. He was hardly drunk at all, with a light, sweet whiskey breath.

"Leslie, everyone will choose that story. You want something that'll be different." He licked his finger and paged through the Chicago Sun-Times. "Here. Look. They say smelt fishing will be great on the Southeast Side this spring because of a quiet winter over Lake Superior." He took his penknife from his pocket key chain and cut the article out. "You and I go after dark every spring, to watch them pull the nets out of the lake, swarming with those little wrigglers. Here. Take this to class."

Daddy was right. Three-fourths of the kids had chosen the frontpage Elvis story. But Gloria DiSecco, Leslie's perennial rival for first place in grade average, presented the smelt fishing article. Gloria's head of strawberry curls stood out against the classroom's wall-sized, deep green blackboard. She batted her eyelashes and smiled, baring her expensive braces.

Then it was Leslie's turn. She had no choice. Although shy, she was a fierce competitor. Confident that no one would have *this* story, she smiled at Sister Agatha Stanislaus and read the headline from a beloved article she had tucked in her catechism textbook: *"Troopers See Saucers in South Pow County."* Leslie read every word. "Not all flying saucers look the same," She raised an eyebrow as she finished.

Sister Agatha Stanislaus folded her arms under the starched white bib of her black habit: "I'm not sure we should believe in flying saucers.

We can't believe everything we read in the newspapers."

"But Sister! Why would *state troopers* say they saw these things?" Leslie waved the article in the air. "They gave all these details!" She could hardly believe it herself: she had dared talk back to a nun for the first time in her life.

The puffy nun fingered the oversized rosary that encircled her waist. "There could be another explanation. Didn't you read toward the end that there could be another explanation?"

By now, Johnny Kovach and a few of the other boys were booing and holding their noses and pointing at Leslie, thumbs down. Sallyann and Cheryl giggled, so most of the other girls began giggling, too. Fuchsia blotches popped out on Sister Aggie's cheeks.

Leslie couldn't take the disdain one more minute. She held her chin up: "Sister, my own mother saw a real flying saucer last week. A huge, silent, creamy-white globe, hovering over Elm Avenue on a quiet night. I have that clipping, too." Leslie drew the article, wrapped in Saran Wrap, from her pocket and held it high for the class to see.

"Leslie Lujak," said Sister Agatha Stanislaus, "I am surprised and disappointed that *You, you* above all others, a model student, should talk of such nonsense. Please take your seat."

Leslie got quick revenge that afternoon by winning a classroom spelling bee and getting the only "A" in the class on an Indiana history pop quiz. Sister Aggie certainly couldn't dispute that.

***

"Are you going to tell your mother what happened in school?" asked Betty-Lou Stavros. The best friends were teaching themselves to ice skate on the shallow frozen marsh behind the metal smelting plant

"Absolutely not!" said Leslie.

She and Betty-Lou held on to stiff cattails for balance as they picked their way along by the floodlights from the factory. The January sun had already set.

"Did you promise not to tell anyone about the flying saucer?"

"I didn't have to, Betty-Lou. I am expected to keep our family secrets." Leslie grumbled.

"Well, it was worth it," Betty-Lou laughed. "Sister Aggie was so red faced I thought she would pop a vein in her forehead and blow her veil off. Or that the frames of her wiry spectacles would sizzle and melt. I think that's what the girls were giggling at—the look on her face."

"I never talked back to a nun before, Betty-Lou," Leslie replied, holding both arms out to keep her balance on her blades.

"Wow," said Betty-Lou. "Now you're like the rest of us. Imperfect. But you're still my friend." She put her heels together and tried to spin around but fell. She had longer legs than Leslie.

Leslie thought she heard Betty-Lou giggle, but since both girls wore two woolen mufflers over their mouths and heavy knit hats that they had crocheted themselves pulled down to their eyes, she couldn't see her friend's dimples deepen. She extended her mittened hand to help Betty-Lou up but fell back down with her.

"Speaking of your mother," said Betty-Lou, finally standing again, "what would our parents say if they knew we were out here?"

"My father tells stories of how he used to skate across here to get to St. Benedict's in the winter," answered Leslie. "And it hasn't been above freezing for ten days, so it's safe."

Not too far off on the forbidden pond of industrial waste, a group of boys from their class, including Johnny Kovach, were noisily playing ice hockey. They pointed at the girls. "That's the sixth time you fell down, Betty-Lou. Ten times and Billy here will get you a free White Castle."

When the girls went to reclaim the boots they had left at the shore, they couldn't find them. After poking around in the frozen weeds, they found a note on a soggy scrap of lined notebook paper: "The little green men took your shoes to Mars."

Of course, Betty-Lou and Leslie couldn't walk home in their white leather ice skates. Thank God they each had worn three pairs of socks to keep their feet warm. They walked the four blocks home shoeless.

***

The next Monday, Father Mike Sespak, the pastor of St. Benedict's, tapped on the classroom door, unannounced, a surprise that often caused the nuns to blush. Not blush as much as when slender, young Father Hovno visited the class, but blush nonetheless. Sister Agatha Stanislaus called Leslie to watch the class while she went into the hall. "Teacher's pet!" mouthed Johnny Kovach. (Leslie's mother said that Johnny had a crush on her.)

Through the doorway, Leslie heard an army of tinkling rosaries approach. Led by the Principal Sister Bridget Patrick, the sisters gathered around Father Sespak, white bibs on long, black dresses, looking like a waddle of penguins.

Father Sespak stuck his kind, square face into the door and summoned Cissy Kolch and Pam Czipsky into the hall and shut the door so the class couldn't hear what the fuss was about.

"Continue working on your book reports," Leslie directed the class, claiming her authority.

It seemed like forever until Cissy and Pam re-entered the room, sniffling and wiping teary eyes, and sat in their seats. Sister Aggie, a name they never called her to her face, explained that the girls had seen the Blessed Mother statue crying in the grotto in the back of the church. Scary. Most of the kids knew that Mr. Zamarsky had once seen the Devil in the back of the church by the holy water fountain and that he had chased the horned figure with his push broom, but it had disappeared into that very side grotto. Which was why children were never supposed to turn their heads away from the altar during Mass.

That afternoon after school, all the girls took turns in groups of four to kneel in the tiny grotto, designed to look like the grotto at Lourdes. Sure enough, Leslie saw a blur around the virgin's head and her cheeks seemed moist. But tears?

"*Not really,*" thought Leslie. "*Definitely not.*"

She didn't for a minute think that she wasn't holy enough to witness the apparition. She just knew she was more sensible. She had read about the women and teens in Salem who were falsely accused of witchcraft after suffering mass hysteria.

Apparently, most of her classmates didn't see tears, either, though they didn't admit it. After a few days, the Weeping Queen of Heaven phenomenon faded away.

***

Two mornings later, unannounced again, Father Sespak came to the classroom door and motioned to Sister Aggie to come out.

Thirty seconds later, Sister Aggie stepped back into the classroom with a super-stern look on her pasty face. It happened almost in slow motion. The nun walked toward Leslie, towering like Godzilla over her star pupil, who always sat in the front row. She looked down at the girl.

"Leslie Lujak," she announced in a stentorian voice, "Father Sespak would like to see you in the hall."

Leslie popped out of her seat and found that she was shaking. "Yes, Sister," she answered and slowly walked into the hallway. *Would Sister reprimand her for doubting the Virgin's tears were real? How could she have known?*

Father Sespak's jaw was set; his expression was stern. Yet she detected a glimmer of amusement in his light blue eyes.

"Leslie, Sister Agatha reported that you upset her class last week when you said that your mother saw a flying saucer over Peacepipe."

"Upset, Father? I'm not sure they were upset," said Leslie. She remembered Johnny Kovach making fun of her and felt angry and upset herself. "Momma's story was in the Peacepipe Press, Father."

"Can you explain this to me, Leslie?" He spoke softly, like when he was hearing sins in the confessional. "Trust me, Leslie. I know what a good student you are and how hard you work." He smiled down at her.

Once a year, her parents would take her and Father Mike to dinner at Helen's Fish House for a feast of boned lake perch in drawn butter, so she was comfortable around him. She composed herself and smiled back. "Yes, Father. It was in the paper last week, on the obituary page, when people we trust, like state troopers, were seeing flying saucers. Only hers—my mother's—wasn't flashing, dancing red, blue and green lights in the sky. Hers was alone. Round, like the moon."

"Was it the moon, then, Leslie?" he whispered as if he were trying to calm and settle the situation.

"There was no full moon that night, Father. The next full moon is the Full Snow Moon in early February, next week. My mother checked."

"You are gifted with a wild imagination, Leslie, but others might not understand what you say sometimes." Father Sespak spoke in the tone with which he gave a post-confession penance. She thought for a moment he would tell her to say five Our Fathers and three Hail Marys, but he didn't.

"You are more poetic than most children your age, Leslie," said Father Sespak. "I suggest you reserve it for writing stories in English class. Now go back inside."

"Yes, Father. Thank you, Father." She quietly walked back in and slipped into her seat, while Sister Aggie continued to teach a 1950's Midwestern fifth-grade version of the Emancipation Proclamation.

When Leslie came home that evening, Momma broke the news:

Father Sespak wanted both parents at the rectory for a conference.

"About what?" Leslie tried to play it cool.

"Father Mike said that it's something about your belief in flying saucers. And then Johnny Kovach's mother called to tell me that she believes in flying saucers, too. Where would she get that in her head, LezzzLEE!"

"Calm down, Momma. Johnny's the one who stole our boots, so it's none of her business."

"I told you, Leslie. Boys do foolish things when they have a crush on you. But don't change the subject. What did you say in school about me?"

"That you saw a flying saucer," Leslie droned.

"What did I say about family secrets, Leslie?" Her mother's mouth twisted; her eyes were slits.

"Momma, you've been pulling that article out of your purse everywhere you go without Daddy." Leslie stood her ground. "Besides, I had to outshine Gloria DeSecco who was reporting on that story about smelt season. Everybody else did Elvis. Daddy's always right, anyway. It's all your fault. You shouldn't've called the cops that night. When you gonna meet with him?"

"Father Mike asked for the three of us to come together. But you know I have nothing to do with those priests in their cushy rectory that they decorate with our weekly offerings," Momma clenched her small, pearly teeth. A bit of lipstick was smeared on them. "Your father will go alone with you. Next Wednesday after school. It'll be at 4:30, so with any luck he won't be soused."

***

Leslie met Daddy at the drugstore soda fountain across the street from school. He was, of course, in full business suit, striped blue tie and polished leather shoes. He wore a black tweed topcoat and a felt-brimmed charcoal hat. Best of all, a miracle. He was sober. They sat at the counter and had milkshakes—he, chocolate; she, strawberry—then walked the short block to the rectory, across the street from the church.

"It's been a while since I was in here," Daddy was wistful. Momma was right. He was so interesting when he wasn't drunk. "When I was in grade school and there was a snowstorm, Father Mike, his brother Leo and I used to get up in the winter when it was still dark, and we would shovel a path for whichever priest was saying six o'clock Mass that morning. That's how the three of us got scholarships to seminary."

The three-story, 80-year-old wooden building, dark brown with carved eaves like something that Heidi would live in, loomed before them in the winter dusk. Leslie knew that the Knights of Columbus did their best to keep up with the warped window frames and peeling paint. It looked like a big job. Maybe that's why their daughters deserved to be the Lightkeepers. Holding on to opposite railings, father and daughter mounted the steep, creaky steps and rang the doorbell.

Mrs. Dubrov, looking every bit an officious church housekeeper from central casting with a frumpy dress, apron and her gray hair in a bun, let them in. Father Mike stood at the door of his office, shook Daddy's hand and invited them to sit across from him at his burnished mahogany desk. The gray carpet was frayed, the embroidered lace curtains looked as old as the building itself. There must have been more dust particles in the room than there were words in the hundreds of books that crowded the bookshelves. Wow, she'd like to read those books. But did she detect the slightest sour smell, the scent that lingered in the Corner Tap where Daddy took her to play pinball when he had to babysit her?

"I'm so glad that you both could come." Father Mike smiled. She noticed that both men had similar haircuts and thought that the priest must go to old Mr. Hrnczyk's barber shop, too. She didn't dare change the subject to ask to read the books. "You know, Leslie, your dad and I went to St. Benedict's grade school and Maryvale Seminary together."

"I know, Father. He's shown me pictures," said Leslie politely. She wondered why he had said that, since he said the same thing every year when they took him to Helen's.

Father Mike looked straight at her father. "Tommy, you were the star of our class at the seminary, I always thought you should've stayed at Maryvale, and I prayed that you would come back to your vocation."

"It wasn't my vocation after the war, Mike."

"You were the most gifted among us, don't deny it. Well, it's clear that God had other plans for you, and your gift is sitting right here."

Father Mike smiled sweetly at Leslie.

"I understand you called me here about some flying saucer stories, Mike. Well, you know, my darling wife Lizzie has a wild imagination. She even married me because she thought she could reform me, and

God knows she's tried. Well, I'm afraid that Leslie has inherited some of that. She'll write stories someday. Go to New York…"

Father Mike interrupted: "I called you two here because I don't think there's anything wrong with having a wild imagination, but sometimes, Leslie, you have to know who to share it with. Your father's a politician and a good lawyer. He can help you with that."

Leslie bowed her head and studied her fingernails.

"I've seen things myself," said the priest. "Remember, Tommy, when we all were allowed to lie on the hillside at Maryvale in the middle of a summer night and watch a meteor shower? And do you remember what happened when you and I were assigned to check out the noise in the barn one night in January?"

Daddy slapped his thigh. "I do, Mike. The animals must've sensed something. That mysterious, shape-shifting light in the sky, swooping up and down above the fields."

The priest was animated, laughing with his old friend. "We thought it was an angel, telling us to shape up."

"Might've been the Northern Lights," said Daddy.

Father Mike broke into a soft song: "There were shepherds, abiding in the field, keeping watch o'er their flock by night."

"Lo, the angel of the Lord came upon them, and the glory of the Lord shone all about them," Leslie finished singing the verse. "Should I be sore afraid, Father?"

"Not if you hold your tongue in the company of people who aren't as clever as you are," chided the priest.

"That was a night, Mike," said Daddy. "The stars were bright, my hands had frostbite and we shared a cigar that you'd smuggled from the monsignor's bookcase."

"And then there was that illusion, Tommy, dancing through the night," sighed the priest. "I think there's a reason that you and I were allowed to share that vision together. I've never forgotten it. It wasn't the Northern Lights, Leslie. It was something from a world beyond ours. I've prayed about that."

Father Mike sighed and sat back in his worn leather chair. He reached below his desk and placed a bottle of Chivas Regal on top of it. "Want a drink, Tommy?"

"No, thanks, Mike, er, Father. It's not 5 o'clock yet," Daddy chuckled.

"As I was saying, Leslie, there are things seen and unseen in our world, in God's world. Not every earthly soul sees the same things. Have you thought much about that, Leslie?"

"Indeed, I have, Father," answered Leslie. "And since Cissy and Pam saw the Weeping Queen of Heaven and my own mother saw a flying saucer, I've been wondering, Father, is it a sin to believe in flying saucers? Or fairies? You believe in angels, don't you? Is there a difference between angels and flying saucers? Some say the saints were creatures from other planets because they were so much wiser than most people..." Leslie paused to catch her breath.

Daddy took the opportunity to interrupt his daughter. "She spends her summers and weekends reading anything she can grab off the shelves in Peacepipe Public Library."

"Well, Leslie," Father Mike folded his hands atop his desk and leaned forward. "Your questions are probably best answered and explained by your father. Right, Councilor? Maybe your mother will even sit in on your discussion."

"Yes, Father," said Leslie.

Daddy smiled proudly. The grandfather clock in the hall chimed five. Daddy reached for two highball glasses on the bookcase. Father Mike twisted open the Chivas with a pop and poured some of the bronze liquid into each. "*Nasdrovja*," they said and clinked glasses and downed the scotch in one gulp. The priest poured another round.

Leslie sneezed.

"Bless you, my child," said Father Mike. "You know, it's quite drafty in this old house. We're launching a major capital campaign to build a new rectory, across the street in the parking lot. The diocese will give us seed money, but St. Benedict's kids are going to be selling almond chocolate bars for the next three years to help. I hope you can talk us up at the VFW, Tommy."

"For my old schoolmate, why not?" Daddy said. "We can hold a mutton roast at the gun club and sponsor a skeet shooting competition when it gets warmer."

Father Mike swirled around the scotch that was left in his glass and got a faraway look in his eyes.

"All this talk of visions, Tommy. My mother had a vision when Leo was killed in the war. She just knew, days before they knocked on our door."

"I miss him to this day, Mike," said Daddy. "The guys at the VFW still talk about him. He was a real athlete."

"A daredevil and a chaplain," said the priest. "Probably ran straight at the Germans, hollering his head off. My mother saw him plain as day in her dream.

"And, Jesus," he continued, "what Rudy Dudak says he sees at night downstairs in his mortuary. That funeral home was opened 70, 80 years ago, when the German land barons came to buy up land and sell it to the Rockefellers to build the refinery. Dudak's embalming room, before his time, of course, became the final stop for so many of those early guys who lived in those rooming houses and drank themselves into the ground. The plant had a running account to quietly dispose of those who fell asleep on the train tracks or slipped off a still that was being constructed. And the funeral home over in Stilltown collected the remains of those who fell into glowing vats of bubbling steel. It's no wonder Rudy feels a presence. Jesus, Tommy."

The yummy smell of home cooking wafted into the office. Mrs. Dubrov hovered in the doorway.

"I guess it's time to go, Mike," Daddy rose from his chair.

"Yep. I'm calling bingo for the Rosary Society right after dinner. Please. Visit more often, Tommy," said Mike.

"Let's hope I can personally deliver those building funds," Daddy chuckled. He grabbed his coat and hat.

Father Mike helped Leslie on with her fur-trimmed blue coat and whispered, "You know, Leslie, there was a problem a few weeks ago with the steam heat in the ceiling of the grotto. Mr. Zamarsky noticed it and fixed it."

Leslie snapped her fingers. "Yes! I *knew* she wasn't crying, Father!"

"That's between us, Leslie. If you stay out of trouble and don't get called in to the rectory again," he winked, "I'll see you and your parents at Helen's after Easter."

"Easter..." thought Leslie. She held Daddy's hand as she negotiated the rickety rectory steps in her patent leather maryjanes. If she gave up something really significant for Lent, like French fries or wearing a ponytail, maybe Daddy would stop drinking by Easter.

The Girl from Bethel Park

Kathy Bashaar

All Frankie's friends knew right off that there was something wrong with that girl. First off, she never met your eyes. She was always looking over your shoulder or down at your feet or, according to Roxanne, at your chest. And she never had nothing to say for herself neither. Tony's brother Joe got that outtasight new car with his combat pay from 'Nam, a Shelby Mustang, acid green with black interior. Everybody else went crazy, climbing over the hot vinyl seats, begging for rides, admiring the all chrome blinding us in the sun. Even if it wasn't a really boss car, you'd make a fuss over it because you knew Joe wanted you to and he just got back from 'Nam and you wanted to make the guy feel good.

But not Frankie's new girlfriend, not Erica. She hung back, with her arms folded, and looked at the Mustang kind of sideways like she was thinking how to steal it or looking for something wrong with it. When Frankie's turn came to get in it, he talked her into sitting in the front seat with him and then she did smile, all simpering and embarrassed-looking like she just got offered some great honor that nobody else had, even though the whole neighborhood just got done sitting in that car. And then she just sat there while Frankie pretended to drive and hardly said anything to Joe when she got out.

"She's shy maybe," I said. "She don't really know us, so she don't know what to say." The girls just rolled their eyes.

Oh, sure she was cute: straight brown hair like a curtain falling down to her waist, weird green eyes, big boobs—which, Roxanne pointed out, she showed off in tight sweaters every chance she got. Not only was she cute, but she was from Bethel Park, and that just made her even more not right. What was a really cute girl from a cake neighborhood like Bethel Park doing with Frankie?

Everybody loved Frankie, sure. We all went through St. Casimir's together and stuck together now at South High, but you loved Frankie kind of like you loved your dog. He was never any competition for the girls, with those thick glasses and that mill-hunk build and those wild-colored nylon shirts he was always wearing. The girls flirted with him because they knew he didn't mean no harm and they knew that he knew that they knew.

It was me and Paul and Tony and Frankie almost all the time hanging out, and usually Roxanne and sometimes Patty and Donna. Roxanne and Tony were kind of going together. We lived within a couple of blocks of each other all our lives, in the South Side Flats of Pittsburgh, around Eighteenth Street, right after Brownsville Road wound up the Slopes to make its way through Mt. Oliver to Brentwood and Baldwin and all the way to Bethel Park where all the houses had rec rooms and two bathrooms.

But last year Frankie got a crazy crush on Melody Moskiewicz, a senior for crying out loud, and Melody Moskiewicz to boot, with her blond hair and her white teeth like a mouthful of jewels and her straight A's that would get her right into a good college. She had a boyfriend from Baldwin who was already away at Penn State.

Mr. Moskiewicz had gotten moved up to supervisor at the J&L mill, but he still treated all the guys square, everyone said so. The Moskiewiczes were good people, never put on no airs. When Mr. Moskiewicz got the promotion and Mrs. Moskiewicz came into money from selling her father's bar in Mt. Oliver after he died, they could have afforded to move to Baldwin or Bethel Park. But they stayed in the South Side and built a nice new split level on the vacant lots where the houses the hippies used to live in burned down. The Moskiewiczes never forgot where they came from, and everybody respected that.

So, Frankie had no chance with Melody and everyone except him knew it. We just shook our heads when we saw him following her through the halls at school, carrying her books, bringing her Milky Ways and packs of Juicy Fruit from the corner confectionary. Melody was nice to him because the Moskiewiczes were nice to everybody. That was how they were.

Then he said he was taking her to the senior prom.

"Get out. You ain't taking no Melody Moskiewicz to no senior prom," Tony said.

"Yeah, I am. Her college boyfriend can't come home. He has tests that week. So, I asked could I take her and she said 'yes.'"

And damned if he didn't take her, dressed like a pimp in a blue crushed velvet tuxedo with a black velvet bowtie on the hottest night of the summer so far. Mr. Moskiewicz drove them in his Caddy.

Melody went away to Penn State a few weeks later for the summer semester. So, nothing ever came of it, which everyone knew nothing would, but Frankie got bolder with the girls after that, and over the summer he met Erica.

We had nothing to do one Saturday night, so we got on a trolley and went to the Grove dance hall. You were supposed to be eighteen to get into the Grove. Tony was the only one who was there before, with his brother one time, but he said it would be OK, they never asked for ID. It was a hot night. The storm that afternoon didn't cool things off at all, but it left muddy puddles all over the gravel parking lot of the Grove, which we had to step between to keep our shoes from getting wet.

The dance hall sat on stilts above this muddy lot. As we climbed the rickety steps to the door, we could already smell the damp old wood, like the leaky rowboats at summer camp.

A little guy with tattoos and a Fu Manchu mustache stood at the door, toothpick working in his mouth. "You boys eighteen?" he asked.

"Yeah," Tony said.

"Yeah, yeah," we all echoed.

"Let's see some ID."

"We don't have it."

"You're all eighteen and none of yinz has a driver's license? Uh-huh. Get lost."

"Come on, man, give us a break," Tony pleaded. "We came all the way from the South Side. I got in before."

He glanced into the dance hall. "Not tonight. Sorry." He didn't look sorry.

We went clumping back down the stairs. I was last and heard him giving the same treatment to the girls behind us.

"They're packed tonight; that's why he was being an asshole," Tony said. "If they wasn't so crowded, he'd have let us in."

"We wasted our carfare for nothing," I complained.

"Hey, sorry, Andy man! How was I supposed to know?"

I saw the three girls that were behind us, coming down the stairs with their heads hanging.

"Hey!" I yelled. "That guy turn you away, too?"

"Yeah," Erica said. She walked towards us, her girlfriends trailing behind her.

"Well, wanna go do something?"

Erica turned to her two girlfriends. I could see one of them making a face like "no," but the other one shrugged and said, "Might as well."

"What's around here? We're from the South Side."

"There's Mama Lena's, that's about it."

"We don't have the money for some fancy Italian restaurant."

Erica's friend laughed. "Mama Lena's isn't fancy. Come on. We can walk."

Erica was the only cute one. The one girl, Jill, the one who tried to mouth "no" to her friends, was fat, and the other one, Linda, who knew about Mama Lena's, might be cute someday if she developed a little and straightened her hair. So, right off, you wondered why a cute girl like Erica was wasting her time with those two dogs.

Plus, there was four of us and only three of them anyway, so you knew nothing would come of it, but it was something to do, hanging around at Mama Lena's with them.

We picked our way along the side of the main road, with cars flying past us, blowing more hot, wet air on us, walking to Mama Lena's.

When we got there, we saw what Linda meant about it not being fancy. It was just an old-style diner, with stools at a counter, and greasy booths along the side. We crowded into one booth, put all our change on the chipped linoleum table and figured out we had just enough for each of us to have a Coke. The waitress banged the glasses down on the table and didn't smile, like she already knew she wasn't getting no tip.

Erica, Linda and Jill were all going into their junior year, same as us. They went to Bethel Park High School. Erica and Jill were sixteen; Linda was seventeen. Linda had a driver's license but couldn't borrow her dad's car that night because he had his Moose Lodge meeting, so they wasted carfare riding the trolley to the Grove, too.

We talked about what kind of cars were cool, and what kind of music we liked. Linda and Jill liked Bread and The Carpenters. Erica said she liked Black Sabbath, and Paul and me kind of looked at each other: druggie music.

"Best song! Baddest song ever: 'War.'" Tony said. "*War! Mmmph! What is it good for? Absolutely nothin!*' "

Then Tony, Paul, Frankie and me all started singing it, and the girls just sat there with little smiles on their faces, well, except Jill, because the whole time Jill just looked like she couldn't wait to leave.

"I have a whole dance routine made up to 'War'," Frankie said. I'm going to the WIXZ Summer Music Festival and I'm going to jump up on the stage and dance when Edwin Starr comes on."

Paul and Tony and me looked at each other. Frankie had been talking about this dance routine all summer, trying to get us to go up and do it with him. It was a total waste of time. He was never getting into no WIXZ Summer Music Festival, where the tickets cost, like, ten bucks, and then, even if he did, no way was he getting on stage with Edwin Starr. He still had a big head from taking Melody to the prom.

But the girls acted like he was really going to do it, and said they'd like to see the routine some time, and then, thank God, we got off on other things, like were we for or against the war. Jill and Linda weren't sure. Erica was against. Tony, Paul and me all agreed, yeah, it was ugly, but we had to stick it out to show the Communists they couldn't just take over the world. Then Frankie came out and said he agreed with Erica. I never heard Frankie say a word about the war one way or another before that, but pretty soon we're leaving Mama Lena's and walking the girls to the trolley stop and it's Frankie hanging back with Erica in some deep discussion about the war, while me and Paul and Tony are walking in front listening to Linda yap about Bobby Sherman's new record.

So, Frankie got Erica's phone number. We bet he'd call her a couple of times and she'd shut him down and that would be it, but no. Pretty soon he's meeting her at the trolley stop a couple of times a week, walking her back to the South Side, then walking her back to the trolley again later. We were curious if he had ever been to her house and what it was like. I liked to think about her parents sitting in their living room, her dad maybe smoking a pipe and reading a newspaper and her mom wearing high heels and an apron and a pearl necklace and knitting or playing the piano or something. Frankie said he went there a couple of times. They had two bathrooms upstairs, a powder room on the first floor, and a rec room in the basement with a pool table. I asked him why they didn't hang out at her house, and he said he didn't know; she just would rather hang around here with us.

I don't know why she wanted to hang with us, since she hardly said anything to anybody. The girls couldn't stand her right off, because she just hung on Frankie all the time and didn't talk to them.

If we had money, we would buy Cokes and hang around in the

corner confectionary for a while, but usually, we just sat on Tony's stoop. Nobody had a house we could hang around in. Everybody's house was the same: a row house with a front living room and a back kitchen with stairs to the upstairs bedrooms. Our dads sat in their recliners in the living room in their undershirts watching "Mannix" and "Hawaii Five-O" and studio wrestling. But at least Tony's dad let us sit on the stoop, where the concrete still held the heat of the day and black soot collected in the corners and between the Belgium-block alley pavers.

If it wasn't too hot, sometimes we would take a walk up and down Carson Street or down to the river. It was pretty to walk along the river at night and see the sparks flying out of the steel mills and the reflections of orange flame swimming in the water. We could hear the shriek of metal on metal and the hiss of hot steel being poured. By day, the soot from the mills left black streaks all over everything. But, by night, the Mon River snaked its path through the flames like the road to either heaven or hell.

We sang sometimes. We did our old "In Gadda Da Vida" routine for Erica, where Tony had the whole drum solo down pat, tapping his foot for the bass drum, beating his thighs for the snare, and slapping Frankie on the head for the cymbals.

Frankie used to really get into it, but now halfway through he got up and moved away and Tony had to slap the air where Frankie's head used to be. Erica followed Frankie, mooning up at him, rubbing his back. She flipped her hair behind one ear, and I noticed she had a yellow bruise on the side of her cheek. It made me feel like she needed to be protected or something, and I liked her a little more.

Roxanne and Donna and Patty would sing with us or sing on their own, "Close to You" or oldies like "Angel Baby" or "Blue Moon." They weren't afraid to go in Wagner's and ask to try on the most expensive pair of shoes, pretending that they had some fancy party to attend. They laughed out loud, told you what they really thought, and let you see them cry if a teacher yelled at them, or their parents had a fight or a boy they liked gave a ring to another girl. They were like our sisters and we harassed them like sisters and would have protected them like sisters. They treated Frankie like the family dog, sending him down to the confectionary to fetch Twizzlers for them, patting and praising him when he performed tricks for them.

Frankie would clown for the girls. He had this thing he'd been doing since we were in seventh grade where he'd peek out from behind something and say "Verrrrry innnnteresting," like the guy on "Laugh-In" from back in 1967 or something. That always got a laugh. All the black chicks were crazy about "Shaft" that summer, and Frankie did an imitation of a black girl group singing the "Shaft" song, where he did all kinds of spins and went "Shaft!" in a real high-pitched voice and simpered and waved his wrist.

"Do Shaft! Do Shaft!" Patty and Donna would plead, and after a while the rest of us got sick of it because we knew they were kind of making fun of him. We all loved Frankie, but we loved him in that way that let us laugh at him at the same time we were laughing with him. He never seemed to mind, which made us do it more, but in a way made us feel worse.

But the night when he moved away in the middle of "Ina Gadda Da Vida," it seemed like something had changed. Tony kind of petered out on his drum routine before he was even finished, and we all stood there with nothing to say, trying to think what to do next.

"Hey, it's Tuesday. Whoever has a buck, ten pins is only a buck at Bowling City tonight," Tony said.

"Yeah, but how would we get there?" Roxanne said.

"I'll see if my brother will take us. Hang on."

"Want to go bowling?" Frankie whispered to Erica, squeezing her waist.

She twisted her mouth and shrugged. "I'm not that good at bowling."

"Figures," Donna muttered.

"You don't have to be good," Paul insisted. "We just go for the laughs."

Erica shrugged again. She looked like she didn't want to go but couldn't think how to get out of it without looking like a bad sport.

Tony came running out of the house. "Yeah, Joe'll take us."

"Yes!" Paul yelled, and the girls started jumping up and down about getting a ride in the Mustang.

Now, don't even ask me how nine people fit in a Mustang all the way to the Bowling City in Baldwin, but we did it.

We decided to bowl boys against girls. Even though we had five boys and four girls, the girls had Donna, who was the only really good bowler.

Erica wanted to bowl last, after the other girls. When her turn came, she picked up the ball and it took her a minute to claw her fingers into the holes. Then, pressing her lips together, she walked up to the alley and kind of dropped the ball. It wandered down the lane for a few feet and then gave up and thunked into the gutter.

Erica stuck her finger in her mouth, then popped it out and shook her hand. Her face was red. "Ow," she complained. She went and sat on Frankie's lap and he patted her ass and kissed her cheek and whispered "That's OK" to her neck. The girls all rolled their eyes. Where Erica couldn't see, Roxanne mimicked her putting her fingers in her mouth then shaking them, mouthing a babyish, pouting "ow."

Tony and I bowled spares, Joe knocked down eight, Paul knocked down only five, and Frankie bowled another spare. Donna bowled a strike and Roxanne and Patty got spares. Then it was Erica's turn again.

"Can I help her?" Donna asked the rest of us.

"Yeah, yeah," we all agreed quickly.

Donna walked up behind Erica. "Here. Walk all the way up. OK, now, bring your leg way back and bring your arm back… No, the arm on the same side. Now, swing it forward and let go."

Erica's ball hit the ground, bounced a few times and almost made it to the pins this time before it dropped into the gutter.

Donna rolled her eyes. "Have you ever bowled before?"

"Yeah," Erica said, flushing again. "I told you I wasn't good."

"Well, at least you're not a liar."

Erica went and sat on Frankie's lap again, but this time he didn't encourage her, just patted her ass absent-mindedly, looking around the bowling alley.

The girls were creaming us, even so. The next time Erica's turn came, she said, "I don't want to play anymore. I'll just watch."

"But then we'll have three girls and five boys!" Donna exploded.

"Well, I'm not good. I'm just messing you up."

"Frankie, if she quits you have to come on the girl's team," Roxanne said. "She's your girlfriend."

Frankie whispered to Erica. "Come on. Keep playing."

"No, I'm not good. I told you I wasn't good."

"Frankie, come on," Roxanne insisted. "She don't want to play, fine. Let her sit there. But you have to play for the girls now."

Frankie sighed. "Okay." He got up and rolled his ball kind of sloppy, but still bowled a spare.

With Erica out of the picture and Frankie in her place, the girls started beating us even worse and Donna's mood improved. Erica sat back not saying much, but looking happier now that she didn't have to bowl no more. She even complimented Donna on a beautiful strike once, but she said it so soft that I couldn't tell if Donna didn't hear or was ignoring her on purpose.

We were setting up for another game when a gang of pretty girls came in and started putting on shoes two lanes over. One of them called over, "Erica? Hi!"

"Oh. Hi," Erica replied flatly, and turned back to Frankie.

"Do you know those girls?" Roxanne wanted to know.

"Yeah. They go to my school."

"Then why don't you go over and talk to them?"

"I don't really know them that well."

"Maybe you don't want them to see you with us?"

"Roxanne," Tony cut in, "cut it out. Leave her alone. She don't know them that well. She said."

"Or maybe they know things about you that you don't want us to know?" Roxanne pressed.

Erica's face was very tight and pink, like she might cry.

Tony got up and put his arms around Roxanne, steering her away from Erica. "Come on. Leave her alone. Let's play."

We bowled another game. Erica was even quieter than usual, holding her arms close to her body, like she was protecting herself from something. Her back was to those girls she knew, but her eyes kept shifting to the side like she wanted to look behind her.

And I noticed something else. Frankie wasn't always sitting right beside her, pawing at her like he usually did. In between his turns, he sometimes stayed standing, horsing around with us, flirting with Patty and Donna like he used to.

We were going into the last frame and the boys were winning. Donna had bowled a strike in the last frame and, if she could get another one this time, the girls would pull ahead. She picked up a ball, squinted, bit her lower lip a little and took her step. Her arm swung in a sure, smooth arc, and the ball released like a bomb, headed straight for its target and crashed into the pins.

"Aw, shit," we moaned, and Donna smiled a little triangular smile and curtseyed.

Frankie slapped her five, and they did a little hoochie-koo and bumped hips.

"Hey, guys, guess I got on the right team," he taunted us.

He and Donna were still horsing around, now bumping shoulders and asses. I glanced over at Erica, who was watching them tensely.

"Hey, man," I whispered to Frankie, "you better pay some attention to your girlfriend."

"She's okay," he said.

Erica got up and went over to the Coke machine. She came back with a Coke while Frankie was taking his turn.

"Nice how she offered to get anybody else anything," I heard Patty mutter to Roxanne. "Hey, Erica," she said, louder. "Since you're not doing anything, how about you go get us all Cokes?"

Erica flushed. "Do you have money?"

"I have money," Joe spoke up. "Come on. I'll go over with you. I already finished fucking up bowling."

By the time Joe and Erica came back with cold, dripping wet bottles of Coke for everyone, the game was over, and the girls had beat the boys by forty points. Donna and Frankie danced around bumping various body parts.

Erica didn't call "goodbye" to those girls she knew from her school as we left the bowling alley.

We crammed ourselves into the Mustang again for the trip home. I thought Erica would give Frankie the cold shoulder after how he flirted with Donna. Donna was not as cute as Erica by a long shot. She had a cute face and she wasn't exactly fat, but she was one of those short, round girls whose stomachs always look pregnant. You just knew she'd be a load like her mom when she got older. And last year she started dyeing her hair blonde, which didn't look so good. So, she was no competition for Erica in the looks department, but I still thought Erica would teach Frankie a lesson. If the situation was reversed, Donna would teach a real good lesson.

But, no, we squeezed into the Mustang, and Erica sat on Frankie's lap just like always, and they started making out. They made out in front of us before this, but never in a car so close up. I was kind of grossed out and at the same time, I'll be honest, turned on. I could see him trying to snake his hand under her sweater, and her slapping him away, and I was actually kind of rooting for her, but wondering what it would feel like if he did get a feel.

Since we weren't that far from her house, Joe said he'd drive Erica home, and the rest of us were pretty excited to see what her house looked like, I can tell you that. It was the kind of house I'd like to buy someday when I'm married: nice lawn, two-car garage, lots of space between houses. Her parents had bushes planted in front of the house, and pots of red flowers on the two steps leading up to the little front porch. We got a look into the living room through one of the windows. We could see her dad, sitting watching TV, same as our dads at night.

Erica unfolded herself from the Mustang and thanked Joe. Frankie didn't get out and walk her to her door, but Joe waited until she was in the house to pull away. She went in the door and we saw her walk past the living room window. Her dad waved his arms at her and it looked like he was yelling at her, but she just walked past him. He got up and grabbed her by the arm. I saw her glance out the window to see if we were still there. Then he smacked her.

Joe pulled away.

We was quiet until then, just sitting there staring at the house, but I burst out, "Joe! What are you doing, man? What if he beats her up? We gotta go back there and make sure she's okay."

"None of our business," he replied.

"Come on, Joey, man, we all saw it! We gotta go back there. Frankie, it's your girlfriend, man. Tell him."

"I go along with whatever Joey says," Frankie said, and, I swear to God, he grinned. I felt like punching him.

Joe stopped the car, turned around and looked me in the eye. "Andy. She don't want us to go back."

"What are you talking about? How do you know?"

"I know, man. She don't want us to know her dad beats her up. Didn't you see her look out the window? She didn't want us to see. Leave her alone. Save her pride. You'll be doing her a favor." He paused. "Plus, did you ever think of this? We go back and try to act like heroes, right? But we can't do nothing. That's her dad. So, he just beats the shit out of her worse as soon as we're gone, for making him look bad. Did you ever think of that?"

I couldn't answer that. For once, even the girls were quiet.

"Forget it, man," Joe said gently.

I didn't see her for a while after that. We'd be hanging out on Tony's stoop or in the confectionary, and no Erica. I asked Frankie a couple of times where she was and he said, "Just didn't feel like calling her today. I need a little space."

Finally, one evening a couple of weeks after the bowling, Patty had a sixteenth birthday party at her sister and brother-in-law's apartment on the Slopes, and Frankie brought Erica.

The apartment building was built into the hillside and Patty's sister' and brother-in-law, Val and Eddie, had the basement apartment so you went into their place from the back of the building. A rusty glider covered in black soot sat on the cracked concrete patio outside their door. Val made pizza, greasy with bright-orange cheese, and Eddie had bought us a few bottles of Ripple wine as a treat.

The apartment was small. We sat around on the lumpy couch and on the floor, eating pizza, listening to records and drinking wine out of jelly glasses.

After we had a little bit of wine, we got out Eddie's "Magical Mystery Tour" album and tried to hear whether Paul was really dead, but we couldn't get it. We tried playing it backwards and at all different speeds, but we couldn't hear nobody saying, "Paul is dead."

"Wait, try it backwards on sixteen again," Patty said. "I think I heard something."

We all tilted our heads towards the record player while Eddie played the record again.

"There!" Patty insisted. "I heard it that time."

"Me, too," Erica echoed.

"You didn't hear nothing," Tony argued.

"Play it again," Patty told Eddie.

Eddie played the record again. Nothing.

"See, you didn't hear nothing," Tony said.

"A little case of overactive imagination, Pat," Eddie teased.

"Or too much wine," Roxanne added.

Patty flushed. "I didn't really hear anything. I was just trying to see if I could jag Erica into thinking she heard it."

"Yeah, sure," Val teased. We all laughed.

"I had her going," Patty insisted. She gave Erica a mean smile. "You really thought you heard something."

Erica blushed. "Maybe I was just being nice."

"I doubt that." Patty swung her hair and started flipping through Eddie's records. "Let's hear something good now."

She put on "Dance to the Music" and Roxanne and Tony started dancing. Wine glass still in hand, Donna grabbed Frankie's hand to get him to dance with her.

After "Dance to the Music," Val put on "Oh Girl" and Roxanne and Tony shifted to a slow dance. I thought Frankie would come get Erica for that one, or just sit down, but Donna grabbed on to him and he started slow dancing with her. I glanced over at Erica. She was still sitting on the thin, stained rug, hugging her knees, her back leaning against the couch, a phony little smile on her face, sipping her jelly glass of Ripple.

When the song was over, Frankie came back and sat on the floor beside her. "We've got to get going," she told him.

"I'm not ready to go," he argued.

"I have to be home by eleven. I have to go."

"Go ahead then."

Even though the lights were low, I could see Erica's face tighten and flush like someone slapped her.

"Hey, Eddie," Frankie called, getting up. "Is there any more of that wine?"

"Yeah, in the fridge. Remember, if you get caught, just don't go telling nobody where you got it."

"I won't, I won't," Frankie replied, heading to the kitchen.

I slid closer to Erica. "Do you want me to walk you to the trolley?" I asked.

She looked into my eyes for once. "That would be great," she replied.

"You ready now?"

She nodded.

"I'm going to walk Erica to the trolley," I announced to nobody in particular.

"I'm telling Frankie," Patty teased.

"Don't look like he cares," I said.

"Bye, thank you," Erica said. I guess she was talking to Eddie and Val, but she was looking off at one of the walls, so it was hard to tell.

It was one of those nights in September when you get a little cold snap, and neither of us was dressed for it. Erica just had on jeans and a ribbed blue body suit that laced up the front, no jacket. She walked with her arms crossed over her chest.

We walked along without talking until we got down to Carson, then I thought I should say something. "I don't know what's wrong with Frankie."

Erica shrugged.

"You're the best-looking girl that ever looked at him," I told her.

"Seriously. He's being a real fool."

"Thank you."

"I mean it I don't know what he's fooling around with Donna for. She's not really interested in him. Donna and Patty and Roxanne always used to make fun of him."

"I know."

We walked in silence a while longer. Finally, I said, "You have a nice house."

"Thanks."

"I'd like to have a house like that when I'm married. You know, with a yard and a garage. What does your dad do? For his job, I mean."

"He's a chemical engineer."

"Sounds like something I wouldn't be smart enough to do." I paused, seeing an opportunity. "You get along with your folks?"

"My mom's okay."

"How about your dad? You get along with him okay?"

She looked down at the ground, walking along, like she thought she might find a hundred-dollar bill there if she just stared hard enough. "He's okay."

"My dad's a little hard on me," I said.

"My hands are cold," she said. "Can I put my hand in your pocket?"

"Yeah, I guess."

It was a little awkward, walking with her hand in my back pants pocket. She had her other hand in her armpit. It had to be awkward for her, too. But I won't lie, it felt good. When we got to her trolley stop, I hesitated then pulled her to me and kissed her. I thought she'd stop me, but she didn't. Her lips were full and firm, and she didn't take her hand out of my pocket. I dared to put my hands in her back pockets and she still didn't stop me. I could feel the edge of her underwear under her jeans and got an instant hard-on. She didn't push away when I slid my tongue between her lips. Somewhere way in the back of my mind, I felt a little dirty, like I was taking advantage of her, but I didn't feel bad enough to stop.

I was starting to think of trying to feel her up, when I heard the rattle of the trolley coming. I broke away from her. Her lips were swollen from our kissing. She still didn't look me in the eye.

"You okay?" I asked, surprised that my voice sounded hoarse.

"Mm-hmm," she replied brightly.

I kissed her another time before she got on the trolley. She gave me a little wave from the inside as she walked back to a seat.

Frankie never called her no more after that. I didn't tell him I made out with her. I asked him one time about her, and he shrugged. "I just got a little tired of her," he said. "I needed to play the field a little." I didn't know what field he thought he was playing.

I seen Erica again downtown a few months later, holding hands with an older guy in a polyester suit. I was so surprised that at first I wasn't sure it was her. But it was her, alright. Her eyes kind of skittered over me, then she looked back at her new boyfriend and pretended she didn't see me. I was shocked to see her with a guy who had to be about thirty, but when I thought about it later, I realized I didn't ever really know her, and I remembered how easy it was to make out with her even when she was still supposed to be Frankie's girl.

Nothing ever came of the little thing between Frankie and Donna, which I knew nothing would.

But Frankie was different after that summer. He quit clowning for the girls so much, and he quit for good being Tony's cymbal for "In A Gadda Da Vida." That was getting kind of old anyhow. He got a job behind the counter in one of the pizza shops on Carson Street and bought himself contact lenses and lost weight. He started going out with another girl who was too cute for him, Marie Vespucci. Guy still dressed like a pimp, though. Made all kinds of tips at the pizza shop and bought new clothes and still looked like a fuckin' pimp.

Granny's Traveling Trunk

Karen Banks Pearson

Route 101 that ran through the five-block shopping district of Moreland Heights was closed to vehicle traffic, rerouting tankers and 18-wheelers, cars, and buses. Streets and sidewalks were peppered with vendors' sale signs atop stacks of wares, local amateur entertainers—comedians, singing groups, and restaurateurs preparing their specialty dishes of barbeque, tamales, corned beef and pastrami, burgers, Chicago hotdogs, and all the fixins'. Even ole' Mr. Archer, the baker, had a table and managed a smile and conversation, something that was difficult for him to muster when we stopped after school to buy a to-die-for apple slice pastry. Residents, young and old, came to feast, play games to win first-prize teddy bears or colorful thingies that twirled on a stick for a consolation prize, and also to stock up on new winter school clothes, hats, and gloves at a discount.

This was what Annual Street Bazaar day looked like every year, always held at the end of the work week, the last Friday before the beginning of the new school year. It outshone Christmas and the Independence Day parade, the other two special times that got the Heights buzzing. Days before the event, businesses stayed open longer so families could run their typical Saturday errands. The high energy and town's pace was felt in grocery store aisles where rushing mothers nearly bumped into each other with their baby buggies, in long lines at the bank, at the barber shops and beauty salons, dry cleaners, and the public utilities office.

On Bazaar day, one street over from the main attractions in the Serbian Orthodox Church parking lot, teenage boys challenged now-grown men who used to play on the championship high school teams to a high stakes basketball game. Girls either watched, played dodgeball, or jumped double dutch on the elementary school grounds. The younger kids sat in a circle listening to a freckled Howdy Doody, reading a Treasure Island story. There was a chorus of "oohs and aahs" when Clarabell, the clown, showed up ringing his bell.

"Hey kids, what time is it?" Howdy asked.

"It's Howdy Doody time," they shouted, then broke into the show's theme song.

Not wanting to break their spell, parents never told them that their principal and kindergarten teacher were in costume.

Bardensburg Steel Works, Moreland Heights' major employer and lead sponsor of the event, pulled out all the stops; it was the company's appreciation day to give back to the community.

Highlighting the festivities was the speech given by one of the Bardensburg family's founders to welcome the residents and thank employees. Daniel Stockman was the grandson of the state's first Jewish representative, a stout man, standing all of 5'6". His slumped-over posture did not match his deep, baritone, booming voice that, without a microphone, reached people standing in the back row. The way the stairs were set on the podium, Stockman, flanked by the chief of police with his shiny, gold-decorated lapel, the muscular fire captain, and owner of a chain of five-and-dime stores, seemed taller and more imposing than he was at street level.

"Good afternoon everyone. It is Bardensburg's distinct pleasure to host this annual event but it is you, the residents of this fine community, that make it a success. Each year, I proudly walk along the streets with you and meet fine business owners who make this city a vital beacon. Moreland Heights belongs to all of us; it's my home and the headquarters of the largest steel producer in The Region with a bright future. We're all in this together."

A rousing round of applause followed. A few mumbles could be heard in the back row,

"Bet he runs for mayor someday."

"Yeah, well, hope he signs our union contract before he leaves. I can use the extra money with cold weather coming and the high cost of coal—same coal we shove into those furnaces at the mill every day. We earned it."

A co-worker within earshot moved up close to whisper. "Hey, shhh, don't want any of the foremen or supervisors in the crowd to hear ya. 'sides, I hear the guy's on our side, wants to do the right thing."

It was a long day for my grandmother, a member of the Order of the Eastern Star that volunteered to staff the Bardensburg table every year. They distributed leaflets about the company and answered questions about civic matters such as where to vote in local elections, how to contact city councilmen, school holidays and such.

The Order's table was right next to the bakery. My grandmother and her friends helped Mr. Archer bring out trays of bite-sized apple slices, cinnamon twists, cookies, and other delicacies the bakery was known for. They were tempted to taste each one after breathing in the sugar-flour-butter mixtures wafting outside from the large commercial ovens.

Wiping their mouths and straightening their skirts, the ladies sat back to greet the visitors all the while their minds were on Mr. Archer's recent struggles. My grandmother remembered when Mr. Archer and his wife first opened the store. She also remembered their delight when their two children were born; she and Mrs. Archer would share niceties and family recipes when they ran into each other at the meat market. Not so much anymore. The Archers were still struggling with their youngest daughter's double pneumonia treatment.

The table-mates were reluctant to start a conversation with the baker. They were just glad that he agreed to participate in the Bazaar.

In hushed voices, "How do you think they are doing?"

"I don't know. I hear from the grocer that they aren't at church very often, and I don't see the Mrs. either."

"Is the daughter back in school?"

"No, she's probably going to miss this whole school year—was always a sickly child."

"Maybe the Order can make a donation. Do you think they will accept it? Some people are too proud to accept charity."

"Maybe they will feel better about it if it comes through the church."

"And, now that I'm thinking about it, we better tell the kids not to soap his store windows at Halloween if no one comes to the door. I think that might be why he's not too keen about them coming in the bakery after school. Still holding a grudge."

At 7 p.m., a voice through a bullhorn announced the Bazaar was nearing its end. Steelworkers, my uncles among them, along with police and firemen, lined the exits to hand out gift bags with movie tickets, baseball cards, Tootsie Rolls and penny candies, Kleenex, lotion, St. Joseph's aspirin, and a few other items that every family wanted to have on hand. The day-off from work or other responsibilities that the entire family looked forward to would soon be in the past—until next year.

"Here you go, little one, now don't eat too much candy all at once."

"Goodnight ma'am. It was good to see all of you. Hope you had a good time."

"See you Monday, Frank. I'll be working nights with you."

This community-minded spirit was evident throughout Moreland Heights. Bardensburg and a few other smaller industrial companies made it a *land of opportunity;* welcome signs reached far and wide to Western and Eastern Europe, for instance, from Serbia, Poland, Hungary, Czechoslovakia and in America's Deep South, Mexico, and Puerto Rico. The steelworkers worked side-by-side toward the same goal: make a decent living for their families. For the most part it was steady work for unskilled laborers inside the mill, also hard, hot, and dirty. Management employees enjoyed the benefits of a typically clean office environment along with prestige. Nevertheless, the familial connection associated with Bardensburg spilled over into the schools. Some elementary school students spoke their native language at home and learned English at school. They were translators for their parents. Children whose families moved from the places like Mississippi or Alabama were the translators of the ways of urban life. Isolation, though, was obvious as steelworkers walked different directions to and from their homes and different directions to and from their churches, depending on their ethnicity and, usually, slight differences in social class.

The segregated neighborhoods in Moreland Heights did not mirror the shared experience within the mill and in the integrated public schools. After work or school, each ethnic group went to their respective corners of the city, like boxers when the bell rings at the end of a boxing round. Churches and synagogues marked the people who lived in surrounding areas—restaurants and Spanish-Speaking residents on the west side, Blacks or Coloreds (1950-60's nomenclature) on the east, Jewish and Europeans on both the south and far north sides. Families with less means, economically, lived on the fringes, further isolated. In this respect, Moreland Heights was no different from many other American cities before the laws promoted by the Civil Rights Movement took full effect.

On the bright side, families lived and shared the tradition they brought with them from the "old world" to the "new." Shopkeepers helped blend cultures by the foods they sold or prepared; ingredients for a meal with Mexican-style chorizo and concha sweet bread, Polish cabbage rolls, goulash, collard greens, and more were easily found in most grocery stores. Babushka-wearing grandmothers on front porches could hear children on their way from school in unison,

"uno,"

"dos,"

"tres,"

"cuatro,"

"cinco,"

"seis,"

"siete,"

"ocho," and so on, practicing in Spanish the numbers their friends taught them. In elementary school, the children were immune to a separated way of life.

Since arriving in Moreland Heights from the Deep South when it was a young town with aspirations to be an industrial leader, my grandmother, Granny to us, saw the opportunity, to help build a good life for her family. She put her good instincts to work and went about integrating herself in community through church and volunteer activities, creating a network of friends and relationships with business owners that offered services like hairdressing, real estate renting, painting, plumbing, and other essentials. She was well acquainted, too, with Bardensburg operations through her husband who worked as a contractor.

Granny was well-known throughout the Heights' civic circles and a valuable resource. She and her Eastern Star colleagues ran clothing drives and delivered meals to the elderly. When a fire broke out on the dock, she organized a group of off-duty steelworkers who didn't have telephones to take over a shift at the mill while on-duty workers helped firefighters fight the blaze. During inclement winter weather, she coordinated a childcare service for children whose parents couldn't make it home from work.

"Reverend Hinton, Celia calling. Doing fine… but we need the recreation center tomorrow and maybe a coupla' days. Big snow storm coming, and the kids need someplace to go after school so they don't have to stay home and miss."

"It'll be ready, Miss Celia." It was a rare occasion when Reverend didn't come through. After all, Granny was prompt with her tithing even if she didn't make it to Sunday worship.

Granny knew what education meant. Helping out on her family's farm had interfered with her schooling, and the sting of not finishing high school was ever-present. You wouldn't know it, though, by her air of confidence, evident by her community connections. They came in handy as one-by-one younger family members "down South" expressed an interest in moving Up North. Over about a 12-year period, she, made numerous trips South and returned with relatives, sometimes husband, wife, and children. Through her network, newcomers to Moreland were able to find housing and start work immediately, usually at Bardensburg Steel or retailers in the area. A few started their own trucking or construction businesses—and a few returned South. Others got married and moved on to other states, taking their new-found confidence and awareness of living outside the South with them.

As she slowed down with age, Granny enjoyed rocking on her front porch swing, watching children play hopscotch and riding their scooters alongside their mothers walking to the corner store. She had plenty of visitors who stopped by with updates on goings-on in the town.

Granny was in the 10th decade of her life when she passed on quietly without much fanfare, until her funeral. The service was a joyous celebration in her honor and in remembrance of the lives that she helped change for the better. A single white rose sat in her place in the front pew next to her Bible. Some voices quivered as family members shared their memories.

The choir uplifted everyone when it belted out Granny's favorite soul-stirring gospels, a song by the Five Blind Boys of Alabama and Mahalia Jackson's "Move on Up a Little Higher."

"Gonna put on my robe in Glory,
I'm going home, one day, tell my story.
I been climbing over hills and mountains,
will drink that ol' healing water.
Meet me there, early one morning,
somewhere 'round the altar..."

Toe-tapping church members waved hand-held fans portraying Reverend Hinton's family rose up out of their seats and clapped in tune with the piano and drums. "Amens" pierced through the music at, "Meet me there, oh, when the angels shall call God's roll."

***

It was a hot August day but to accommodate all of the guests, dinner was served outside after the service rather than in the small church's basement. White circular tables seated six and were spread about on the lawn behind the church close to the trees to shield us from the sun's piercing gaze. As I took my seat at one of the tables, I joined an uncle close to Granny's age and several cousins deep in conversation. They were reminiscing about living with Granny when they first arrived Up North. Someone referred to her as "the conductor of the *above* ground railroad." My ears perked up, since the "*underground railroad*" was a specific reference to Harriet Tubman, known as the "Moses of her people" and her heroic travels, and I had never heard that version of the term used to describe my grandmother. Her birth name was Celia, but the family had a few different nicknames—Big Sister, and Cee-Cee, but I had never heard "conductor of the *above* ground railroad." I settled into my seat, hoping they would say more. Everyone seemed to be talking at the same time, thoroughly engaged and oblivious to my arrival.

Uncle Emmett, bald now and stooped over, making him appear shorter than the six-foot frame of his youth, quieted the separate conversations when he asked in his quiet, unassuming voice, "Did you all see that old, green trunk?"

I looked at each of their faces and saw eyes with far-away looks, but no one offered an answer. They just held onto the half smiles that memory brought. I suddenly had a memory of my own. I could see an army-green colored trunk in the hallway between two bedrooms with stacks of quilts and pillows neatly arranged on top. It suddenly occurred to me that I never saw anyone open that trunk and, even as a child, was never curious about its contents.

The clanging of dishes and belly laughs brought my attention back to the present as plates of food arrived. Sugar and ice twirled around in the bronze-colored iced tea. Uncle Earl had Gloria doubled over as he told a particular story about how he could never fool Granny. It didn't take much to get Gloria going; she could be counted on for a hearty laugh even when others only smiled politely at a joke.

"Celia was always one step ahead of me," he said in between gulps of laughter, "especially when it came to money. She knew my paydays and kept a good record of what I owed. One day I told her that I got paid on Fridays, that she had me mixed up with my brother's payday.

She looked at me long and hard and said 'And exactly when did your brother even work long enough to get a payday?'"

Granny held the special distinction as the only female in her immediate family. A Southern girl who married at 18, she moved to Moreland Heights with her husband, a lead man on a construction crew that built coal-fueled steel plants near the shores of Lake Michigan, Ohio, and as far east as Connecticut. Granny's long life answered my prayer that the children I would eventually have would get to know her.

I knew as a young child that she answered other prayers, too. She was the center of attention in the family and on our side of town. Relatives and friends stopped by to visit on a regular basis; some had a particular day of the week, like Miss Emma, who visited Granny every Tuesday after "doing her banking business." Miss Emma always brought some sort of sliced meat, cheese, and crackers. Granny would take a break from ironing—Tuesday was her ironing day—and she and Miss Emma would eat lunch and talk for hours which sometimes lasted until near dinnertime. We children thought Miss Emma a mysterious woman; we never heard about children, a husband, or any details about her life. We only knew about her friendship with Granny who didn't share anything about Miss Emma either—true to the times when children didn't inquire about grown-folks' business.

Granny was short and serious about most things but loved a good story and a good joke. Her facial expression always seemed to be grimacing, like she had a difficult matter on her mind, especially when cleaning, laundering, or cooking a meal. To her, those were not just chores but responsibilities, "Seemed like they were handed down to her by the Good Lord," I once heard someone say, "and the day was not a good one unless the chores were completed and done well."

The pride she felt was evident when she yelled over the clothes line to her neighbor, "Just finished two loads of clothes. Have to get them on the line before it rains and got ironing to do, too, before putting dinner on the table."

If all was well, Granny's conversations always seemed to be about production… work to do, work that was finished, or work that was going to be done the next day. Only when someone had a problem that needed attention or an illness of some sort, did I hear a casual, "Hi, how are you, how's the family, do you need anything today?"

After settling in the North, Granny took trips as often as she could back home to where her mother, father, and siblings and other relatives still lived. Uncle Earl, now in his 80's, was one of the first relatives to ride the "above ground railroad" on one of Granny's return trips Up North. He would accompany her many times over the years to transport other family members and was describing one of them when my mind circled back into the present conversation. I noticed that several more people had joined our table. Their chairs formed a balcony.

"We boarded the Regal Express Line train out of Chicago and road it all the way south to the last stop closest to the Alabama state line," Uncle Earl told the crowd as he shifted his body to a comfortable position and rested an elbow on the table.

"That trip took over 24 hours, but Celia's....most folks started calling her Granny after she took in the grandchildren...her fried chicken, tea cakes, and lemonade kept us going. She always packed the food in a brown paper box and carried it into the passenger section with us, but that large green trunk a..." he pointed to church porch where the trunk stood with its gold metal caps on each of the four corners "...that went to the baggage compartment to be unloaded when we got to Reynoldstown. You know, Celia always carried a gift or two for her parents and brothers, but she never would let us pack too much because we had to have room in the trunk for whoever was coming with us on the return trip. When we got off the train, Celia would stand quietly with her hands folded, waiting and watching as the porter unloaded the trunk before we went into the station. She was making sure the train wasn't going to move an inch with that trunk still on it."

Uncle Emmett lifted his frame just high enough to peer beyond shoulders to get a good look at the big green structure sitting stately on the porch. Uncle Earl moved over slightly to give him a better view and then continued reminiscing.

"By the time we pulled in front of Junior's house—you all know Junior," Uncle Earl continued. "We weren't hungry but were ready for a good night's rest. We had to get up early to finish our journey. The next day, Junior arranged for someone to drive us to Celia's folks' house in Oakville, another 30 miles."

The ride to Oakville took my grandmother and her traveling companions down a two-lane highway through the outskirts of rural towns, one mirroring another. They passed cotton, corn, pecan trees, and vegetable gardens on small farms, sometimes with a grazing cow or chickens running underneath the houses raised on stilts. Tractors and other farm equipment and, maybe, a car was visible through open, sagging barn doors. Barefoot children stomped in water puddles recent heavy rains left behind and swung from huge walnut tree branches. These scenes reminded them of their childhoods, the many days they spent planting and harvesting on those small farms, and what they left behind to create new lives.

"When we got there, one of Celia's brothers, a cousin or two, or maybe even a friend of the family were waiting, belongings in bags and crates, sitting next to the door ready for the next week's travel or whenever Celia gave a signal that it was time to go," Earl remembered.

"Anyone who left with us came away with mixed emotions, leaving behind a sharecropping life, no real chance for a good education but they had close family ties, and what they knew as *home*. But, their minds were made up, and they were stepping out on faith that there would be a better life in the North. That's what made for feeling less guilt."

"So, for about a week, me and Celia would make the rounds, visiting family, friends, worshipping at church, and helping out with chores 'round the house. Many evenings after supper, we would sit on her mother's and father's porch in steamy, hot nights and Granny would tell stories about city life, towns folk from foreign countries, all over the world, who spoke different languages, cooked different foods, and who grew up much further away than the South. We told them about all the work people could find. Yes, they washed clothes, cooked, and worked as janitors but there were also teachers and nurses, too, doctors even. Celia even told them that they got friendly with a Pullman porter they met on several train trips."

We listened intently as Earl described how my great-grandparents received these tales. Though Granny and my grandfather offered, they never had any interest in making one of those trips North.

"With the mention of the Pullman porters, a pleasant look came upon her mother's and father's faces," he said. "If they knew about it, they didn't say anything about the Pullmans striking for better pay and work conditions. Always sitting quietly, the relatives who were about to make the journey back North were wide-eyed and anxious-looking. I knew all the thoughts running through their minds."

I imagine most of the conversation on that porch must have sounded like fantasy to my great-grandparents, nothing like what they knew or must have heard from their own parents and grandparents about life during Reconstruction after the Civil War.

Earl continued to tell the group about how the days went before it was time to make the return trip: Celia made arrangements to get to the train station. Like a real railroad conductor, she made a last call for everyone to put their belongings at the front door next to the trunk. One by one, she placed their sacks with a few personal possessions down in the trunk, closed the lid, and placed the lock on the large metal hinge. The key went into her bosom.

The next day, Celia put her brown-striped sweater around her shoulder, placed the flat straw hat on her head and with those motions, everyone knew it was time to go. There were hugs and moist eyes as one of Celia's brothers—not the oldest who helped her father run the farm—a cousin, his wife and toddler all climbed into the borrowed car, courtesy of the department store owner who employed many in Oakville. Word had passed that another trip Up North was taking place that Sunday morning so from neighboring farms, young girls, boys, and new fathers and mothers with babies on their hips stood in the front yard waving goodbye.

As Earl continued, there wasn't a sound from the funeral-dinner guests.

"We rode the 30 miles back to the train station, and when we arrived, Celia handed the driver a few folded bills, then went into the train station to buy the tickets. Then we all sat quietly, just waiting. Cousin B and his wife and young child sat clinging to each other. Everyone watched Celia, but no one moved unless she moved. Even though they were still in the South's familiar surroundings, they were already having new experiences… riding in a new car, sitting in a train station with scribbled lettering directing colored and white folk to their assigned drinking fountains and bathrooms, and about to board a train for the first time.

"I knew exactly what they were feeling because I remembered well my first trip. It wasn't an easy feelin'," Uncle Earl said, almost in a whisper.

One of the college students, hearing about life and times that must have seemed like ancient history, excused himself while he reached over empty bowls and a half-empty platter of cornbread to grab a white paper napkin to take notes of the conversation.

"Well," in a louder voice now, as he looked around and nodded to the minister and his wife who had pulled up a chair. "We made it that trip and I don't know how many more. Emmett over there was that toddler I spoke of. He went on to make the family proud, went to college, and retired from teaching. Most of us went to work in the steel mills and made a good living, married, had children, bought homes. One close friend of mine got on with the Pullman's, rode the train for a while, then moved back South. He did okay farming as things began to change in the South… still came Up North to visit, though, from time to time."

After people were full of cake, pie, and homemade ice cream and were ready to escape the heat, they began to say their goodbyes, hugged, and made promises to keep in touch. On the church porch, they filed past the large, green, weather-beaten trunk one last time, pausing to look at photos and mementos of a full life. Some saw themselves in family photos lying next to a now-frayed apron they saw Granny wear on many occasions, a voter's registration card, a newspaper clipping with a photo of her son receiving his U.S. Army officer stripes, a candle with "92" from her last birthday cake, a page announcing the Bardsensburg Christmas party she helped organize, and a 1952 receipt for a train ticket on the Regal Express Line.

Smokestack Polka

Patrick Michael Finn

My older cousin Irene—we called her Reenie for short—got married six months after my father died.

The three of us—me, my mother, my older brother Jimmy—were still living on Landau Street then, two blocks from the Joliet railyards where my father had worked, and where, many years later, my brother and I got jobs when we finished high school. I know things could have been much worse for us. There hadn't been any agonizing months or even weeks of a gray, thinning illness with my father, but a stiff heart attack that kicked him flat as he walked home from work one night two weeks before Halloween. The railroad union relief fund and life insurance checks started coming in right away, so there weren't any worries about food, clothes, or housing. My mother, a nurse at Mercy Hospital, had only taken a week off work after the funeral, and still made sure we got our meals, and our asses out of bed in the morning to get to school on time.

Still, things were far from calm. I was only eleven, and the loss I felt was rooted in confusion, though I clearly remember knowing that my father was gone for good. I knew this even when I took to sitting on the stoop at dusk those first few weeks (something I'd never done when my father was alive), just to see what the sky above the neighborhood looked like at the time he should have been walking home from the yards. It was almost winter and the sun was gone by five, leaving the air purple and cold behind the rickety skyline of bare trees, phone poles, smokestacks, and steeples.

The tired, steady shuffle of yard workers would pass in their oily blues, coughing over filterless Camels and Pall Malls they clutched in their dirty fists. A few of them would wave or nod when they saw me, but most would hush and look at the ground, frightened by me, the little porch orphan who might have mistook one of them for his dead father and tried to follow him home. I wasn't waiting for anyone, but my mother thought I was being melodramatic.

"Come inside," she finally told me. "This is the hardest time of the day for me and I don't want to be in the house by myself. Besides, it's not healthy for you to sit out here in the cold like this every night. It won't change anything."

I think dusk was even harder on my older brother, Jimmy, who was fourteen and hadn't been home for those hours in weeks. Father Zajc had told our mother to let Jimmy have extra time with his friends, so long as he tried to keep up with his studies and chores. But Jimmy wasn't keeping up with his studies; he'd just started high school a few months before and the deficiency notices were already coming to the house. My mother hadn't found these letters, since Jimmy always got to the mail while she was still at work. I watched him burn them in the dirt behind our garage, and he said if I told our mother about them he'd knock me into next month.

After my mother made me come inside that night, I followed her into the kitchen and watched her rinse cabbage in the sink. I realized she wanted me to be there with her, but I didn't know what I was supposed to say or do, so I stood by the table with my hands locked behind me and stared at her back, the floor, her back again, tense and thankful that at least the sink water was filling our silence. She shut off the faucet, braced her hands on the sink, then looked out the window and shook her head.

"The hell with Father Zajc," she said; I flinched because I'd never heard anyone, especially my mother, say something like that about a priest. "Jimmy's my son," she said. "Mine. I don't care what Father Zajc says. My son belongs at home."

She turned from the window and stared at me for a while, as if she was waiting for me to either agree with or argue what she'd just said. "Go find your brother," she told me.

"Right now?" I said.

"Yes," she said. "Go find him. Please. Get him home for dinner."

I was glad to get out of that kitchen, but I hated having to take Jimmy away from his friends because I knew he'd get mad and probably lose his temper. He knew how to channel his rage into painful abuse that didn't leave any marks, that never left black eyes or split lips or bloody noses. He'd grab a lock of my hair and pull until I squealed, twist my arm behind me and yank so that my wrist was only inches from the back of my neck. I never told on Jimmy, but not because

I was afraid of what he might do to me if I did. I never told on him because he always made up for what he'd done before I had the chance to get him in trouble.

"Hey, hey," he'd say if I started to cry. "Come on, I'm sorry. I'm sorry."

As angry and hurt as I was, I'd believe him, especially when he'd point to his gut or cheek and say, "Go ahead, hit me back."

I took him up on his offer a few times. He squinted, yelped, fell over, even though none of my weak punches deserved that kind of response. I knew he was faking the pain, and even that made me feel better.

Jimmy hadn't touched me since our father's death, and I wanted things to stay that way, so that night I looked for him at all the spots where I knew he wouldn't be: Andy and Sophie's, the corner tavern packed for Monday Night Football; the Hrvatski Kulturni Klub, a place where the neighborhood's oldest men played jukebox polkas and coughed war stories over games of barbudi and cards and short glasses of red brandy. Then I went to the Laundromat, bright, empty, and warm, and though I was freezing I didn't dare go inside, since I knew that Mrs. Kodiak, the crazy, starving widow who lived in the apartment above the place, would cram me into a dryer the second I stepped inside; Saint Sabina's, my family's parish, where I sat in a pew in the back long enough to warm myself, then got scared of the way the vigil candles made wavy shadows on the faces of the painted statues, so that their eyes and mouths looked evil and animated under thorns and drops of blood. I ran out of there and headed home so I could tell my mother I couldn't find Jimmy.

Two blocks from the house I cut through someone's yard and walked down the alley between Landau and Dearborn. I knew my mother would be waiting for me at the front door, and I didn't want her to see me coming home empty-handed. I stepped on the cold, cracked alley pavement slowly, stalling the moment when I'd have to disappoint my mother, when I'd have to lie to her face and tell her how I'd honestly tried to find my older brother. I knew she'd ask where I'd looked, and as I shuffled alongside the darkened rows of garbage cans, I made up a dishonest list of answers: Aladdin's Arcade, the schoolyard, Cheney Drug, and, where I actually did find Jimmy that night, the alley behind our house.

I saw him about half a block ahead under the white glow of a streetlight that hung from a phone pole near the corner, and I immediately ducked behind a garage and watched him from the shadows. He was with five of his friends, all of whom were crouched in the circle around something I couldn't see. Jimmy stood above and behind them, smoking. I thought at first that his friends were trying to set something on fire; whatever they were doing in the circle was a struggle that made them curse and jerk. Then the largest of them, Mike Rhomza, held a brick above his head and brought it down with a grunt that made the others laugh. My brother took a quick last drag off his cigarette, flicked it away, then crossed his arms and said, "Okay, for Chrissakes, quiet. Now bring it up."

The boys in the circle hushed, stood straight, and backed away. Jimmy already had another cigarette going. In charge, giving orders that were followed without question, casually smoking like a champ of old habit, my brother Jimmy had assumed the role of a grownup: maybe a cop or a railyard hack—maybe our father. I felt like running out from behind the garage and begging to be included in whatever they were doing, to be told what to do, to have unreasonable orders barked at me. I would have done anything he'd asked. But when Mike Rhomza turned from the circle and dropped the brick so that his other hand was free, he was covered in the glow of the streetlight, and I could see everything: his red winter cap, maroon coat, and the wounded, shaking gray cat he clutched with both hands by its neck.

"Hurry up," Mike said. "This fucking cat stinks like shit. I don't want to get its goddamned germs."

One of the boys picked up the brick and another produced a hammer and rusted rail spike, and again the group gathered in a circle around the illuminated phone pole, this time to nail the cat to the wood through the loose skin on its back. The animal's head shot back and its mouth stretched open, but only a dull hiss came from it. By then I was huffing the kind of hot breaths someone has right before he throws up, but I didn't look away until after the boys backed up to pitch rocks and bottles at the dangling cat, didn't leave my hiding spot until I watched Jimmy wind up a horrid brick pitch that crushed the cat's head and ended the game. Then I lost it, ran through another yard and back onto Landau. I thought I might puke and didn't want to get caught from the gushing sound. Only a small part of me was sick from watching such a graphic torture. The rest of me was sick simply from knowing my older brother Jimmy was capable of such a thing.

My mother was waiting behind the front door when I got home. "What's the matter?" she said. "The color's all gone from your face."

"Nothing," I said, trying to get past her. "I couldn't find Jimmy is all. I looked everywhere."

She stopped me, anyway, turned me around by both shoulders and lifted my head up with her thumb under my chin. "You're a sheet," she said, touching my cheek to check for a fever. I didn't think I was tough enough to hide what I knew from my mother and waited for her to pull the truth from me with a long list of questions.

But she never did. "I shouldn't have sent you out running in the cold like that," was all she said. "You're sick now," she said, and I knew I was off the hook. She made up a plate of crackers and sent me upstairs to bed, assuring me I'd have to stay home from the school the next day, a kind of gift, I believed, for enduring the chaos of searching and scheming and lying on behalf of my big brother, who should have been caught and brought home in the first place.

I lay in bed for an hour before Jimmy finally got back. Though our house had two floors, it was small enough to tell from upstairs where exactly people were talking, especially if they were arguing, and my mother hadn't let Jimmy get any further than the front door. They were at it down there, yelling, shouting, yelling, back and forth and over each other so that I couldn't even make out what was said. Then I heard Jimmy march upstairs, and when he slammed the bedroom door behind him I jolted, pretending he'd woken me up, though he didn't notice one way or the other. He dropped his coat on the floor and sat on his bed without looking at me. His black hair was dirty and hung an inch over the collar of his red flannel shirt. I sniffed the air he'd brought in with him for cat blood, but I only picked up the salty yellow smell of cigarettes. I was propped up on my elbows, watching Jimmy and waiting for him to regard me, but he only stared at the floor, sucked on a finger stained by smoke, shook his head and muttered, "Shit," drawing the word out in a long whisper like he really meant it.

"Where were you?" I finally asked him, ready to catch him in a lie.

"Back in the alley," he said. Then he looked at me with his gray eyes that had grown deeper and more circled in the short time since our father's death. "We found a cat in the garbage back there, a stray. And we killed it. It was my idea to kill it and we did. I don't even know why."

"How did you kill it?" I said.

"Does it matter?" he said, very empty and defeated. "Just don't tell Mom. Please. She's already on my ass for being out all the time."

I nodded, and Jimmy got up to leave. He opened the door, looked in the hallway, then closed it again and said:

"Mom says you're sick from running around looking for me. I know you could have found me. Why didn't you look in the alley?"

"I did."

"You did," he said, and crossed his arms. His circled eyes got narrow and hard. "Then why the hell didn't you say so? Why the hell did you have to ask me what I did?"

I got scared when he walked over to my bed. "You saw what I did?" he said.

"Yeah," I told him.

He asked me in stiff whispers why I hadn't told our mother, why I'd lied to her, and in my frightened silence, Jimmy started to look nervous. He crossed and uncrossed his arms then put them on his hips. He turned around in a half circle and ran his hands through his hair. And then he turned to me and said:

"Did you lie because you're scared of me, or because I'm your brother?"

Of course, I'd lied out of fear, but by then Jimmy's regret had convinced me to believe that he wasn't completely a monster, convinced me to see him as someone, however brutal and careless, to look up to. Why I'd lied wasn't important to me. I only wanted Jimmy to see that I had, and he did, and knowing this made him squirm. In the end, I never answered his question.

"I don't want you to lie for me," he said. "I'm not worth it." He turned to leave, shut off the light, and opened the door. But before he walked through it and closed it behind him to leave me alone in the dark, he stared at me for a second and said:

"But if you have to lie, do it because I'm your brother."

***

Most nights my father came home from work with hardly enough energy to talk, but I still don't blame his distance. He worked outside for ten-hour shifts in the vast open railyards. And season after season, he was battered by choking humidity, and by sub-zero winds that froze the ground solid as rail steel. He was a big man, but never awkward or lumbering, and his nightly six packs of Old Style at the kitchen table never made him soft. Neither did the hot, rich breakfasts he had every winter morning, those enormous platters that probably killed him: biscuits drenched in pork gravy, fried eggs and sardines covered with ketchup, salted sausage and home fries, gallons of whole milk and black coffee. None of that stuff—his beer, two-pack Camel habit, bad food—ever made my father look wrecked and stuffed, like most of the men on our block. He cared about the way people saw him: scrubbed, trimmed, and filed his nails; pressed his own shirts and slacks for Sunday Mass; kept his black hair (the same shade he gave to Jimmy) set neatly and slicked back against his head with two fingertips of Royal Crown hair dress.

As strong and dapper as he was, those railyard shifts kicked the hell out of him, made him so quiet, so gone even with us that I feared him, and wish that he'd at least raise his voice when Jimmy and I made too much racket. "Oh, Christ on His throne," was sometimes all he'd say, if he said anything at all, a mumble like someone talking in his sleep. He brought home those mumbles and groans each night with his cigarettes and beer, and kept them in the kitchen with the hands he rested his face in, with the elbows he kept propped on the table, until he knew, after two or three hours, that he was seconds from falling asleep like that, right there with the salt and pepper, the napkin dispenser, his beer can and ashtray. If my mother was at the sink, he'd get up and finish his beer next to her and stare out the window, his other tired hand rubbing her back. Then he'd pad away to bed, where he'd drop out for nine hours of numb, thoughtless sleep.

My father wasn't the kind of man who gave any form of daily credence to religion. The only time I saw him pray was in church, and even the acts of crossing himself and mumbling responses and taking communion were too quick and mechanical for someone who made any effort to attend, let alone for someone who never thought about Christ or the Virgin one way or the other. He went to church for my mother, who went to church for her children. The cross was just wood, and the body on it plaster, and my father never said a single word to us, his boys, about why any of it mattered. And so I'm still confused, baffled as all hell, really, when I think about my father's relationship with Christmas, how the tinsel and tacky strings of lights came over him, how gullible he was to get lifted in spirit by little more than a month wrapped in silver green plastic.

I don't know what went through his head to make him love the red sweaters and dopey songs; he simply did, and just about every December night after work he was moved to turn the kitchen into a Christmas party. Jimmy and I could have gotten sick on all the candy he brought home for us, bags of chocolate bars still cold from the drugstore icebox, red vines, snow balls, and chunks of brown powdered nougat. And other nights there were bags of wonderful, useless things he'd bring us from the job, like mesh railroad caps, union buttons, pens and pocket protectors, tape measures, rulers, keychains, inch-long squeeze lights, all of these things colored red, white, and blue, etched with crests and insignias and slogans from the Local Brotherhood, *Ten Decades of Dignity* printed around tiny images of eagles and black fists clutching hammers.

My father certainly didn't drink any less that time of year, but his six packs failed to drag him into the exhaustion that usually pulled him away from the rest of us. The beer put a pink warmth in his face and hours of easy laughter in his chest, and it made him want to slow dance around the kitchen with my mother while they took turns sipping from the same can, the only time I saw my mother drink. His Christmas beers turned him into a magician who knew how to make a cigarette vanish in his ear or up his nose, then appear with a snap from the corner of his mouth before he lit it to blow a long row of smoke rings, perfect and round as quarters, white rolling circles that Jimmy and I would poke with our fingers and struggle to catch in our hands.

Upstairs in bed, our heads buzzing from all that chocolate, Jimmy and I would lay awake and listen to our mother and father laugh together in the kitchen, a sound as distinct and memorable as the silence that would follow, when I knew they were kissing. I'm sure they took each other to bed every one of those nights, and since Jimmy and I both have birthdays in September, I'm sure that Christmas was what urged our father to make us.

And that's why that first one without him was so goddamn miserable. The three of us spent a Saturday putting up the tree and the ornaments, and my mother played holiday albums on the stereo. Other than the few times we spoke to one another that afternoon, we worked in a disconnected, joyless quiet, which seemed ridiculous next to the Como, Crosby, and Sinatra carols, those stupid songs that never seem to care about people in pain.

Once the last ornament was placed on the branch, and once the string of lights went on, my mother held her arms out before the tree and said, "There," as if telling Jimmy and me to behold some greatness we'd created in that box of a living room. "There," she said, and shook her head. Then she let out a sob and went to her bedroom.

"What happened?" I said.

Jimmy shut the stereo off, and through the silence that was left we could hear our mother's muffled crying from behind her bedroom door.

"What the hell you think happened?" Jimmy said. He leaned against the stereo and lit a cigarette, pretending he didn't care about getting caught. He took tough, obvious drags and blew the smoke up toward the ceiling.

"You know you could get in trouble for that," I said.

"So what?" he said. "Why don't you go get Mom and tell her what a bad guy I am?" He cupped the ashes in his hand and puffed away. Soon there was a smug little cloud of cigarette smoke above the Christmas tree.

Then Jimmy got tired of this arrogant show and put on his coat to leave. "Stop being such a little goddamn girl," he said, and slammed the front door on his way out.

Then it was just me and the tree, a mean, towering thing that blinked and took up too much room, an unwanted guest we'd brought in ourselves to remind us of how badly things were going. I wanted to pull it down and drag it into the street, lights, ornaments, and all, but I didn't want to wake my mother. There were no more sounds from her bedroom. I knew she'd cried herself to sleep.

***

My mother never made a habit of breaking down and hiding in her room. But I'm sure she wanted to, especially when life with her oldest son became a daily trial she was forced to hold up on her own. She found out about the whole cat ordeal right after the first of the year, from a mother of one of the younger boys who'd been back there in the alley that night. The kid had finally cracked and spilled the story after weeks of nightmares and a dangerous loss of appetite. Jimmy had made him do it, is what the kid told his mother.

"Why on earth?" was all my mother could say to Jimmy before she reluctantly took him to see Father Zajc. She didn't even yell at him. Jimmy is a boy without a father, she must have thought. Why else would he do such a thing? And she didn't yell when Jimmy's burned and buried deficiency notes caught up with him, when the school finally called one night to see why she hadn't responded to the several warning letters they'd sent to let her know that Jimmy was failing all of his classes.

"Jimmy, you've got to try harder," she said, then took him again to see Father Zajc. *Jimmy's a good boy,* she must have thought. *A good boy in a slump without his father.*

Or maybe she scolded him more once they left the house, on the three-block walk to and from the parish, and maybe Jimmy cried, or simply fooled her into thinking he was better than he actually was, just like all the times he did the same after twisting my limbs and yanking my hair. But I don't know for sure, since both of them worked hard to keep these matters from me. Night after night I'd get sent to my room after parents, teachers, and God knows who else would call to tell her about something Jimmy had done, and from my bed I'd hear the murmured pleas and whines between my mother and older brother downstairs. I'd only catch corners of what they said, hopeless questions about broken windows my mother would have to pay for, skipped classes, shoplifting, fistfights. And when Jimmy would finally make his way upstairs I'd try to find out what had happened, but he'd only stare at the ceiling from his bed and say, "Nothing," or pull the blanket over his head and turn to face the wall without saying a word.

Then most Saturday afternoons the two of them would go see our priest. "Going to church," is what my mother called it, but I knew this wasn't actually true since she never invited me to go along. I know she never wanted to listen to an aging man who'd never had children tell her how she should raise one of her own, tell her why her boy was acting the way he was, but by then everyone in the neighborhood was watching, and most were shaking their heads behind her back, this poor young widow who didn't know how to control her boys. So she gulped back her anger and did what she was supposed to do. She kept her head and her pride and walked those blocks each week to show the world that she knew what was best for her children.

But something in my mother swung wide open one Saturday afternoon in March, the day we got the invite to my cousin Reenie's wedding. The three of us had just finished lunch when my mother went to get the mail, and when she got back to the kitchen table I could tell something was wrong. The invitation came from my father's side of the family, and it was addressed to us, but under my father's name. It might have been a dumb mistake, or a stab at the way my mother had handled Jimmy. Either way, seeing her dead husband's name on the envelope made my mother cry. Her tears were slow and quiet, but they still welled up and rolled.

Jimmy grabbed the envelope and read what was written on the front. "Reenie," he said. "What a stupid fucking cunt."

My mother gasped. Her final strain of reason had been snapped. She reached over the table and slapped Jimmy flush across the face.

"Don't," she said. "Don't ever say that, goddamn you."

Jimmy held his face wide-eyed for a moment, stunned.

"Don't," my mother said.

But Jimmy ran right out the front door. He didn't come back for three long days, and even the cops seemed worried. My mother didn't sleep the first night, and a doctor she worked with at Mercy came the next day and made her take tranquilizers. Aunts and uncles and older cousins, Father Zajc, all crowded our house, came and went searching the streets on foot, and in cars throughout the city. Everyone told my mother to stay put, and for three days she did just that, dark-eyed, doped up, then frantic, until finally she couldn't take another minute of that house.

"What are you doing?" my Uncle John asked from the kitchen table.

"Looking for my son," she said.

"Hold it," he told her, but it was too late. She slammed the door and marched down the sidewalk. I ran after her, but she told me to get back inside and wait with Uncle John.

"I'm going to find him," she said. "I promise. That's it."

Two hours later she was back at the house, her promise intact. Jimmy was dirty and looked three years older. He saw her from wherever he'd been hiding, and her futile, searching look had moved him to give up and come out.

"You can tell everyone to quit looking," she told Uncle John. "Go tell them. I'll thank them all in person when I get the chance."

Jimmy was guzzling water at the sink, glass after glass until he broke a sweat.

"Maybe Jimmy should stay with us for a while," said Uncle John, who looked more angry than relieved.

"No, thank you," my mother told him. "I don't think he should. I don't think that would be right at all."

***

It was settled: we were going to Rennie's wedding, and my mother didn't want to hear another word about it. And not only were we going to the wedding, but to the reception at the V.F.W. Cantigney Hall later that night. We'd been invited, and we were going. Jimmy and I even got new shoes and suits from Goldblatt's downtown, and from the time we got up that Saturday morning until the time we left the house later that afternoon, my mother was rushed in the act of priming herself and her boys for this event. Jimmy was terrified of facing everyone after all he'd done and begged my mother to let him stay home.

"Just tell them I'm sick," he said. "I can't go. They're all going to stare at me."

"They probably will," she told him. "I don't really blame them, either."

We finally left and walked up the block toward the church. The sidewalks were already crowded, since just about everyone in the neighborhood had been invited. People who saw us seemed surprised, even shocked, but they hid this with forced smiles and greetings, asking if we planned on going to the reception.

"Well why wouldn't we?" my mother said. "Of course, we're going."

A block from the church, my mother took us around a corner to tell us something nobody else would hear.

"Now listen to me," she said. "We're going to this wedding because nobody here thinks I can take care of you on my own, and I need them to see that I can. Because I can. Have you boys gone without a meal since your dad died? I gave you a good Christmas and your clothes are always clean. So for God's sake, don't do anything that'll give these people something else to say behind our backs when we pass them. Do you understand this?"

We nodded, then walked on for the church.

An hour later, my cousin Reenie was a truckdriver's wife.

***

After Mass, the sun set while we waited in the reception line that stretched around the corner of Cantigney Hall and halfway down the block. Since we'd sat at the back of the church, we were the last to leave, the last to walk over to the hall, and among the last in the long line. Jimmy and I wanted to take our ties off, but our mother said we had to look our best to congratulate Rennie and her new husband, Norb Dzurko. I could tell Jimmy was nervous; with a lowered face he bit his nails and looked around to see if anyone was watching him.

"Stop with the nails," my mother told him. "And stand up straight."

Jimmy stopped and straightened without hesitation, without rolling his eyes, without a word, and I wondered what she'd told him to whip him into such obedient fear. Though he might have looked older when he came back from running away, he'd cowered like a child ever since. He even seemed too scared to talk to me, and in a way I felt like I'd become *his* older brother. But I didn't like looking at Jimmy this way. I felt embarrassed for him, this tough older brother I'd looked up to for so long, suddenly soft stepping and frightened like a bullied playground runt.

The line around the hall finally started moving, and the last pink hint of dusk darkened to show stars and a full moon over rooftops to the east. We passed the back of the building, and then the guzzling rumble of a rowdy car sounded from the street behind us, and I turned to see a glitter-black Monte Carlo tear into the small lot behind the hall, a White Sox night game blaring from the radio inside. The driver was Jack Tomczak, who had worked with my father at the yards. I'd heard my father talk about Tomczak, how he'd choke down pills with whiskey during lunch, and how he'd sit in his car and do coke before he clocked in for his shift. There were other rumors about Tomczak, even darker ones that dealt with the beatings he gave his wife before she finally left him, and so when he pulled himself from the car that night, parked by itself in back beside the rusted red Dumpster, I knew he was some kind of enemy.

Tomczak called my mother's name, waved, then jogged over to wait with us in line. "Private parking," he said, motioning to his Monte. "Just got the paint touched up. Don't want nobody to fuck with it." He laughed then and covered his mouth. "But pardon my French, boys," he said.

Though it was a different color, Tomczak's green suit seemed to have the same flashy glitter of his Monte. His teeth and slicked blonde hair even sparkled. He was a loud, fumy parade, way too much to have to stand with. "Just got the paint touched up," he said again. "Why don't you come and take a look?" He didn't seem to notice me or Jimmy when he asked this and spoke with his back to us.

"No, thank you," my mother told him; she was trying to be polite. "We've been in line for almost an hour."

"Okay," Tomczak said with that sugar-white smile. "But damned if you don't owe me a dance."

At that the blood came back to my older brother's face. "She don't owe you shit, man," he said.

My mother snapped Jimmy's name, but Tomczak said, "No, no, that's good. That's real good, man. You watch out for your mom."

Then Tomczak said he'd see us inside and strutted away to the back of the building.

"I don't believe this," my mother said to Jimmy. "What did I tell you?"

She had much more to say, but we were in the hall and it was our turn to meet the bride and groom. Rennie's wedding dress looked wrinkled, and her new husband's tux was undone at the collar so that the bowtie dangled from his thick, sweat-soaked neck. They were both pink from drinking. Reenie kept saying, "You made it!" while her husband nodded, sized up the guests, and slugged back a can of Schlitz.

"We made it, all right," my mother said.

"You boys look like a pair of heartbreakers tonight," Reenie told us.

"Oh, they are," my mother said. "So do yourself a favor and wait ten years before you decide to have your own."

This should have hurt my feelings, but it was good to see my mother laugh, even if she did have to force it from herself.

***

The hall's main floor was hot and packed with dancers who spun one another to the wild horn and accordion polkas that blared from the stage where the Joliet Jugoslavs played—ten gray neighborhood guys who had a jukebox record in every tavern from Plainfield to Preston Heights, and who worked weekend tours of weddings and church picnics that stretched from Milwaukee to East Chicago, Indiana. The local polka radio station, WJOL, played their songs at least five times a day. And the Jugoslavs were even regulars on *Eddie Korosa's Polka Hour*, the television program that aired Saturdays at three in the morning. Their biggest hit, the song I loved to watch them play the most, was the "Smokestack Polka," a traditional instrumental about the place where we lived, the place where all ten Joliet Jugoslavs came from as well. But I was too young to understand local pride back then. I just liked to watch the trumpet player, Joe Novak, fill his mouth with cigar smoke before he blasted out a line of the tune, so that the end of his horn had smoke blowing from it, just like the stacks that surrounded our world in every direction we looked.

But I didn't enjoy the band too much that night. I was worried about Jimmy, and the way people looked at him as our mother lead us through the crowd searching for our table. Almost every glance Jimmy got that night was the same: strained, pitiful, and waiting, it seemed, to watch how badly he'd fuck up next.

They seated us with people from the groom's side of the family, and just as we got settled, Jack Tomczak strolled over and gave Jimmy a playful tug on his ear that made him redden and scowl. "Hey, tough guy," Tomczak said. "Let's you and me go knock back some shots." There was an open bar, and Tomczak smelled like he'd already made ten trips to it before he got to us. His laugh made its way into a wet cough. "Maybe later," Tomczak said, then held out his hand and winked at my mother. "I requested this one," he said. "I requested it for you and me. Come on. Let's get a dance in."

My mother's smile was genuine. She blushed a little, but turned the offer down. "No, really. Thanks, Jack," she said. "We just sat down. But thank you."

Tomczak's smile got thinner and keeping it in place seemed to take a lot of effort. "Maybe later," he said as he started walking away. Then he made little guns with his hands and pointed them at Jimmy. "And later you and me'll do some shots, tough guy," he said, and winked a bloodshot eye.

***

For dinner, they served the local wedding favorite: red cabbage and meatballs and two slices of bread with pats of white butter. The Jugoslavs were still roaring on stage, and I waited for them to kick in with the "Smokestack Polka." The band never took breaks but slowed now and then with a solo so the sweat-soaked dancers could catch a breath. The dinner didn't stop the dancing, either. The floor stayed crowded and the guests only broke from their reeling to take quick bites from their plates, or to hit the bar for shots and cans of Old Style they'd take back onto the floor. With these drinks they toasted the band, Reenie and Norb, their parents, the hall, the neighborhood, anything, over and over until they were staggering. "*Na Zarowie!*" they yelled. "*Na Zarowie!*"

Meanwhile, I'd guzzled down three Cokes and had to take a leak.

"Take your brother to the bathroom," my mother told Jimmy. "And don't take too long. I'm timing you."

I followed Jimmy past the bar, where Tomczak was arm wrestling the bartender in a circle of men who'd put five bucks on either side of the match. Tomczak lost and the crowd laughed at him.

"Fuck off," he told them. "Your sisters and fucking mothers, too."

There was a long line waiting for the toilet. Jimmy took me by the arm, told me to follow him, and I asked him where we were going.

"Just come on," he said, and lead me past the kitchen, then past the old coat check nobody used anymore, then to a short, dark hallway with a door at the end. He opened it and showed me the steep stairway that went up into another, deeper darkness.

"No way," I said. "I'm not going up there."

"Don't be a pussy, man. You're not going to fall. I'm right behind you."

He closed the door, flicked his cigarette lighter, then guided me up the stairs. There wasn't a railing, so I balanced my steps by touching the narrow walls. We finally got to the end, another door that Jimmy told me to open.

"It's stuck," I told him.

"Then push it," he said.

We both gave it a shove, another, then stumbled out onto a wide place cluttered with stacks of bricks covered in plastic that rustled in a strange breeze, and with wrapped pipes, and cans of paint under stars and a full moon.

We were on the roof above the hall.

"Man," I said, then walked over to the ledge and looked at the streets below. We were up pretty high, and to the north I could see the Union refinery torches that reflected on the moving surface of the sanitary canal behind it. I could see everything from up there: the smokestacks that towered over Commonwealth Edison to the south, and over Olin Chemical to the west.

"How did you find this?" I said. "How did you know this was up here?"

"Dad," Jimmy told me. "Dad took me up here one day when I was your age." He nodded at the covered bricks, the pipes and paint. "They were planning on building another floor, but the old commander died, and the new one said one floor was enough."

Mercy Hospital was in the distance to the east, with the landing pad light that turned and turned in green and red from the very top of the building. The railyard was a few blocks over, the slow-moving lights of passing freight engines, the dim red switch lamps, the watchtower.

"This is where I came when I ran away," Jimmy said. He stood next to me and lit a cigarette. "I stayed up here the whole time. I snuck down into the kitchen at night for food, but the only thing they had in the fridge was pickles. Big jars of pickles," he said. "All I ate for three days were those fucking pickles." He laughed at this, and I laughed with him. Then Jimmy stopped and got quiet. "But when I saw Mom down there looking for me, calling for me like that, I knew I had to come out," he said. "You should have seen her."

I made out the steeples of five parishes from up there. The tallest was Saint Raymond Nonnatus, the cathedral west of the canal; Holy Transfiguration in Rockdale had twin silver steeples; Saint Bride's up in Lockport was the oldest, with a network of renovation scaffolding that held the ancient bricks together; the giant red and green onion domes on the Byzantine parish rose above clumps of trees on South Briggs, and looked a little foreign and out of place; Saint Sabina's was right next to us, two streets over—but that steeple towered over us every day, and didn't seem that impressive from our spot.

A roar of cheers came from the crowd underneath us. The Joliet Jugoslavs tore into the first beats of the song I'd waited for all night, the first proud sounds of accordion and horns that played the "Smokestack Polka."

"Let's go," I said, and ran for the door to the stairway.

"Wait," Jimmy told me. "Just stay up here with me for a minute."

"We're going to miss the song," I told him. But I could see Jimmy needed to tell me something, so I stayed and leaned on the ledge next to him, looking down on the streets where we were raised.

Downstairs, the whole crowd must have been dancing. The thunder of their steps and yells almost drowned out the band. And they all danced with such purpose because they knew the song belonged to them. The song was about them, and no matter where the Jugoslavs played it, Kenosha, Oshkosh, Calumet City, Gary, or Hammond, it would always be about them, about us; our identical brick houses topped with green shingles; our uncles and fathers who worked in the yards, power plants, refineries, and who drank in the taverns; our grandparents who were buried in the Protection of Our Savior's Five Wounds Cemetery; our mothers who made sure we got religion, even if they didn't buy any of it themselves.

"I'm in big trouble," Jimmy finally said. "I screwed up too much, and now I'm all out of chances."

He lit another cigarette off the first, then flicked the old one away; I watched the ember flutter down to the sidewalk, where it landed with a small burst of orange sparks.

"I'm all out of chances," he said. "If I mess up one more time, Mom and Father Zajc are going to send me away."

The music and dancing, the roof, the stars, the sky, it all flashed away, and the only thing that mattered then was that I was with my brother, who had reached the worst of his troubles. "Where?" I said. "Send you away where?"

"Some priest school," he said. "A place way up in Wisconsin for fuckups like me."

The song ended, and the applause pushed through the roof and echoed across the entire city.

"So will you help me?" Jimmy asked.

"How?"

"Just don't let me fuck up anymore," he said. "Watch out for me. And I promise I won't pull your hair."

***

I finally got to use the bathroom once we were back down in the hall. Jimmy went, washed his hands, then told me to meet him by the kitchen. I was in a stall by myself, and some guy in the next one was on his hands and knees throwing up. "Christ wept," he moaned. When he was done, I heard him stumble to the sink to wash his mouth and face, heard him gag and spit and blow his nose. Someone else came in and, with a boozy slur I recognized at once, asked the drunk if he was okay, and if he wanted to do more shots, since they were free, and since free shots didn't come along every day.

"No fucking way, Tomczak," the sink drunk said. "You're a pig with that booze. Look at me. I'm an hour from dying, you fuck."

Tomczak laughed. "That bitch's stomach you got can't take a real drink."

"Your ass, Jack," the guy said, and Tomczak, who was at the urinal, laughed even louder.

After a moment, Tomczak moaned and said something about my mother; I froze when I heard him use her name.

"I keep asking her to dance, but no dice," Tomczak said.

The guy at the sink wasn't sure who he was talking about.

"You know, the nurse," Tomczak said. "The nurse with the two kids? Her husband died about six months ago."

"The nurse."

"Yeah, the nurse," Tomczak said. "Hope I get sick while she's on the clock. Bet she hasn't been cracked since her husband died. That's six months and no dick. Goddamn if she don't need it…"

The rest of whatever the hell Tomczak said got pushed under by the loud flush of urinal water, but I didn't need to hear another word. They both left. A weight of great toil hit my stomach, since I knew I couldn't tell a soul.

***

Tomczak was hovering over my mother when we got back to the table. "Hey," he said as soon as he saw us. "I'm gonna drive us all for ice cream!"

"Jesus, Jack," my mother said. "How much have you had to drink?"

"I'm at a wedding, it don't matter. Come on, let's dance," he said, and started pulling my mother away from her seat. Jimmy had to look away to hide his anger. If he'd known what I'd heard Tomczak say in that bathroom, he'd have jumped right over the table and made straight for his eyes, and that night would have been Jimmy's last in our house for a long, long time.

"No, Jack," my mother said, but Tomczak didn't stop.

"We're dancing," he said. "Right now."

My mother finally had to get forceful enough for others to notice. She yanked herself away and said, "I'm not dancing, Jack, and that's that."

Someone laughed and told Tomczak to go have another drink before he got into any more trouble, and he stood there for a few seconds with a dumb angry look on his face. "Well, screw it," he said, then tossed up his hands and stormed away.

We all watched Tomczak make his way to the bar, where he pounded back a beer and glared at the spot he'd just left, at the three of us—me, my mother, my older brother Jimmy.

"Let's go," my mother said. "I'm sorry I made you boys come here."

***

The three-block walk home in the dark seemed way too long. My ears rang and my mind just couldn't hold all that was on it. I was dying to tell Jimmy what I knew, dying to get him to do something about Tomczak, but by keeping it from him, I was the only person left in the world who could help him from getting sent away.

"Was I good?" Jimmy asked.

"Not really," my mother told him.

"Are you going to send me away?"

My mother said it was late, she was too tired, and didn't want to talk about it or anything else until morning.

We all went to bed as soon as we got home, but there was no way I could get to sleep. I thought I might never sleep so long as I hid what I'd heard. The things Tomczak had said about my mother sounded over and over in the ringing between my ears.

"Jimmy," I said. "Are you asleep?"

"Yes," he groaned. "What do you want?"

"What would you do for mom?"

"Jesus, man," Jimmy said. "Just go to sleep."

"Would you do anything?" I asked.

"I'd let her sleep," he said, then pulled the blanket over his head. Within minutes he was deep into his snoring, leaving me no choice but to take care of the problem myself.

***

The hardest part wasn't dressing in the dark, sneaking out of the house, or even getting back into the hall, since the band was wrapping up and everyone else was too drunk to notice or even care that we'd left, and that now, an hour later, I was back. No, the hardest part was making that walk up the stairs to the roof by myself. Since that night, I've never been in a darkness blacker than the stairway once I closed the door behind me. By the time I got to the door at the top, I felt like I'd walked up one thousand stairs, and breathlessly pushed the door open and collapsed onto the roof. After I got my breath back, I took a brick from the stack and went to the ledge that overlooked the space where Tomczak's black Monte Carlo was still parked, and I waited. People were leaving, staggering home on the streets and sidewalks below. The Jugoslavs said goodnight and thanked everyone for coming, and the leftover handful downstairs made a few feeble whistles and claps. Reenie and Norb drove away in their rented white Caddie, with tin cans tied to the back bumper that clattered on the cracked asphalt. A train whistle sounded from the railyards, and with my eyes I made the route my father once walked each night, through the gates, down the sidewalk, then onto Landau Street to our dark little house, where Jimmy and my mother were now sleeping, while I waited for my one chance to do what I could to protect them.

And that's when Jack Tomczak came out right below me and stood on the steps by the back door, steadying himself on the railing. My heart was going, and I saw spots from all the blood that rushed up to my head. Tomczak just stood there, lit a cigarette and watched his car, as if he was waiting for someone as well. I had one chance, and Tomczak didn't budge, so I brought the brick high above me, concentrated on the top of his head for measure, then thrust the brick down with everything I had.

And as the brick left my fingers, rushing in a fall toward the ground, Tomczak took one step forward, one step, and saved his own life. The brick missed him by an inch and crashed on the steps into fifty thick pieces by his feet.

"The hell?" he said. I ducked down behind the ledge, and Tomczak never saw me.

Then whoever Tomczak had been waiting for came out of the same back door. "You driving?" he said.

"I don't care," Tomczak told him. "But let's get the hell out of here. This fucking place is falling apart."

Toe Picks and Hoar Frost

Sharon Hale Hotko

The winters of my childhood in northwest Indiana could best be described with one word—miserable. The icy waters of Lake Michigan added a damp chill to the air, a cold that sliced through winter garb and froze you to the bone. And I was dressed for a stint in Siberia. My mother was a big believer in layering. Winter wear was two sweaters stuffed inside a hooded coat, gloves covered by mittens, day clothes stuffed into snow pants, heavy duty socks, rubber boots and two large scarves wrapped around my face. I was sure I was going to die from carbon dioxide poisoning from breathing my own breath. Only the blue of my eyes could be seen. Mobility was a slow waddle. But what made winter so unbearable was the sheer bleakness. Steel mills gave life to the region (as it was known) in the form of jobs—grueling work that broke the body down and pollution was just a way of life. Coke furnaces bellowed out their filth turning the sky a hazy, dismal gray covering the landscape with ash. Adding to the pollution, homes heated by coal furnaces with their attached coal bins made a slushy black snow to make nightmarish snowmen. In contrast, movies and songs portrayed winter as a wonderland of glistening white snow, joyful children on sleds, and best of all—figure skaters dressed in sparkling outfits made of silk adorned with rhinestones. I wanted that kind of winter. All I needed was a pair of skates.

The wretchedness of winter was intensified when the steelworkers went on a prolonged strike. Dad handled the stress of unemployment by taking lots of naps on the Davenport and watching television. He was a tall man, taller than the Davenport was long, his feet dangled off the end. The television was just a few feet away. "Jane," he called. I kept quiet, hoping he would think I was outside. It was a ritual. He liked giving orders. He repeated my name several times before I answered in an annoyed voice, "What?" But I knew "what". It was always the same.

"Come here!" he replied. The television was just out of his reach and I was the official channel changer.

It was always, "Find me a cowboy." It didn't matter which western anyone would do, a horse just had to appear on the small black and white screen. He would be fast asleep before the first shoot out. But childhood is best seen through the clouded lens of cataract covered eyes than it is through the clear eyes of a child. What I took as laziness was just a body and lungs worn out from hard mill work and years of breathing pollution and smoking cigarettes.

Mom was the opposite of dad. She was as short as he was tall and was the one who worried about finances. Dad was much too quick to give us kids change for candy and pop. With money short and Christmas just a few days away, mother added lots of starchy foods to our meals and was preparing for what she called a "bleak Christmas". I was at the age where belief in that gift giving old elf, Santa Claus, began to wane and I had a sneaking suspicion that presents actually came from parents. Mom made it clear that I was not to expect our usual bounty of colorfully wrapped presents. But my younger brother, Danny was still a fervent believer and waited for Santa with all the excitement a five-year-old could muster. So, to soften our disappointment, our mother created an elaborate story of collaboration between Santa and parents. The union and the mills could have used my mother's negotiating skills. Still, I held the secret desire that Santa was real.

It was Christmas Eve. Dad had stoked the furnace and shoveled the walkway—all before sitting down to a breakfast of biscuits and gravy, a lumpy brown mixture of flour and grease. It was a cheap meal that filled the stomach. But instead of settling down for his usual nap, Dad put on his coat and gloves and grabbed the snow shovel. He went outside where a bunch of neighborhood men waited. They were all steelworkers. The mills provided affordable housing for the men with families; houses built around a block all having a common back yard-no fences. They were discussing some strategy and waved their arms, pointing to different areas of the common backyard. Then they all began to shovel until a large rink was formed. The women supplied them with thermoses of hot coffee and soup. It was late afternoon when they formed a garden hose brigade and filled the rink with water. By evening, the water froze. Flashlights and lanterns were placed around the rim. A transistor radio provided music. They had built an ice rink. It was the most wonderful skating rink ever built. All I needed was a pair of skates.

Mother called us in for a dinner of fried chicken, mashed potatoes and more gravy. After dinner, dad went into the living room and called us to the tree decorated with ornaments of paper straws, string and glitter that we made in Sunday school. "Presents from us," he said giving a bright red package to me and a blue one to Danny.

"Open now," said mom, as she dried her hands with her flowered apron. I was filled with anticipation—this had never happened before. We were Christmas day people. I carefully unwrapped my present hoping I wouldn't show disappointment if it contained pajamas or a dress for school. Danny just tore his paper off in a delighted fury. But I'm sure I stopped breathing as I lifted my present out of the box.

I held the object of my desire in my hands; my face reflected in the bright steel blade. I stroked the soft white leather. Danny was holding a pair of black training skates in his hands, not quite sure what they were. But my excitement was unrestrained.

We went outside. It was a different kind of winter night The air was cold and crisp. A freshly fallen snow covered the ground. Everything looked as if it was covered in crushed diamonds. It was the winter of movies and paintings. It was a hoar frost. Dad helped Danny with his skates and guided him onto the ice. Mom helped me don my skates. Suddenly, I glided gracefully onto the ice. A full moon was my spot light. I was wearing a blue and silver skating outfit adorned with rhinestones. I performed figure 8's and tight spins. Using my toe pick, I came to a perfect stop and took my pose as the audience applauded. The judges held up 10-10-10.

"Okay," said my mother as she pulled the legs of my snow pants over the top of my skates. My beautiful skating outfit was actually snow pants and my hooded coat worn over two sweaters. I wore mittens over gloves, and I had one scarf wrapped around my neck and another wrapped over my face. I looked down at my poorly fitted oversized skates. My mom explained that they would have to last more than one winter. Ice skates weren't cheap and I would grow into them. To make them fit, I wore two pairs of socks and a pair stuffed into the toe area. My mom helped me wobble to the edge of the rink. I took my first shaky step. My feet turned outward and I found myself standing on the inside of my ankles. I struggled to stand on the narrow blades; I fell but I was well cushioned by my snow pants. I managed to slowly skate across the pond but my dreams of Olympic stardom had vanished. I looked around at the beaming faces of the men, especially my dad, who had built the ice rink. My mom was just happy that I got the present that I wanted. I knew she had sacrificed something she wanted, but I didn't know exactly what that was, to get me my skates. I realized that my memories of miserable winters had been replaced with memories of toe picks and hoar frost. It was the most beautiful and best winter of my life.

The Other Side of the Fence

Curtis Mazzaferri

The early sun was already hot as he stepped off the porch and walked down the gravel drive toward his car. The sudden change in temperature from the night before had left a thick layer of condensation on the inside of his old Buick's windshield, so he reached up, wiped off a small section above the steering wheel with his hand, and started the engine.

It wasn't long before he reached the winding state route that ran through the Shawnee River Valley, leading out to the steel mill's property. He rolled down his window to let the cool morning air in, quickly, filling the cab with that familiar stench of sulfur that seemed to permeate the town during the humid, summer months. It was a smell that always reminded him of his grandfather, who had spent the better part of three decades on the coke battery as a night-shift manager. Even after being retired for years, beneath his after shave, his skin still retained the faintest hint of it.

A few miles down the road, after the wooded switchbacks, he found himself stopped at the traffic light just outside of the plant's rusty gate, and he quickly realized the severity of the situation as fold-out-picnic chairs lined both sides of the road, and fifty or so protesters huddled around in small groups. Some were talking amongst each other while others marched around holding signs and waving at passing traffic. He felt a lump accumulate in his throat as he flicked on the turn signal as the words of the apprenticeship director flashed through his mind: "Ya raidy ta git ta work?" Dan, the silver-haired, old briar had asked him as soon as he walked into the office. "Sure am," he answered, trying to contain his excitement. He had been waiting the better part of a month to find out whether or not he had gotten accepted into the apprenticeship. "Where am I heading?" he asked.

"I got ya startin' out at the meel on Mundee," Dan replied, leaving him wearing a countenance of confusion. Dan noticed the change in his demeanor. "Well, do ya wanna git ta work or donchya?" he asked bluntly. His white eyebrows rose up to his hairline as he stared at the young man.

"Well, yeah, but I thought that with whatever is going on out there," he started. His voice grew soft as his mind attempted to process this new information.

It quickly became clear that his response had frustrated Dan, who cut in before he had finished. "Lissen key-ud," he spoke, leaning forward and resting his forehead in the crook of his palm and thumb. "If we don't go in 'ere, they jus' gone replace us with some scab outfit like they deed with them steel workers, 'cept unlike them, wer gunna lose that work fer good. We got bruthers at dapend on what little work we get in 'ere. So, I'm gon' ask ya 'gain, d'ya wanna git ta work or nawt?" His voice had grown weary by the time he was finished, and he peered curiously over his desk as he waited for an answer.

The young man let out a deep sigh and glanced down at his feet. He knew some of those steel workers from town. He didn't understand the politics of the situation, and the uncertainty of the situation left an uncomfortable pressure pushing on his chest. But he knew there wasn't an alternative. "I want to go to work," he answered firmly.

Now, as he sat in the turn lane of that intersection, feeling the glare of those disgruntled steel workers fall on him, he found little satisfaction in the rationalization that had so easily convinced him to take the job. A bead of sweat started to run down his forehead as the light changed to green, and when he turned across the intersection, the crowd began to scream.

"Scab!" yelled out one of picketers.

"Screw you, you piece of shit!" screamed another.

"You're taking food out of my child's mouth!" a woman chided. He kept his eyes forward as he drove around them.

By the time he made it through the crowd and found a parking spot around the corner, his hands were shaking from the adrenaline. He thought back to what his step-father had said about the matter, in a drunken outburst, several months back when it all started. "Those lazy communists don't deserve those jobs, anyway," he hollered from his recliner as the evening news ran a story on the local backlash, resulting from an instance in which one particular member of the machinists' union decided to cross the picket line and take a management position shortly after the lockout began. The action by this rogue individual had a stifling effect on the union's pressure on their members to stay true to the cause, and they reacted by blotting out his face from the billboard they had bought near the highway to gain support in their endeavor. That man had lived down the street from his parents for as long as he could remember, and every time he would pass his house after that story ran, he thought that man must be the most hated person in all of the city for the news to think him worthy of discussing at night. What would they think of him, now? The young man shook off the thought.

Across the lot, he noticed the office for the company, a single-wide trailer with a "Webber Electric" sign hanging above the door, and he got out of his car and made his way toward it as a tall, older man with sun-dried skin walked out onto the deck and lit up a cigarette. Leaning on the handrail, the man watched the young stranger make his way toward him. "You the new apprentice?" he called out.

"Yes, sir," the young man answered, extending his hand, awkwardly, as he neared him. "Name's Cole."

"Steve," the man spoke, grasping his hand. He took a long draw from the cigarette and flicked the remainder of it out into the parking lot, where its flight came to an end next to a small patch of dandelions sprouting up through the gravel. "Let's get this paperwork filled out real quick, so I can have John come get ya," he spoke in a hurried tone as he walked back inside. Cole followed him in. Steve took a seat at a desk in front of the door, reaching into the cabinet underneath. "Got your own tools?" he asked as he rummaged through the drawer.

"I got everything that was on the list they gave me at the union hall," Cole answered. His eyes darted around the cramped room, taking in the thin, faux-wood paneling of the walls and noticing the thin layer of grainy soot that covered every horizontal surface in the room. He swiped his finger across the corner of Steve's desk and rubbed the substance between his thumb and forefinger.

"That's good, but you're prolly not gunna need most a that stuff. We're gunna have you workin on a special project for a while," Steve spoke with a smile. "Here, go ahead and have a seat over there and fill this stuff out," he spoke, handing Cole the stack of paperwork and pointing toward a table across the room.

It took him a while to figure out the tax forms in the packet. He finished just prior to a middle-aged man with a well-groomed mustache walking in the back door. The man wore a thick pair of coveralls over a gray polo shirt and blue jeans. The pants of which, being too short, left several inches of the man's jeans jutting out of the bottoms.

Steve addressed the man without getting up from his desk: "John, there's your new apprentice—uh—what's your name again, kid?"

"Cole," he spoke, handing the paperwork back to him.

Steve stood, motionlessly, in the door way, staring at him with a concerned look. "Jesus, kid, how old are you?" he muttered.

Cole felt his face flush. "Eighteen," he said meagerly.

John shook his head and glanced down at his watch. "Well, we better get goin. I'm sposed to be at the hot strip in fifteen minutes for a meetin.'"

"I'll go grab my tools out of my car," Cole stated, starting toward the front door.

"Don't bother. You won't need em," John chimed. "Come on, I'm parked out back."

"Don't forget this," Steve said as the two walked past his desk. He tossed up a shiny, gray hardhat, which Cole caught in stride. Printed on the front of it was a label with his name: *Cole Rosenthal.*

As they walked outside, John pointed at an old, orange, Chevy truck. "That's me," he stated; his hand fighting to get the keys out of his jean pocket from beneath the coveralls.

Cole stared the truck over. It looked as though it had been sitting in a junkyard since the day it came off the assembly line. The wheel wells were so corroded that dish-plate-sized holes had formed in the quarter panels surrounding them, and the same soot that had thinly covered the inside of the trailer was splashed all over the hood and doors.

"Yeah, I know," John said, noticing the look on his face. "Trucks out here don't last very long. It's the coke dust—it eats away at the paint. Now get in. I gotta hurry and drop you off at the compound."

When they pulled up to the security gate, John rolled his window down and stared at the old, thinly-whiskered man sitting in the shack. The old man stared back for a few seconds before pressing the button that raised the gate and waving him on. As they passed through, Cole slid the hardhat on and twisted the knob on the back until it fit snugly.

"You don't need to put that on right now. You only need to wear that when you're in the mill," John said with a chuckle.

Cole loosened the knob and took it back off, rubbing his hand over the back of his head where the plastic strap had bit into his scalp. "I thought we were in the mill?" he replied.

"Sort of," John responded. "It helps to think of this place as its own city and every department out here, as its own little neighborhood."

"Where's the coke plant at? That's where my grandpa used to work," Cole asked.

"Way over there, on the other side," John replied, pointing to a tall, candy-striped stack off in the distance; its mouth, covered in soot, bellowing white smoke into the blue sky above. "Thankfully, we don't do a lot a jobs over there. At's a nasty place."

"What exactly do they do over there?" Cole asked.

"Make the stuff used to melt down the pig iron over at the blast furnace," John replied.

"Oh," Cole responded. John's response had opened up a dozen other lines of questioning, but he remembered the advice his mother had given him when he got accepted into the apprenticeship: "Act like you belong, and you'll be alright," she instructed. "Where's the blast furnace?" was the question he settled on.

"You got plenty of time to figure all this stuff out, kid," John answered. "Now, you see this place right here?" He was pointing at a long, red building that ran perpendicular to the security gate road.

"Yeah."

"That there's the hot strip. It's where all of the steel slabs get flattened out and rolled up. We do a lot of work in there. If I got time, later, maybe, I'll take you over and let you watch." He, checking his watch again, began to pinch at his mustache, anxiously. "Now explain to me why they're sending you, first-year apprentices, out here. What, they can't find any volunteers to cross the picket line?"

Cole shrugged. "I don't know. The apprenticeship director said that we didn't have a choice and if I wanted to go to work, I had to come out here."

John shook his head. "They shouldn't be sending you kids out here. It's too dangerous, right now," John answered. He seemed perturbed by the fact that he was burdened with responsibility for the young man.

"You talkin' 'bout the people out front?" Cole asked.

John nodded. "They're locked out and pissed off, and rightly so, too."

"They sure gave me an ear full when I drove through the gate this morning," Cole muttered. "I don't even know what's goin' on. What are they so mad at me for."

"Those steel workers got screwed out of their raise and some of 'em were gunna lose part of their retirement in the next contract, so they threatened to strike, and when the company realized it, they kicked 'em out, and hired a bunch of scab workers to replace em. Every time one of us crosses that picket line, we're helpin' keep 'em outta work. Probbum is, we don't have a choice but to do it. It's in our contract."

"They just kicked 'em out? They can do that?" Cole asked.

John responded with a patronizing smile: "you got a lot to learn about the politics of places like this, kid."

Cole nodded and refocused his attention on his surroundings. He stared out of the window in awe as they passed one massive, looming, red, corrugated-steel-sided structure after another. He'd lived near the mill all of his life and had never realized just how big everything was on the inside. "These buildings are enormous," he thought out loud.

After traveling a few more miles, John pulled the truck off the road and into a parking lot in front of another single-wide. It was a dilapidated little building. Half of its windows, alone, had been broken out and replaced with pieces of plywood. To add to its lack of appeal, the garbage cans near the staircase overflowed with trash, and the sparse patches of grass, jutting out of the gravel lot, were knee high in most places. "What is this place?" Cole asked, trying to hide his concern.

"This is where you'll be working for a while," John answered. "Now, I got somewhere to be, so just grab a broom and start sweepin' out that trailer, and I'll be back when I can, alright?"

"Okay," Cole replied. He stepped out of the truck and watched as John backed out of the parking lot and stomped the accelerator, leaving a trail of dust in his wake. After John disappeared, he walked over to the staircase and opened the trailer door. Before his eyes had time to adjust to the dimness of the interior, he was hit with the musty odor of mildew and stale cigarettes. He had walked into a mostly empty room where a shelf, housing dozens of pairs of the same coveralls that John had been wearing, was wedged between a broken closet door and a small desk. A handful of cheap, folding chairs were scattered around the perimeter. Through the doorway, to the right, was a dining room, containing a pair of plastic picnic tables, covered in garbage, and the room on the other side of that seemed to contain a scattered array of boxes of power tools and various wire reels. He shook his head and chuckled under his breath as he walked over and set his hardhat down on the desk. "Special project," he muttered.

He began to organize the shelf with the coveralls, first. He had only been at it about ten minutes when the front door was suddenly flung open, and a mullet-wielding man came charging in, wild-eyed and red in the face. He paused like a deer who'd been spotlighted as the man stormed past him and into the dining area. "I knew I shouldn't a come back out here!" the man yelled angrily, ripping off his coveralls and revealing a sweat-soaked, white tee-shirt and blue jeans underneath. "Everybody was saying how happy they were to see me, too!" he continued to shout, seemingly, unaware of Cole's presence.

Cole stayed in the corner of the front room, trying to make as little noise as possible as he arranged the coveralls in neat piles on the shelf, hoping that the man would leave without noticing him, but his hope was dashed when the man walked over and threw his coveralls on the floor next to his feet, and took a seat in a chair by the front door. He sat quietly for a few moments, breathing heavily and staring at the ground before directing his attention to the young stranger. "I shouldn't be saying all of this stuff in front of you. Don't pay any attention to me," he spoke. "Who are you, anyway?"

"I'm Cole, the new apprentice," he answered.

"Well, I'm Greg," the man replied, monotonously. "When'd you get out here? I ain't seen you before."

"Today's my first day."

"Makes sense," Greg responded with a snort. "Probably my replacement."

They both sat in awkward silence for a while until the knocking sound of a diesel truck could be heard outside.

"Guess that's my ride," Greg remarked, grabbing his dirty lunch box from the floor. As he reached the door, he paused briefly. "Don't trust anyone out here," he spoke before walking out. His gaze never leaving the ground in front of him. Cole watched the door shut behind him and listened as the sound of the engine faded away. He went back to his task with the words of the stranger reverberating in his head.

Several hours passed before anyone else showed up. He had just sat down to eat his lunch at one of the plastic tables around a quarter to noon when he heard several trucks pull into the parking lot, outside. Shortly after, a flood of guys came rushing through the front door, talking loudly over each other. They all grew quiet when they noticed him at the table. The tallest of the bunch, a man with a buzzed head and a goofy countenance, spoke first. "Who the hell are you?" he asked. His question provoking a laugh out of the rest of the crew, who all stood in the doorway waiting for a response.

"I'm Cole. I'm the new apprentice," he answered. He could feel his face turning red as he tried to act casual.

"Oh, well why didn't you say so. My name's..."

"Dumbass," one of the other guys quickly interjected, gaining a snicker from the rest of the group. Cole pursed his lips hard in an attempt to hide his smile.

"Shut up, Bucky!" the tall guy lashed out. "My name is Jaron, and that asshole's Craig, but everyone just calls him Bucky, on account of that bucket-sized head a his," he spoke, pointing to the younger guy with the smart mouth. He proceeded down the line introducing all of the other men: there was Joe, the oldest of the group, a salt and pepper-headed old man; then there was Mueller, a chain-smoking Appalachian, with an infectious belly laugh; and finally, there was Jake, a legacy in the brotherhood and apprentice in his fifth and final year.

"How long you been in?" Joe asked after Jaron finished with his introductions.

"Today's my first day," Cole responded.

Everyone sat quietly for a few moments before Mueller chimed in. "Damn kid, who'd ye piss off ta get sent in hare?" he asked.

"No one I know of, why?" Cole replied with a look of confusion.

"It's a general rule of thumb that the hall ain't 'sposed to send apprentices into the mill until they're at least in their third year," Joe answered.

"That's bullshit. They sent me out here when I was a first year," Bucky responded.

"That's because you're an asshole, Bucky," Jaron answered. Bucky nodded and shrugged his shoulders.

"So what do they have you doing?" Jaron asked.

"I don't know. John dropped me off and told me to clean out the trailer. I haven't seen him since."

"Good, it needs it," Jake chimed in.

"I bet they're gunna put him with Ed," Bucky said with a chuckle.

"Who's Ed?" Cole asked.

Bucky's face grew serious. "You mean you ain't met the Catholic crusader, yet?"

Cole shook his head. "No, you guys are the first people I've met in here, well, besides Greg." The group grew quiet and glanced around at each other at the mention of Greg's name.

"So you met the drunk, huh?" Jaron asked.

"He just came in here, took off his coveralls, and left," Cole answered.

"And what'd he have to say?" Joe asked.

"Nothing really, just seemed upset about something," Cole replied. He thought about those last words that Greg had spoken, but decided it was something that was better off not being mentioned.

"Well, don't believe anything out of that guy's mouth," Jaron said. "He's been arrested about ten times for DUI."

"Yeah, how many times has old uncle Greg been arrested, Jake?" Bucky shouted.

"Shut up, Bucky," Jake shot back.

"Greg is Jake's uncle," Jaron told Cole with a smile

"I don't know. I'm still convinced that Greg is Jake's real dad. Look at that face," Bucky quipped.

"Why don't you pick on the new guy and leave me alone for once!" Jake yelled across the table.

"Because he hasn't given me a reason to, yet." Bucky turned to Cole and winked before continuing: "I'm honestly surprised he made it a week this time before they gave him his walkin' papers. I woulda thought that they'd spin him at the gate as soon as he showed up. Must have been someone even dumber and lazier on top of the book."

"So who is Ed?" Cole asked after Bucky went back to stuffing his face and the room grew quiet.

"He is our resident farmer, and devout Catholic, and I am pretty sure that he is still a virgin," Bucky answered.

"He's one of the foremen out here and kind of a hard ass," Jaron added.

"That's who I'm going to be working with?" Cole asked.

"You better hope not. You know what they say about them Catholics," Bucky spoke.

Joe, who had pulled out the morning paper and unfolded it upright, spoke out from behind it: "You know, if Ed hears you talking like that, he's gunna get your money, Bucky."

"Pfft, the hell with him," Bucky sneered back.

"Bucky and Ed don't get along if you couldn't tell," Jaron informed Cole.

"Shit. Member en them two gat into et out 'ere in the barn,"

Mueller asked, causing a stir of laughs.

"I woulda beat his ass if Jake wouldn't a broke it up," Bucky replied.

"Yeah right, he would a sent you up to the front trailer with your tail between your legs like a whipped dog," Jaron responded. Bucky shook his head in reply.

The crew continued to talk about Ed for quite some time until the knocking sound of a diesel engine could be heard outside, again. Jaron looked at his watch. "We need to get back, Bucky," he said, hurriedly. As he turned to grab his hard hat from the shelf behind him, footsteps started clanking up the staircase outside and through the front door, a slender, weathered-faced man walked in.

Jaron spoke as everyone else grew quiet. "How's it goin, Ed?"

The man walked closer to the table. His blue eyes, contrasted by a soot-blackened face, were as uninviting as Cole had ever seen in a man. "You tell me, Jaron—you boys taking a long break or what?" he responded in a cold tone.

"No, we, uh, took a late one," Jaron answered, nervously. *It's strange for such a large-bodied man to seem so intimidated by a slight one*, Cole thought.

"That right?" Ed replied. "Well, then, don't let me interrupt your all's leisure time," he stated before turning around and walking back outside. Everyone sat motionlessly, waiting until he was out of earshot before saying anything.

"Speak of the devil, and he'll appear," Bucky chimed. Everyone stood up and grabbed their hardhats and headed for the door, and Cole sat there, admiring the mess they had all left for him as their engines sounded and faded away.

After cleaning up the table, Cole walked outside to get some fresh air. He took a seat on the staircase and glanced out at the horizon where a dozen red buildings were scattered around the large candy-striped stack. He found the way that they contrasted with the blue sky to be pleasing for some reason. As his vision scanned across the parking lot, he recognized John's beat-up Chevy approaching from the road. It came to a stop about ten feet in front of him, and he reached up and shielded his eyes with his arm as the trail of dust, that followed, washed over him.

John rolled down the window. "Go put some coveralls on, grab your hard hat, and get in!" he yelled over the engine.

Cole ran back inside and grabbed one of the faded, denim jumpsuits from the shelf and stuffed his foot in. He bounced around for a while, fighting to get his clunky metatarsal boot through the pant leg before falling to the dusty ground and working them through. But as he jumped up and rushed for the door, he caught a glimpse of himself in the dusty, broken mirror that hung by the closet, and he paused, for a moment, to admire his reflection.

John grinned at him as he pulled the creaky, truck door closed behind him. "Them blues look good on ya, kid," he said.

Cole smiled. "Where are we going?"

"I told you that if I had some free time, I'd take you over to see the hot strip, so here we go."

As they pulled out onto the dirt road, Cole rolled down his window, watching and listening to his surroundings as they traveled. The whistling of steam-pipe relief valves; the howling of crane sirens; mixed in with the groans of train cars moving iron slabs, from the casters over to the hot strip—all harmonized into some sort of industrial symphony.

"What's that thing?" Cole asked in amazement as a massive tractor-like vehicle, carrying a cauldron of black, steaming muck, drove past them.

"Slag hauler," John replied. "When they melt the iron down at the furnaces, all of the impurities boil to the top, so they haul it cross the road and dump it."

"Bet that stuff's good for ya," Cole replied, sarcastically, as the aroma of burnt plastic and rotten eggs wafted passed them, in its wake.

John shrugged his shoulders. "Ain't anything out here at's good for you, kid."

They turned back onto the section of road that Cole recognized from their drive in. He hadn't initially noticed the parking lots, full of bright-orange trucks, just like John's, lining the side of the long building, which extended so far he couldn't see the end of it from where they were. They pulled into the nearest lot and, quickly, found a parking spot. As he watched John grab the keys from the ignition, Cole could feel butterflies starting to form in his stomach.

"Alright, listen up," John spoke, harshly. "Put your hard hat and safety glasses on before we walk in here. Don't ever forget those, ok? Otherwise, the safety department will kick you out of here faster than you can say 'unemployment.'"

"Okay," Cole responded.

"And follow what I do, don't go wanderin' off. It's gonna be loud and dirty and just about everything inside here can kill ya. You understand?"

"Yeah."

"All right, then," John said with a grin. He stepped out of the truck and headed for a small doorway cut into the side of the building. As he followed closely behind, Cole noticed three men standing next to another truck, conversing and smoking cigarettes. They all wore the same kind of coveralls as John and him, but had pulled them down to the waist, revealing large, sweat-patterns, drenching their undershirts. Except for where the perspiration had plowed flesh-colored lines, all of the exposed parts of each man—hands, neck, face—were blotched with that familiar soot that he had come to find ubiquitous around here. One of the men, noticing the way he was gawking at them, shot back a stern look, causing him to quickly avert his vision back to the doorway. As he got closer to the entrance, the wail of a siren, from inside, grew louder, and after watching John walk through and disappear into the darkness on the other side of the doorway, he took a deep breath and followed.

Inside, the noise was deafening. He stuck fingers in his ear canals as his eyes slowly adjusted to the dimly-lit interior and looked for John, who was pointing to a shelf next to the door where a small cardboard box sat. He hurried over and grabbed a pair of ear plugs from it and shoved them in. The sound of the siren slowly began to fade away as they took form, and he headed back over to where John was waiting for him and glanced up to the source of the noise—a crane that spanned the width of the building sat fifty feet or so above them. Every time it shifted left or right, it emitted a whooping howl.

John nudged him and headed toward a staircase that led up to a walkway above the main floor, but just as they reached it, a loud "CLANK" sounded behind them, and Cole turned to watch as a large, oven door opened up next to the conveyor that ran down the center of the building, exposing a glowing, foot-and-a-half thick, twenty-foot long, slab of steel. He quickly lifted his hand to shield his face from the intense heat and light that it put off as a pair of arms lifted the slab up and out of the oven and pushed it out onto the rotating steel drums of the conveyor. Beads of sweat start to roll down his forehead as it moved closer. He had never felt heat like this before—it was as if the skin on his face would dry up and peel off like old paint. Paying close attention to the expression of awe on Cole's face, John motioned for them to head up the stairs as the slab slowly began its journey down the line.

Every time the slab collided with a press, a thunderous concussion rang out, and the high-pressured jets of water that were sprayed onto the slab's glowing surface as it was squeezed through each series of presses, caused a thick cloud of moisture to hover throughout the building before escaping through a gap in the ceiling halfway down the line. Cole pointed up to the opening and yelled out to John, "What happened there?"

John smiled. "A couple months ago one of the slabs hit a press wonky, and the ass end of it shot up and knocked that hole in the roof!" he yelled back.

They continued down the walkway and watched as the slab grew thinner and longer after each press, going from nearly two feet in thickness to less than a half an inch by the time it completed its journey. John pointed out the large machine at the end of the conveyor it neared it. "Down coiler!" he shouted over the deafening sound of the steel ribbon colliding with the mechanism, which quickly wound it up into a perfectly round coil and banded it tightly before flipping it over and setting it down on another conveyor that led underground.

They watched several more slabs make their way through the process before John, who had had enough of the heat, finally, nudged him and pointed at a door that led back outside. As they made it through the exit, John pulled out his ear plugs and turned to him. "Well, what'd you think?" he asked with a grin.

Struggling to find the words, Cole just shook his head. "It was fascinatin'."

"Sure is," John replied. "I always love bringin you new guys over here and watchin' your faces when those slabs roll down the line." He glanced at his watch. "'Bout time to head home, though, so I'm gunna go ahead an drop you back over at the trailer."

"Okay," Cole replied. They didn't say much as they made their way back across the mill. Cole's mind was too pre-occupied with trying to process what he had witnessed—the searing heat of the re-heat oven still pricking at his cheeks. When they pulled into the lot, John finally spoke, breaking the silence. "Well, kid, you gunna be here tomorrow?" he jovially inquired.

Cole hesitated, unsure of John's meaning. "Yeah," he answered cautiously.

"Good," John replied. "Catch a ride out to your car from one of the guys, and I'll see you in the mornin.'"

"Sure," Cole replied, "See you tomorrow." He stepped out of the cab and navigated his way toward the trailer through the maze of trucks littering the lot, and when he reached the staircase, he set his hardhat down, unzipped the stuffy coveralls, and folded the top down around his waist. The warm, summer breeze blew against his damp shirt, sending a shiver running through him as he glanced out to that candy-striped stack peeking over the tree line. He wondered what his grandfather thought the first time he stared up at that towering structure from this side of the fence. Inside the trailer, the crew let out another roar of synchronized laughter, and a crooked grin crept across his face as he listened. He combed aside his matted hair with his fingers and grabbed his hardhat from the stair before walking in and joining them. Off in the distance, the blast furnace erupted, sending a forty-foot cloud of tish into the sky as hundreds of first and second-shift workers shuffled through the rusty gates, below. In a few hours, the wind would push the phyllitic-looking debris over the town and evenly distribute it onto the bungalow rooftops.

These are the circumstances of industry.

Consumed

Barbara Dubos

Olga thought about her marriage to Roman. She remembered the day of her wedding and how her grandmother gave her three gold coins wrapped in a lace trimmed handkerchief and told her never to tell anyone. She clutched the handkerchief as if it were the last piece of security. The thought of Roman nauseated her now. He promised a better life in Slovakia and never delivered. What could she do? She gave birth to two children in a small village of Splinski, Slovakia. As time passed, the gold became a source of comfort. Again, Olga clutched the handkerchief that contained the gold coins tightly as if she were holding her future in her hand. She was afraid. Roman did not meet her at the station in New York, and she was unnerved. She felt a sharp pain in her stomach. The pain felt like a hot poker going deep into her core. Her thoughts raced about what her future in America was going to be like for her and her family. She looked over at Johnny and Mary, her two small children, and slowly drifted off to sleep.

Every once in a while Olga caught a glimpse now and then out the train window at the rolling green pastures and mountain ranges. They brought back memories of her village landscape in Slovakia. The journey was long and tiring. She melted into the wine velvet seats. She ran her fingers over the worn seats, and she wondered how many other passengers dreamt of a new life in America. She continued to run her hands over the seats and then across the foreheads of her sleeping children. She took a deep breath, relaxed, and realized things will be better as soon as she gets off the train in Camville, Ohio. The gold pieces, other than her two children, were the most important possessions she brought with her to America. She clutched the handkerchief and settled back into her seat as the train coasted along the tracks.

A gentleman across from Olga noticed the nervous tension with

Olga and he cleared his throat and attempted to attract her attention. She purposely tried to avoid a conversation with him.

Finally, he asked, "Are you alright, Miss?"

"Tired," answered Olga.

"Let me introduce myself, my name is John Langely... I'm heading home from business in Europe, I'll be getting off at Camville. And you?" replied Langely.

"I'm also going to Camville," Olga sighed.

"My, you seem exhausted, and what darling children, I have a child," he continued, "I can't wait to get home."

"My husband did not meet me in New York, so I hope he will be at the station in Camville." Olga answered.

After she said that, she thought it too much information to give to a stranger; especially a man she knew nothing about, a complete stranger on a train. She was so tired and frustrated that any sense of privacy evaded her. She wanted to burst and scream to the world how sad she was, how tired she was, and just how disappointed she was with Roman.

Langely replied, "Well, he would be a fool not to be at the train station."

Suddenly the train porter announced, "Next stop, Camville."

Olga gathered the children. She walked off the train and entered into a crowded smoke-filled city. The trains were running constantly along the tracks and the mills were in full swing twenty-four seven producing steel. She looked around the crowd. Her heart raced, and she was anxious.

Thoughts were running through her mind.

Is he here?

What do I do now?

Oh, suddenly she spotted Roman.

"Roman, here I am, I am here!" she shouted.

Olga was so excited she rushed towards Roman and almost forgot the children. She grabbed Roman and she realized the children were not by her side. The crowd at the station was shoving and pushing. Travelers were in a hurry to exit the train and baggage was thrown around. Everyone was in a state of confusion and excitement. Roman realized the children were missing.

She said, "My God, Roman what have you done?"

She heard children screaming in the background and frantically she pulled away from Roman and recognized the shrill voices of Johnny and Mary.

***

Exhausted, Olga was torn with opposing emotions. Roman was hugging her, but she sensed distance, and she pulled away from him. He was a stranger to her. She hadn't seen him for six years. She's lived on promises of a new life and a new beginning. She experienced the cries of the frightened children, the distance of a husband she hadn't seen for six years. Where was this all going for her?

Roman looked so different. He was heavier and had some gray hair along the sides of his hairline. On the other hand, Olga and her children were thin and worn. While back in Slovakia, she birthed a second child, she had lived in poverty, and protected Roman from having a nagging, complaining wife. She took care of problems so Roman could have peace. Olga now questioned her efforts. He looked well-fed. She and the children were thin and pale. Roman guided his family to a waiting trolley car.

On her way to the company house, she passed remnants of the simple wooden shacks steel mill workers lived in prior to the strike of 1916 when the workers tried to unionize. Roman tried to assure her that their living conditions were much better. She wondered what new life had Roman brought her to?

As she rode through East Oldstown on her way to Camville, it was a contrast to the rolling hills and green pastures from her train ride from New York to Camville. The street was dirt and the shops were close together and there was a pungent smell through the air. Not the fresh breathable air of her homeland. When Olga arrived at the company houses in Camville, she noticed the company houses were a tight slender row of houses consisting of blocks of twelve attached together. Olga looked at the slenderness of the homes and her stomach dropped. She felt as if a two-ton weight pulled it down onto the ground, and she had a hard time lifting herself out of the trolley.

She walked down the short stone pathway to her new home. Somehow all of this was not what she envisioned. It felt as if she were dragging the weight of so many disappointments behind her as she slowly walked to the doorway. She entered the home. The living and kitchen area were two small rooms that one could barely maneuver about, let alone having the children have adequate place to play. In the kitchen there was limited cabinet space. She noticed a gas stove and running water, something she lacked in Slovakia. As she went up the narrow winding steps to the upstairs, she noticed there were two small bedrooms. She he realized that the children would be cramped together. Olga wondered if this would be the better life Roman promised. She began to unpack and settled the children into their new environment. The children were excited about their new home. For now, Olga thought, but in a few years, they will outgrow the room.

Olga turned and looked at her and Roman's room. Suddenly a sick feeling came over her. She will have to sleep with Roman. A task she has not performed for six years. Instead of being excited, she was apprehensive about the thought of it. He looked so well, and she was thin and pale. She was exhausted from the trip. She remembered how exhaustion was not an excuse and not accepted by the men from the married women in the village back in Slovakia. She remembered numerous conversations amongst her married cousins.

"Oh my, again he wants to grope my body," a cousin would say, "then after all the work during the day, I must continue into the night."

The older women would laugh and say think of something else, it passes. Now Olga was faced with the same problem. She really had no desire for sex tonight, but Roman kept looking at her like a lion stalking its prey. The thought was unsettling to her core.

What's happened and why has all of this changed? Was it she or Roman who had changed? she asked herself.

Finally, the children were in bed and asleep. Olga stayed in the kitchen and hoped that Roman would drift off to sleep. No such luck.

"Olga, my love… where are you?" Roman said.

"Here in the kitchen cleaning" Olga replied.

"There will be plenty of time for cleaning…come to bed," Roman answered. Olga felt a queasiness in her stomach and slowly went up the narrow winding steps. Each footstep becomes so heavy and she wished she could just run back down and out the door. Back to the green landscapes she passed riding on the train or better yet back to Slovakia to the familiar language and sound of the horse carts. She could not jump out the window, but if she only could, she imagined herself flying away and never coming back. Slowly she reached the top of the stairs. She entered the bedroom and Roman was naked under the covers waiting for her. Shyly she undressed.

"Come 'on woman! It's been too long! Show me how much you've missed me," Roman anxiously commanded. She slid into bed and felt his hands caressed parts of her that hadn't been touched for six years. She thought, *Was this the way he touched me or have I just forgotten?* What was it that was so different than what they had before. Was it the distance of an ocean or was Roman distant? Olga whimpered and moved with Roman. She followed his lead just as she followed him through the years. As usual Roman got what he wanted. Olga was left staring at the ceiling wondering what just happened. Olga slowly drifted off to sleep and entered into an unknown world.

The drudgery of everyday life settled in. The children were oblivious to what was going on in the home. Olga tried to please Roman, but he was so preoccupied with work they barely ever saw each other. Olga was beginning to feel like a prop used for cooking, cleaning, taking care of the children, and meeting her wifely duties. Roman also acquired a drinking habit and on one or more occasions had brought home little money for household expenses. He forbade Olga to inquire about him or go to the mill office. Olga talked to the neighborhood women and they always picked up the check and were the money handlers in the family. Six months passed and Olga defied Roman and went down to the recruiting office at the mill to see about Roman's paycheck. As she entered the office, she was surprised to see the man she met on the train.

She said, "I remember you from the train."

Langely replied, "I wondered what happened to you… did your husband ever meet you?"

Olga continued, "I need to find out if my husband has a paycheck, we are so hungry, and why is the company not helping us with rent?"

Langely replied, "What do you mean? Tell me your name and address again, and I will check for you."

Olga gave Langely her last name and address, and she finally felt as though someone would finally help her in this new world. Roman just worked and complained, drank the money away, and left her and the children without food.

Langely took her over to the employee who handled the distribution of paychecks. Olga went over to a young woman named Aednat. Once Aednat found out who Olga was she became more than accommodating to her in a covert style. For the last two days Aednat had been with Roman and enjoyed taking gifts from Roman. In fact, Aednat has been in Roman's life for quite a while. She knew Roman had a wife, but never cared. Aednat informed Olga that Roman had picked up his check two days ago. Olga sensed a kindness with Aednat, but something stung her heart when she mentioned Roman's name because Aednat's expression turned to one of a cat that was hiding its prey. Unsettled Olga got the information, but still she had no money. Langely was sympathetic but told her she would have to take it up with her husband.

Olga left the office, and Aednat felt a sense of power. The more struggle Aednat saw in Olga's face the more content she was inside. Even for Olga's children, Aednat had no remorse. After all, it was about survival in this steel mill town of Camville. Aednat remembered her dreams of a good life with a husband and the reality of being locked in a room not permitted to see her child and having to succumb to the supervisor so her husband could attain a better position for the good of the family. Aednat thought Olga would have to learn the dark side of the City of Churches and her children will be just collateral damage along the way. After all, Aednat's child had endured an abusive upbringing in a steel mill town. Aednat had no choice because her husband needed to advance in order provide a good life, and Aednat whether she liked it or not had no choice but to submit to what her husband demanded of her. Aednat thought to herself that Olga should go to church and pray. Most women in Camville prayed continuously in order to cope with life. Especially, when the men worked in the labor pools. In the labor pools, one day a job was available and the next day no work, so many men would meet at the main gate to the mill each morning and waited to see their fate for the day or week ahead. The Irish foreman would pick and choose which men would have work that day. The others were told to return home and come back tomorrow. Aednat's husband in order to move up traded off Aednat to his supervisor. Like all the other men in the mill, Aednat's husband was no different. He tried with desperation to escape the bonds of the labor pool in the steel mills of Camville. All of that started when an Irish foreman eyed Aednat when she worked as a domestic in one of the boarding houses. He promised Langely a position outside of the labor pool for a night with Aednat. The foreman was bored and needed amusement. He was tired of his job, his plump wife, and six children: Aednat was his amusement. Langely traded for a guaranteed position in management for her husband and out of the labor pool. Inside the City of Churches was a dark undercurrent that flowed amongst its citizens.

Crying, Olga walked home. The children tugged at her skirt. She felt as if she wanted to escape and leave, but what about the children. Her thoughts raced about Roman and what was going on with him. As she walked through the streets, she was touted by the men entering and exiting the saloons. Even though she did not understand what they were saying, their gestures were obscene and universal to imply she is not in a good area of town. The children were upset. She quickly tried to walk through the badly paved street back to her home. Her head was spinning with thoughts of home and what this promise of a better life turned out to be for her.

Back home she looked around. Home was a place that a rat could barely survive in and no food in the cupboards. A husband either worked 16-hour days, frequented saloons, or was there for his once in a while sexual pleasure that at most times seemed more like a chore for Olga. Something to satisfy Olga so she did not seek comfort elsewhere. A trap of guilt to make Olga stay. The children were anchors and their chains wrapped tighter and tighter around Olga. She was slowly suffocating.

How could the love of children turn to such a feeling of such entrapment? What had Roman done to her and her children? It was as if she was pitted against her own children. She wanted to be free. Free from Roman and even her own children. A husband who really did not care only to make Olga the scapegoat in their eyes. Whenever Olga tried to mention what the children needed, he shut her down. Olga thought, *What does he know? He is never home.* He dictated what should be done with the children and constantly tried to make her question her ability to raise her own children. What kind of man was he? Roman the ambitious young man with dreams… Dreams for his wife and family, or were they only dreams for his own ambitions? She frantically checked Roman's clothing and drawers. She flipped through his belongings like a desperate animal in search of food as if one's existence relied on just the next crumb of bread. Finally, she heard Roman enter. It had been two days. The sound of his steps dragged and scraped the floor. Drunk again. Quickly she ushered the children up the winding staircase and into their room. She crept down to see what his excuse was this time.

She made it slowly down the narrow winding staircase. Her heart was beating fast and she nervously clutched her skirt. A fine mist of sweat was on her brow. She turned the corner and there he was. He sat at the small kitchen table.

He sensed her and said, "Where is my food?"

Olga replied, "You haven't been home and there is no money to buy food."

"Impossible," he screamed, "I give you money each week… are the little heathens eating that much," continuing, "or maybe you have other interests and keeping the money hidden…from now on I will buy the food and you will make do."

Knowing that Roman was paid, Olga now sensed that something was going on. There was more to Roman than overwork, saloons, and whores.

The next day Olga realized she never lived the life she wanted, but the life others wanted her to live. She compromised herself so many times.

Why?

All she wanted was to live her life the way she wanted and to raise her children. Her world was now upside down. She had trusted Roman, believed in Roman.

Now who was she? She had left her village and she was not a resident of a village anymore. If she lost her children, was she still a mother? Who was she? Roman had gone off and adapted to life in America.

Was Roman a husband?

Was he ever a husband?

So, in this new world everything she thought she was had been stripped from her. In this steel town, she was defined as who or what? It was a melting pot of ethnicity. She was raised one way and was now confronted with change.

Where did she really belong?

Where did her children belong?

In the safe shell of her village, she was defined by her last name and position. Here she was alone. Her last name and position did not help her. Even Roman had stripped her of her role of wife and mother.

Was wife and mother someone who was just seen once a week? Given a small amount of money and left to a lonely existence?

Olga realized so much changed for her and her children. She

became a worn and tired individual bled by others and used until she had nothing left to give.

Then what?

Exhausted she went upstairs and calmed the children. She went into her bedroom and craved to be released from this small town of Camville.

She thought, *Sleep, yes, I cannot make it another day, maybe life will be kind to me and I will not wake up.*

Olga awakened the next day and thought about her life back In the village. She thought about being defined as Roman's wife, mother of his children, and now all of that was being taken from her in this new world.

Was she a mere stepping stone for Roman?

Her trusting and naïve upbringing so worked against her. She was now something to be discarded into the past. I bore his future, gave birth to his children, and now he's destroyed me. Should she be diminished by this new world or rise up and fight for what was hers.

Was it ever hers? She left her old world for the new. In this new society, the residents of Camville were stepping over each other to get ahead. The residents were like rats thrown in a well to drown furiously clawing and destroying each other to stay alive. The tearing apart of the families within this City of Churches, whores, gambling, and drunkenness. All the people did in Camville was quell each other's dreams. Olga learned not to trust.

At that point, Olga realized she was stronger than she thought. She searched for the lace handkerchief that contained her gold coins. She clutched the coins in her hand and realized she did have the strength and the means to escape this situation. She always had it but never realized until now that the heartache and pain she had survived in this new world had given her the character and the strength to move forward. She now realized why her grandmother gave her the coins and told her to keep them a secret from everyone. She opened the window and looked into the horizon. Suddenly there was a knock on the door.

She heard, "Olga, open the door."

It was Langely. She told the children to go outside and play. As she opened the door, she positioned the handkerchief with the coins behind her. Langely wrapped his arm around her waist. Her hand had been forced to seek comfort now with a complete stranger. Langely looked handsome in his suit and she let him in. She knew it was wrong. The children, Roman, and everything suddenly left her thoughts. Langley slid his arm around her waist. She melted into a pool of relief, and the handkerchief that contained the gold coins glided down her skirt and onto the floor. The City of Churches swallowed two more lives.

Lo, the Steel They Forged on That Boundless Lakeshore

Joseph S. Pete

A reddish-orange haze burned over the Lake Michigan shoreline like an eternal flame for fallen soldiers, but it had less of the solemn formality of a war memorial than the damned fatedness of hellfire. The brimstone blast furnaces at Northwest Indiana's steel mills raged day and night, boiling like red-hot cauldrons of industrial heft. They burned so hot they could knock you back if you got too close. Generations of rough-hewn folks, many initially imported from Eastern Europe, Mexico, or the Southern "Jim Crow" United States, sweated it out by the raging conflagration that yielded so much molten iron that was made into steel, wound into coil, hauled off by train, and run through the assembly line.

In that flame and unforgiving heat, hardened steelworkers forged the steel that built America: that raised its skyscrapers, spanned its bridges, and formed its cars and refrigerators and washing machines.

But it seemed like every year another blast furnace got idled, a gilded euphemism of corporate-speak that implied it might someday come back. Sometimes they'd go down for maintenance and never get restarted because the demand just wasn't there. There just wasn't the need for so much steelmaking capacity anymore. Cheap imports were flooding the ports, coils of steel sat rusting in the yard, and you just couldn't count on a good-paying job there the way your grandfather could.

The paychecks were always good at the mill, at least after they unionized, but it wasn't all gravy as the barkeep Nick Papadakis and his best customer Frank Markovic would discover in a rude awakening.

Smoke billowed in seeming perpetuity from the cloud factories on the lakefront. A hazy pall of air pollution settled over the surrounding neighborhoods like a permanent fixture. The stench was so acrid you knew when you were there. Longtime residents got used to the smell but it was strong. So many chemicals poured into the lake they called a nearby stretch of sand "Bareass Beach" because the potent steel mill discharges would put holes into your bathing suit.

The sky would turn black and pink from all the iron oxide the mill pumped into the atmosphere. Flakes of iron oxide dust fell over the parking lot like pink snow, coating steelworkers' cars so they would drive to work in beaters that were known around town as mill cars. People who lived near the mills, like Nick's Greek immigrant parents, were always washing their windows as they were always getting dirty.

But smoke meant jobs, good-paying union jobs that lifted immigrants and their offspring to comfortable middle-class lifestyles, letting them send their kids off to college and maybe even letting them afford a boat to go sailing on the lake.

Hadn't Nick's pappous always pointed at the smokestack and said, "There's your tuition at Purdue Cal, huh?"

The Papadakis family was one of many where fathers, sons, and grandsons all worked at the same mill, toiling away calmly because of that implied promise of security. But they noticed that their mill, once 30,000 strong, back when everything was done by hand, including unloading iron ore boats and shoveling ore into the blast furnaces, had seriously shrunk. Over time, automation gutted the payroll. Someone once remarked that the steel industry was sick and it would never die but it would never get better either. Whole swathes of the mill looked stricken by a wasting disease. Though the trucks and trains continued to roll out nonstop, hauling steel off to points unknown, more and more buildings went dark and rusted away. The equipment aged, rusted, and never got replaced. The mill shut down the oldest cold mill, the oldest galvanizing line, the older ingot cast facilities, the oldest blast furnaces, the oldest hot rolling mills, the oldest plate mill, the only continuous annealing line, the normalizing line, the heat treating lines, the 12' mill, the bloom cast and eventually even the BOF shop in the bar company. The sickly, ever-shrinking mill shuttered the sulfurous coke batteries and the AC power stations, bringing in coke and electricity from the outside.

All those families—from Eastern Europe, the South, south of the border in Mexico, and other parts of the world—dispersed as the mill shrank and job opportunities dried up. They decamped to the suburbs, planted roots in the nearby city of Chicago where careers were more plentiful and better-paying, or answered the siren call of the Sun Belt. The stalwart families that stuck it out always braced for the next batch of bad news. Nick Papadakis carried on the family tradition of working at the mill on summer breaks at Purdue Cal and after graduating but eventually decided to put his business degree to use and buy the bar where he and the guys shot pool and knocked back cold ones after work.

Now the faraway and uncaring bean counters of the steel company idled the tin mill across the street from the He's Not Here Bar and Grill, which hadn't actually had a grill for years and which would normally have been filled with steelworkers after their shift on a night like this.

It was now ever so quiet as Nick stood outside smoking, watching the auburn haze dance like the Aurora Borealis over that infinite lake. He stubbed out the smoke and returned to his only customer Frank, who had been nursing an Old Style and cursing the White Sox for another late-inning collapse in a pitiful, hopeless season full of them.

The bar sat in a neighborhood of planned worker housing modeled after an English village with narrow streets, gabled roofs, and wide porches meant to encourage neighbors to socialize. All the workers flocking there needed somewhere to stay but only a fraction of the homes planned ever ended up getting built. The neighborhood got strip-mined overtime of all the built-in amenities. The hotel that offered lodging to itinerant workers for years was the first to go as the surrounding area developed and steelworkers planted roots in the neighboring communities. The corner store, the coffee shop, the barber shop, the post office and the diner followed and were all long gone. The tavern was all that was hanging on.

Most of the steelworkers had long since moved to surrounding suburbs and now wet their whistles at watering holes closer to home. The same dynamic applied to restaurants serving breakfast or dinner. A food truck that hoped to rope in commuters just before they entered the mill gates made it less than a year. But some still stopped there at the bar out of tradition, to meet up with coworkers after a shift or after a rough day.

It was a far cry from the early days when it was known as the busy corner outside the main mill gate. Workers could find booze, women, gambling, smoke shops, and anything and everything from all the entrepreneurs who popped up angling to get a share of their paycheck.

"I don't know how much longer I can keep this place open, Frank,"

Nick said, pouring himself another Old Style from the tap. "It's bought and paid for, but NIPSCO ain't cheap. Insurance ain't cheap. Kegs of beer ain't cheap. I don't know how I'm supposed to keep the lights on if the mill's closed and nobody's coming through the door. Those bar stools ain't here for decoration."

"The mill will come back," Frank said before cursing the right fielder for flubbing a can of corn.

"Come back you say."

"We still make the best steel in the world."

"Best steel, eh?"

"Yeah."

"You don't say."

"Yeah."

"How we losing, then?"

"Those foreign countries just cheat and dump all their inferior crap here."

"Really?"

"Look, when you look at man-hours per ton, our mills are the most efficient in the world, and that's a fact. You can look it up. Once we finally get some tariffs in place, the mill will come back. It's been here, what, 100 years? It'll come back."

"I'm not so sure," Nick said. "Is the tin mill coming back? Who needs tin? You been to Stracks lately? There aren't as many soup cans on the supermarket shelves as there used to be. Now they got soup pouches, and those, what, see-through plastic containers you can microwave at work."

"Soup pouches," Frank mumbled.

"Look, people aren't even buying canned vegetables like they used to, unless they're giving them to a food pantry. You seen how much bigger the produce section is now? They don't even have as many grocery aisles for canned goods anymore."

"Man's gotta eat." Frank said. "Soup's filling."

"Hey. Half of Strack's customers work at the tin mill. If they aren't buying canned soup, who will? Nobody wants a tin can. Nobody wants steel for a tin can. Things change. Times change."

"Nah, people are always going to need soup," Frank said, shaking his beer at the screen.

"People are always going to eat soup when they're sick or on a cold winter day.

"You sure about that, Frank?"

"Yeah, they just made the decision in Pittsburgh to idle the tin mill because they needed to back up their trade case. The feds won't do anything until after they give a few hundred workers pink slips. That's just how it works. Those Washington types, they need to know the voters are mad or they'll just sit on their duffs and do nothing."

"Ah, I don't know," Nick said. "Even if the mill reopens, it'll be with fewer steelworkers. The next year, there will be even fewer steelworkers. And even fewer the year after that. And the next year after that it could get idled again, and who knows when it'll be for good. You remember how it used to be as well as I do. It's been a gradual decline for years. Those mills are ghost towns compared to what they were. It declines and declines and declines, little by little, until you look around and everything is gone and you can't even recognize it anymore. Hell, this bar is a ghost town. It's a ghost bar. This used to be a neighborhood tavern, but the neighborhood's all gone now. Everybody's moved. Hell, I should move down to Dyer, be closer to the grandkids."

"That would be a sad day," Frank said. "This place is legendary."

"Legendary? What's legendary even mean? Drinking Stroh's is like King Arthur?"

"How many steelworkers have darkened this door and pounded back some brews after stacking up the coil? Think about Stosh and Fat Dan. All those nights yelling at the Sox, griping about supervisors, solving the world's problems. You don't have great joints like this anymore. Definitely not down in Dyer. A steelworker needs somewhere to go for a shot and a beer. An honest day's work, an honest frickin' beer."

"Yeah, yeah, well look, I got to go check on the back… We gotta close up after the game. I'll let you finish it out but, you're the only one here. Guess not everyone goes out to the legendary places. They must not have heard. About the legendariness and all that."

Nick made sure the back door was locked, took a glance at the inventory, and poked his head into the utility closet. He saw a gas can in the corner and tried to remember how much the place was insured for. He hoisted it up; it was light and empty.

He put the gas can back in the corner and stared at it for a good minute.

Indulging in a little fantasy, Nick returned to the dimly lit barroom, surveying the dated wooden panels, the neon beer signs, the jar of pickled eggs no one touched, and the banquet hall chairs and tables. Lately, the bar itself was more than big enough to handle all the odd stragglers who wandered in.

He imagined it all consumed in columns of flame, just more fire lighting the hazy Northwest Indiana sky.

Frank cursed as the last batter flew out to left field in the bottom of the ninth. The previous two hitters went down in a predictable march of futility. With two down, the final batter seemed to make solid contact but outfielder's casual, planted assurance as the ball arced toward him signaled the inevitability seconds in advance. The game's conclusion felt foregone, hope slipped away with every strike but there was always that smidgeon of hope, however delusional, that desperate prayer, however much of a Hail Mary, until the last out.

"We let it get away from us," Frank said, shaking his head. "We had it, but we let it get away from us."

Clockwork

Kurt Samano

Joe stood in the grungy doorway, fumbling through the crab nebula of keys that he kept in his "Good Times" windbreaker. Above him, the air conditioner dripped on his thinning hair. Finding the right one, he pushed open the weathered door with his plump rear and entered the tavern.

Once inside, he sat down the box of napkins on the pinball game and lit up a smoke. It was 3:00 PM and Joe knew that the rowdies were gonna be bustling in right after the 4:30 whistle. He took a long drag off his Camel and wearily gazed at the bar. A skyline of drinks left over from the night prompted the "Proprietor" to put out his smoke and start his work. He was wearing the red flannel he wore last night. His face was covered with a two-day-old beard, and his eyes were watery, with deep bags. He waddled over to the juke to put on the only tune that was not written after 1980: "Spanish Lady."

Joe took his position in front of the twenty-foot mosaic of bourbons, rums, and scotches. He threw last night's dishes into a dark sink of cold, semi-soapy water, and began wiping off the bar stools. He thought of how fortunate he was to have only the drinking glasses to contend with and not the dishes in the kitchen that was shut down two months ago by the state health authorities. After the bar was cleaned Joe began sweeping up the ocean of ciggie butts and losing lottery tix and swabbing up the lakes of spilled beer that deodorized the place for the past twelve years.

After he completed his cleaning, Joe looked around the tavern. Despite his labors the place still seemed dirty. The floor was sticky, the windows were glazed, and smog hung over the back by the pool tables. Noticing this, the "Proprietor" sat down at the bar to treat himself to a bourbon. Reaching into his back pocket, Joe pulled out a picture of his wife and softly began speaking to it. He remembered how the two of them would get in early to clean so that they would have time to cuddle in the kitchen. She made "Good Times" look like it had some class. While he was mixing drinks, she was in the back cooking up her sausage and sauerkraut that would tease every patron's nose.

Those were the days, he thought.

He kissed the picture of her and promised himself to go to her grave Saturday morning, or afternoon if he was gonna be hung over. Business sure has been slow lately. Joe needed cash to replace the felt on the pool table, get the neon serviced because after the last brawl it only read "Times," and fix the bowling machine. The house payment was the next week and the hospital bill from his wife was still hanging over him. Joe polished off his Beam and started to turn on all the lights.

Shorty was the first rowdy to swing in. He and Joe exchanged smiles and the proprietor tapped Shorty his regular medicine. Shorty gulped the concoction and signaled Joe for another, which he promptly produced. Joe could tell Shorty was feeling down by the way he gulped down his gin and tonic. Shorty pulled a letter from his own windbreaker, looked at it briefly, then crumbled it and tossed it at his friendly bartender. At that he guzzled down his second mixer and headed out the door.

Joe uncrumpled the piece of paper. It said that the old timers were going to get an "early" retirement in the blast furnace because of recent economic strains. Joe just smiled as he tossed the letter into the trash.

How lucky, thought the proprietor, *not to have to work anymore.*

Time Hangs a Louie

John Szostek

Photo by John J. Szostek Jr., Aetna, Indiana, 1955.

Bucky Stozak and Postal Boy hunched over their vanilla phosphates at the soda fountain in Aetna Drugs. Postal Boy had this moniker because he worked at the Gary Post Office. He was also known as Sloth Boy due to being as slow as honey in mid-winter. They were just finishing when Bucky felt a buzzing in his pocket.

"Wait a minute Postal Boy; I'm getting a message from the past." Bucky pulled out a phone-like device from his pocket. "Yeah, yeah, what? Oh no! Rats! Right, coach, we're on our way."

Bucky, in a panic, said, "P.B., that was coach Wensel. The Little League All-Star game between Aetna and Brunswick is about to start. The parade is turning up 11th Place in Aetna right now. Alex Karras is singing the National Anthem in Hungarian, and coach wants to know where the hell are we."

"Bucky, you're a lunatic; you've never had a firm grasp of reality or chess. That All-Star game was twelve years ago. Hey, how did coach call you from the past?"

"Well, P.B., while you have been wasting time in your parent's basement reading Hegel and playing that Big-League Manager game, I have been hanging out in my dad's TV shop inventing a portable time phone. I get calls from the past and the future."

"You're nuts, Stozak. Anyway, how are we supposed to play for Aetna in a game that was twelve years ago?"

"Easy P.B., I also invented a time machine. Here, check this out. This little TV is a miniature time machine. I whipped it up late last night. It fits in my pocket."

They stared at the tiny bulbous screen. "The lens is filled with clear oil, P.B., makes it look bigger."

"So, I still don't see how we go back in time to play in the All-Star game."

"Hold on to your pants, P.B. Here, just let me adjust the channel. Ah, there we are. All right, just stare at the center of the test pattern."

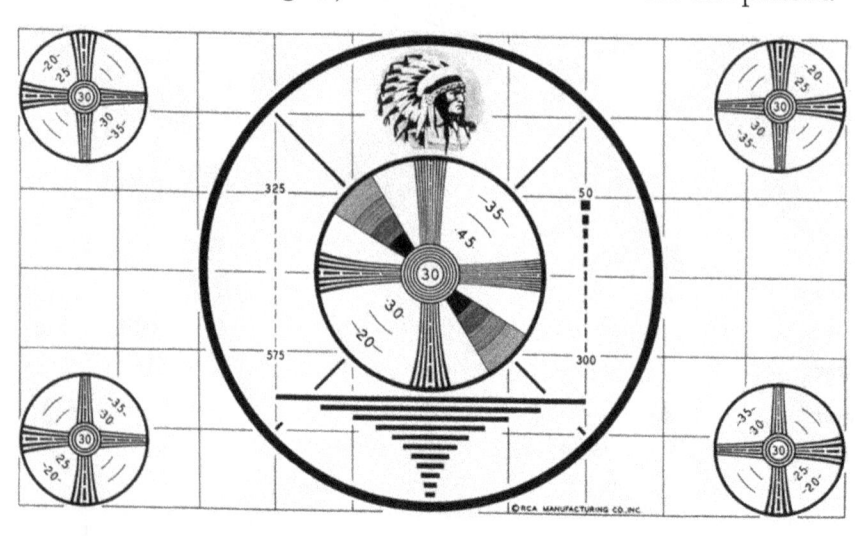

RCA, Public domain, via Wikimedia Commons.

As they stared at the screen, their current reality began to warp and fade, and then something popped, like the uncorking of a bottle of cheap champagne. Quick as a wink, they were smack dab in the middle of the Aetna Little League infield. The announcer's voice boomed over the loudspeaker, "Ladies and gentlemen, boys and girls, labels of gender, catching for the Aetna All-Stars is future Postal Boy!" The crowd roared, and the ground shook. "Pitching today is Bucky Stozak of the Fifield White Sox!" The fans went, "Wha—?" They had expected Louie "The Hook" Rizzo.

P.B. said, "You aren't the only one inventing futuristic gear, Stozak. Check out my latest catcher's device. See here, no-hands catching." He produced a colossal birdcage-like contraption that he strapped to the front of his body. "It works even with balls outside the strike zone. The ball enters the cage through the spring-hinged double doors at my chest level, and the ball then strikes my chest protector; then, the ball drops through the hole at the bottom and out the chute onto the ground. Lookit, my hands are free to interfere with the batter."

"Jesus, Mary, and Joseph," said Stozak.

"Exactly!"

***

Aetna was the home team, so Brunswick batted first. The rest of the Aetna All-Stars ran onto the field to take their positions. Stozak had perfected a two-armed delivery. Two balls in quick succession, one from each arm. His delivery was a veritable whirlwind, and the top of the first was over within two minutes. Sometimes Stozak went through the motions of pitching the ball, and P.B. would palm a ball from his pocket and toss it into the cage, making a loud thwack. Thinking Stozak had thrown the ball and not wanting to be embarrassed, the umpire would call, "Strike."

Danny Cox, playing for Brunswick, was so short the manager had to point out where he was to the umpire. Even when Stozak rolled the ball in on the ground, it was called a high ball. Danny walked on four pitches. After this first at-bat, when Cox came up again, he just went to first base without the formality of Stozak pitching to him.

Stozak moved to third base in the sixth inning, and Wally "Six Finger" Walrus came in to pitch. Cox was up first and went directly to first base. The first pitch to the next batter was a strike. When Wally had released the ball, everyone saw a thin line of dust moving from first to second, then on toward third base. Cox was attempting to steal his way to home plate and score. Ever alert, P.B. signaled to Stozak that something was up and threw the ball to him at third. Instinctively Bucky caught the ball, put his foot in front of the bag to block it, and tagged the incoming dust ball. Bucky thought that Cox, barred from touching the bag, would be called "Out!" The umpire shouted, "Safe." Stozak and the Aetna All-Stars jumped two feet into the air and screamed, "No!" Stozak and the ump went back and forth, spitting and stomping on the hardened clay. Like two Bantam Roosters, they went at it for over twenty minutes. They called each other all the insults men have ever devised since the beginning of time. To the crowd, the scene looked like the cartoon illustrations of Dagwood Bumstead and his boss, Mr. Dithers, fighting amidst a rotating cloud of dust and fury. One saw a fisted arm here, a kicking foot there, hands choking a neck, bulging eyes, and lolling tongues.

Finally, Stozak relented and took his position, protecting third base; Cox stood on the bag. P.B. looked at Bucky, as did Wally. Bucky made a slight gesture toward Wally with his mitt as if to say, "Go ahead." Wally gave a barely perceptible nod, went into his wind-up, and came to the set position. Cox took a several-step leadoff toward home plate. Stozak walked over to Cox and ceremoniously tagged him with his glove. The ball was still in his mitt. He had never relinquished the ball during the dustup. "Yer out!!" cried the umpire, and the crowd cheered and ordered Cokes all around. Stozak had executed the perfect "Hidden Ball Trick."

"Stoz," Bucky's nickname, was no slouch at the plate either. In the third inning, he pointed to the floodlight atop the left-field light pole and, on the next pitch, drove the ball high up into the air and hit the eighteen-inch glass disc covering the lamp. Unfortunately, the ball dropped in play and the Jadorowski Siamese twins playing left caught it. He pointed to a red lightbulb on the center-field scoreboard the next time at bat and promptly hit it on the next pitch. He was, however, called out because of a little-known rule against miracles in Little League.

P.B., who subscribed to the Harmon Killebrew School of hitting and the Ted Kluzewski school of Hypostasis, lofted three balls so high into the air on each of his first three at-bats that they never came down. He was awarded second base for each as a ground-rule double, or stratosphere-rule double, as it became known later. However, P.B. also adhered to the Sherm Lollar School of base running. Sherm Lollar was the slowest runner in the history of baseball. Even though the ump awarded him second base, P.B. never even made it to first base. Fearing the game would be called due to darkness, P.B. was called out for delay of game once and twice for the Zeno's Paradox rule. The crowd screamed in unison, "Sloth Boy, Sloth Boy." Seven years later, all three balls came down in Padua, Italy, and were ascribed as miracles to Padre Pio, assuring the saintly monk a plaque in the Vatican's Saints Hall of Fame.

The game remained scoreless through the first eight innings, not without astonishing feats of athleticism and catechism. No one present will ever forget what happened in the top of the ninth inning. Babe Ruth had, the day before, visited the players of the East Chicago Little League. The Brunswick All-Stars manager met up with the Sultan of Swat and paid Ruth with a case of Old Chevrolet Bourbon to be a ringer for them at the All-Star game.

***

Figuring he would be instantly recognized, they squeezed The Bronx Bomber into a regulation-sized Little League uniform and painted a mustache on his upper lip. No one knew it was the Babe when he pinch-hit in the top of the ninth. On the first pitch, he drove an arcing drive down the left-field line. Stozak made his mind a blank, turned 180 degrees, and ran with his back to home plate as fast as possible. As he ran just inside the foul line, he extended his gloved arm far out in front of him. The ball dropped into his open Al Kaline-styled fielder's glove three-quarters of the way to the left-field fence. After that, the Babe was never the same and left the pro game to become a stand-in for W.C. Fields in the moving pictures.

The next batter was Abbott and Costello. Y'know how that turned out. The third batter was Haystacks Calhoun, and he took the count to three and two. The Aetna manager took Wally out and called the Elephant Man to mop up. On his first pitch, if that's what you call it, Haystacks hit a ball straight up and out of sight. Everyone stood looking up, wondering where the ball was. P.B. called out, "Mine!" and all the infield players and the Elephant Man cleared the diamond. P.B. slowly rhumbaed out to the pitcher's mound, looking straight up, and when he got to the pitching rubber, he remembered what coach Marino taught him about how to catch a pop-up. So, he planted his feet, shaded his eyes with his mitt, and waited. The ball became visible against the clear sky. It appeared to be the size of an aspirin. The crowd stood transfixed, mouths agape as if at the crucifixion. Just as coach had demonstrated, P.B. stood his ground and focused on the ball. It came down with the screaming velocity of a flaming, smoldering comet.

The fans inhaled audibly. The ball missed the catcher's mitt and struck P.B. on the bridge of his nose. He dropped to the ground instantly, and before his mind's eye appeared all the retail establishments he'd ever frequented in Northern Indiana. In an instant, he recalled; Robert Hall, Planter's Peanuts, The Lure, and Calvin's Drive Inn. Images of Cam Lan Restaurant, Snow White Bakery, Pete & Snooks Pizza, and Phil Smidt's flashed strobe-like in his mind at an ever-increasing speed. Then like a kaleidoscope, Coconut Grove, Condi's, Miner Dunn, Coney Island, Tom Oleskers, Flamingo Pizza, Aetna Hardware, Peacock Cleaners, Wiatrolik Realty, and The Palace Theater swirled around a central focal point. A frenzied cyclone of a hundred more businesses followed.

Then he heard a sound like a semi truck's air brakes applied in a panic. The swirling images slowed down like a roulette wheel and paused briefly on a picture of Stozak's miniature time machine showing the test pattern. P.B. had not been aware of his body since the impact. He was, however, aware that he was aware. Now he felt his awareness fading and was beginning to swoon, as one does before losing consciousness. *I must concentrate, focus, focus on the number thirty, concentrate,* he thought. The test pattern transformed into a single, stable image. He opened his eyes. He was awake, or something like it, and no longer lying on the baseball diamond.

He was in his body again. He found himself standing on the southeast corner of 5th and Broadway in Gary, outside ND Lunch. The streets were empty, silent. He was alone except for his shadow, not a black shadow, but a shimmering, iridescent, Peacock tail-colored shadow cast on the wall next to a Pulver Chewing Gum machine. These vending machines typically had a mechanical doll inside a cage, either a policeman or a clown. This one had a clown. It seemed that the diminutive clown spoke to P.B. in ancient Akkadian, which P.B. translated as "Too Choos or Joy Mint?" He searched his pocket for a penny and inserted it into the "Too Choos" slot. The clown turned to face him and gestured for P.B. to come closer. P.B. leaned in, and he heard the clown say, "Bite me." A Joy Mint dropped down the chute. P.B. took it, unwrapped it, chewed it, and as he did, the door to ND Lunch opened, and a hand emerged and beckoned him to enter. He cautiously walked toward the open door and went in.

Postal Boy sat on a twirly-top seat at the counter. His rainbow shadow had followed him. The shimmering light sat next to him, no longer attached to his feet. The proprietor, an old Eastern European mustachio, popped up from behind the counter and said, "Have one of my special black pepper hamburgers while you're waiting?"

So, he did.

Volcanoes of NW Indiana[2]

Hardarshan Singh Valia

From spoon that fetches you food
   To needle that stitches your wound
   All came from my womb
Bloodied, exhausted
Mother of Volcanoes
Yes, I am the Blast Furnace of Northwest Indiana.
Oh! The sons and daughters of this land
Can you spare some time
Ignore Dante's Inferno
Watch Miracle on Cline.
In the amphitheater of life
Along the serene Michigan Lake
Under the shadow of shifting sand dunes
Belching hot lava of steel
That flows, meanders through the uneven land
Erecting houses, bridges, highways, rail tracks
Giving shapes to cars, trains, ships, bicycles
Running turbines, generating electricity
Propelling windmills
Pumping oil and gas.
Yes, I do explode
Yes, I do spew ash
Yes, I do emit noxious fumes
Shed enough tears repenting over mistakes
Took many corrective actions to improve.
I refuse to be boarded up

---

2   "Volcanoes of NW Indiana" poem published courtesy of Hardarshan Valia, *The Hoosier Forty*. WordPress. 10 August 2016. Accessed: 21 October 2023. https://thehoosier40.wordpress.com/2016/08/10/volcanoes-of-northwest-indiana-by-hardarshan-s-valia

I will not let grass obliterate my housing
I have promises to keep
To deliver nature's bounty
To improve lives of masses
So long I can deliver goods
And protect them with an invisible blanket
Woven with steel threads,
I shall survive!

Holy Cross

Connie Wachala

"I ain't gonna be buried next to Leonard," said Hank for the hundredth time that day.

Nettie glared out the passenger side window and, not for the first time, contemplated divorce. The car passed a stretch of small Hammond businesses. A carpet shop. A real estate developer. An auto parts store. The limestone facade of an elementary school. The sun peeked in and out behind fleecy clouds. It was an unseasonably mild day, the first spring day she didn't need a coat. She decided she wouldn't say anything until they got home. She would let him drive her to Holy Cross Cemetery, let him argue, let him chide, let the cemetery manager see him at his pettiest. Then, when it was obvious that she and Hank could not agree on this final issue after duking it out through 54 years of marriage, she would square her shoulders and announce that she was leaving.

Hank turned on the radio to WGN, the sports station. She bristled at the blare of commentators' voices. They boomed out in that same arrogant, irritating way their neighbor's voice, Auggie Juszczak, a retired high school football coach, spoke—as though everyone from the mailman to Nettie were one of his students. The radio personalities debated the pros and cons of the Cubs pitching staff on this, the day of the season opener. She was not a true-blue baseball fan, but she felt sorry for the team. After living with Hank all those years, she knew if anyone did what it felt like, season after season, never to come out on top. They passed a monument store with its sample tombstones sticking up from the concrete yard in front.

"If you want, we can stop at that good bakery on State Line on our way home," Hank said gruffly over the blare of the radio.

So, an olive branch. "You know what the doctor says about eating sweets," she said crisply, staring out the window. She was not going to soften. Not soften. It was true the doctor had told him to watch his diet since he had suffered a heart attack nine months earlier. Against her better judgment, she sneaked a peek at him. His jaw had that familiar stubborn set to it, but even so he was a handsome man. He wore his favorite yellow snap-button shirt and rested his elbow out the window. The heart attack had taken a toll on him, but he had recovered. Still, they were getting old; they were failing. Her arthritis caused her on some days to walk with a cane. Who knew how much longer either of them had? It was the reason they were going to buy their plots at the cemetery. The week before, they had a lawyer draw up wills so their children and grandchildren would be set. She would try one last time, impossible though it seemed, to work out a compromise. After all, a 54-year marriage was not something to throw away without exhausting every possible avenue to a solution. She reached for the radio dial to turn the volume down.

"We'll ask for a plot next to my mother," she said delicately.

"I told you, I don't care where it is," he barked, "as long as we're not next to that jerk."

The so-called jerk was Nettie's brother-in-law, her sister Annie's husband. Leonard hadn't even died yet, but Annie had, a year ago, and Leonard's carved tombstone with the date of death left blank sat next to hers, waiting. Nettie didn't much like Leonard either, but what difference did that make when they were dead? The thought of being buried next to family comforted her, but she knew there was no use arguing with Hank. When it came to their brother-in-law, he was irrational.

Their Buick coasted through the cemetery gates and pulled to a stop before a red brick building. The manager, Mr. Manteno, was waiting for them when they walked into his office.

Nettie was surprised to find him a young man, prematurely bald, with a nice smile and warm handshake. It seemed a job for a much older person.

"So, you want to select your burial plots?" Mr. Manteno said. "That's a wise decision. So many people put it off, leaving their loved ones to struggle with the planning." His manner was polite, even courtly. He steered them toward two leather armchairs in front of his desk.

Nettie smiled nervously in spite of his effort to put them at ease. Hank, too, looked uncomfortable.

"Mr. Manteno," Nettie started hesitantly. "We wondered if any plots are available near my mother."

"Of course, we'll do everything possible to accommodate your wishes," Mr. Manteno said warmly. "But space is at a premium, you understand," he added. "What section is your mother in?" It was obvious that he was a pro. Nettie relaxed a bit.

She did not know the name or number of the section, although she visited the gravesite three times a year—Memorial Day, Mother's Day and her mother's birthday in October. Mr. Manteno assured her that was no problem.

"What year did she die?" he asked.

"Nineteen sixty-four," she said hopefully.

"Nineteen sixty-four," he repeated. "That's a while back." He pulled a large leather-bound book from a shelf behind him. "Her name?" he asked.

"Balbina Wojcik Rogala," Nettie replied. "I'm not sure if she's listed under Wojcik or Rogala. She married twice, you see. She was a widow for many years, and then when she turned sixty-two, Mr. Rogala proposed…"

But Mr. Manteno had already started his search, tracing his finger down the list of names until he found it. "She's in the St. Michael the Archangel section. That closed years ago," he said, a hint of apology in his voice. "Are there any other relatives we can try?"

Nettie looked at Hank for help. "My sister Irene?" she said.

Hank grunted, which she took for an assent.

"Irene Wojcik," she clarified.

Mr. Manteno's finger stopped in mid-page. Nettie looked hopeful.

"She died in nineteen thirty-eight?" he asked, his eyebrows arched. Nettie's smile faded.

"Well, yes, she was five when she developed polio. I suppose it has been a very long time. I don't know what I was thinking."

"Anyone else?" Mr. Manteno asked.

"Lottie, my good friend Lottie Stanczek." She looked at Hank. "You and Edza always got along.

Lottie and Ed would be a good couple to be buried near." Hank scowled but nodded. Nettie turned to Mr. Manteno. "Nineteen seventy," she said and held her breath.

Mr. Manteno raised an eyebrow. "That *was* over thirty years ago," he said, but he started his search down the list. "Mrs. Beda, I'm afraid all those sections were filled years ago," he said finally.

Nettie looked defeated. She stared at her husband, whose face had reddened. "All I know is, I ain't gonna be buried next to Leonard," he said. "He's gonna have his whole family around him, all those Adamowski brothers and sisters, and I can't stand 'em. I ain't gonna do it."

"All right!" Nettie said, overcome with embarrassment. She glanced at Mr. Manteno in despair.

"Isn't there anyone else?" Mr. Manteno offered soothingly. "Someone who passed away, say, within the last two years or so?" Nettie's face assumed a thoughtful expression.

"Why, yes, yes there is, now that I think about it. Lottie's sister, Louise, died three years ago. She wasn't as close to me as Lottie was, but then her husband, Tarzan… er, Stanley, played cards at the American Legion hall with Hank all the time. Right, Hank?"

Hank's face relaxed. Nettie, seeing she was getting somewhere, continued.

"They both died the same year. First him. Then just two months later, she up and died. It was hard to believe as she wasn't sick a day in her life, and it wasn't like they were very close. In fact, she couldn't stand the way he'd…" Hank was scowling and Mr. Manteno's smile looked forced.

"Ted and Louise Golub," she said quickly. "It's short for Golubieski…" She stopped. Mr. Manteno was studying the book. Suddenly, he looked pleased. "Yes," he said. "We've a beautiful spot in the Good Shepherd section. You'll love it there. It's on a little hill with several trees shading the area. Would you like to see it?"

They would. He led them to his car in the parking lot. "It's just around the corner from here," he said. They got in and he whisked them to the site.

When they stepped out, Nettie liked what she saw. A concrete sculpture of the Good Shepherd—Christ cradling a lamb—occupied a central position on the hill. The whole section sloped up gently from the road to an elevation of several feet. They walked up to the top after Mr. Manteno, Nettie clutching her husband's arm for support. A hedge of plum bushes formed a row at the crest of the hill. Stately tombstones stood on the ridge. Mr. Manteno stopped beside a hawthorn tree. A gentle breeze played over them as they stood in its shadow.

"This is a lovely spot," he said, pointing to an empty area between graves. "There are two available plots here."

Nettie turned to her husband, who looked approvingly at the tree and the grassy space. "My mother always wanted to be buried under a tree," he said, his voice thickening. "So when she died, we buried her under a tree."

Mr. Manteno beamed. "Hawthorns are beautiful," he said.

"Then you know what happened?" Hank looked rueful. Mr. Manteno remained silent. "They chopped down that tree. Couple years later." Hank shrugged his shoulders. "Chopped it right down." Mr. Manteno had stopped smiling.

Nettie patted her husband's arm. "Well, dear, you tried. Your mother, bless her soul, knows you tried."

But Hank was looking down. "Well, look at that," he said. Nettie looked to where he pointed. "If it ain't Casimir Kaczka. We used to call him Fibber. And here's his wife, Bertha."

"What a coincidence," Nettie said. "Fibber and Hank used to play the horses together," Nettie explained.

"We'd hit the track once a month," Hank said, a trace of a smile on his face. "He loved to play the long shots." He put his hands in his pockets and stared at the tombstones. "Helluva nice guy."

"If you like, "Mr. Manteno said after a respectful moment of silence, "I can show you where your friend's grave is located."

Nettie nodded and they followed him down a few rows.

"Louise Golub. Here it is." He stood a short distance behind them as they stood with their heads down and paid their respects.

"With Tarzan and Fibber and Louise and Bertha, we'll have some good poker and bunco games in heaven," Nettie said. They both laughed and her eyes skimmed over the neighboring gravesites. On a headstone, she caught the letters "A-D-A-M..." She peered closer. Her stomach tensed. It was indeed her sister's grave and Leonard's tombstone. Dare she mention it, or should she try to steer Hank away? Her ethical dilemma was solved when Hank followed her gaze and saw the stones.

"Leonard and Annie here, too." he said, but he sounded resigned rather than affronted.

"Yes," she answered. Her knuckles tightened on her handbag. Mr. Manteno stood still. Even the birds seemed to stop singing.

"All right," Hank said. "We'll get those graves. Fibber Kaczka—you can't ask for better people than that. You know, he'd give me a cigar—a White Owl—every time I'd see him."

Nettie let out a long breath. "And Bertha was always such a card," she said. "Had me in stitches every time I ran into her." She spoke half to her husband and half to the cemetery manager as they made their way down the slope of the hill to the car, all of them smiling.

On the way home, Nettie interrupted her humming to point Hank down State Line Avenue.

"Let's celebrate," she said, as her husband, following her suggestion, turned the Buick north.

"After all, a little cream horn every once in a while isn't going to hurt anyone."

What the Dogs Knew

Alice Whittenburg

In the fall, after we got back from the first Moratorium March, Edward asked me to move in with him. We went to University Rentals, and they found us a battered old house near the Sheet and Tube. When the agent asked us if we wanted to be house cleaners, we both said, "I do," and then laughed at how this must have sounded.

Sometimes barking dogs kept me awake at night; sometimes it was noise from the mill; and sometimes neither of us could sleep because of Edward's asthma. The air tasted gritty and sulfurous, and I dreamed of places I had never seen.

When we weren't in class or on a cleaning job, we learned to forage. We picked yellow pears from trees in a neglected lot. We helped ourselves to unclaimed grapes, made wine from them, and drank it young from jam jars. We brought in a big stuffed blue chair from the curb and found our work clothes at the St. Vincent de Paul. "Honorary poor," our friend Steve said, and we took it as a compliment.

A small pack of homeless dogs roamed our neighborhood. One morning I looked out the window and said, "There's a brown coat out on the sidewalk." When I got there, I saw that it was a dead young shepherd dog. I had my first panic attack and sat down on the ground.

My mother came to visit us. She looked around and saw that everything was turning gray—the railings of the porch, the floorboards of the house, the tender skin around my eyes. "You should come home," she said to me as though Edward wasn't there. "The dog is pining for you."

"Your mother is very directive," Edward said when she was gone. "That's what makes you have bad dreams." Then he poured us both a glass of our homemade red wine and told me he had lost his cleaning job. "Just as well," he said. "All that dust fucks with my asthma."

The first time those neighborhood dogs came sniffing around, I ignored them. But as the weather grew colder and Steve shipped out to Vietnam, I watched those dogs, tried to befriend them, tried to learn from them how to live on the edge of nearly complete uncertainty.

Steel Valley

Stacy Alderman

I never minded going to my grandmother's house on Eliza Street. Nothing bad ever happened at Grandma's.

Gram and her nine siblings had all been born and raised there throughout the thirties and forties, and as far as I was concerned, the place was like magic, like a house from a fairy tale. It was full of adventure, warmth, and love.

The basement, with its dirt floor and uneven stairs smelled like mother earth and I loved gazing at the jars lining the wooden shelves—stewed tomatoes, whitish yellow potatoes of all sizes, bright orange carrots, all sitting patiently in the darkness waiting for us to crack open the seal one frigid winter day and be added to soup or served with pork roast. All of these vegetables came from the garden out back—the expansive, uneven land with equal amounts of sunny patches and shady spots, where clusters of towering trees swayed in the summer breeze and provided a magnificent playground for me and my four brothers.

Of course, as I grew older on these special Grandma days, I spent more time hiding from my brothers than playing with them. Instead of catching bugs and making mud soup, I fancied myself to be a lost princess, out of place in some far away kingdom. The two younger boys, Andrew and Eddie, tortured me with creepy crawlies and mud-splattered hands, while my elder brothers, Bobby and Ronnie barely acknowledged that I still existed. They were permitted to wander further off into the woods than I was, and spent hours constructing a tree house out of scraps of wood and other detritus, all the while muttering swear words and talking about some girl from school who had "certainly blossomed" since last term ended.

Being caught between the two pairs made me an outsider in my own family, even if it weren't for the fact that I was the only girl.

When I eventually grew bored with the older boys' talk of football and girls and the younger ones' endless desire to get dirty, I'd make my way back towards the house, kicking at dirt and bits of grass and relishing the feel of the hot sun on my neck.

Inside, I knew I could count on finding my grandmother in the kitchen, where she would pour me a chilled glass of lemonade or iced tea and would let me help her with some chore in the kitchen that she wouldn't dare share with my brothers.

"Oh, Frances!" she would call excitedly, as if she hadn't seen me in weeks. "What should we cook today?"

For the next several hours, she let me help her prepare dinner and dessert, perching me on a stool so I could reach the wood-block counter and the old, squat, cast-iron stove.

It was here that I learned the art of cooking without recipes, of measuring ingredients without cups or spoons, and heard endless tales of her homeland, Austria-Hungary. She taught me how to make pierogi from scratch and how to say it with the proper accent, how to make noodles and bread from flour, starch, and yeast, and how to grind nuts in the old-fashioned grinder for nut rolls and cakes.

When it was time for the food to be served, my brothers and my grandfather would eat as if they hadn't seen sustenance in days, and Gram would give me all the credit for how good everything tasted.

After dessert was served and my brothers were made to do the dishes, Gram would cuddle up with me on the floral-patterned sofa to brush my hair and watch Lawrence Welk.

Like I said, nothing bad ever happened at Grandma's house.

One particular night, I lay awake in bed, staring at the ceiling and thinking how lucky I was to have such a magical place to spend the days and nights when my parents went bowling or attended weddings or spent weekends away to celebrate their anniversary. Though the air was sticky and thick, a slight breeze carried through the open window in my tiny room in the corner of the house, a room my grandmother made sure I knew was kept especially for me.

My brothers had carried on well past their bed time, thumping and laughing and shouting until my grandfather threatened them with his belt, while I lay snug and safe in the room next door, listening to the buzz of cicadas and the whistle of the wind cutting through the open windows in their uneven frames.

I'd drifted to sleep quickly after that, biting my lip to keep from chuckling at my brother's mischief and my grandfather's empty threats, delighting in the fact that I had my own room here and that my grandmother had promised to bake chocolate chip cookies with me next time I stayed over.

Suddenly, my peaceful state was interrupted by hushed voices and the bright glow of the kitchen light just down the hall from where I lay.

My parents must have arrived back from their bowling night, I realized sleepily, rubbing my face and sighing contently. Shortly they'd be rousing my brothers and me to take us home to finish our rest, so we'd be fresh for church the next morning.

But the chatter from the kitchen was not light or short-lived. My parents didn't tiptoe down the hallway to stir me and my siblings awake and pack us up in the back of their station wagon.

Instead I was suddenly reminded of a bleak November day four years ago where, at the age of five, I'd woken up from a nap to similar voices in the living room at home.

Then, I couldn't understand why my entire family was gathered around the television. I couldn't understand why my mother was crying over something the man was saying on the screen. My young, innocent brain still couldn't really comprehend it when my father, haltingly, explained that our president, John F. Kennedy had been shot and killed. Assassinated, he said, and I puzzled over the word itself more than its hefty meaning.

Now, like, then, my father was doing most of the talking, and his strong, usually jovial voice sounded ragged and hesitant. My mother kept saying things like "I can't imagine" and "it's so horrible" and I thought I caught the name Mary Sedlak. Mary was a quiet, kind woman my parents bowled with who had two daughters a few years older than myself. Her husband worked at the steel mill in Homestead with my father, and I remembered Daddy saying something about how he'd volunteered to work an overnight shift that evening even though it was league night.

My heart pounding in my ears, I quietly swung my feet to the floor and padded to the doorway so I could hear better. Being left out of my brother's conversations and adventures had made me an excellent eavesdropper, even though I knew it was incredibly rude.

"My God," Grandma was saying. "I knew the work you boys did there was dangerous but I never…"

"We all know it's a possibility," Daddy answered, "But this is the first time it ever happened. I can only be thankful I wasn't there to witness it."

I heard a sniffle. "I keep picturing Tom coming into the bowling alley to get Mary. I'll never forget the look on her face."

"All we can do is pray for her," Daddy said. "At least we know that the foreman will take care of her, financially anyway. Mill widows don't want for money, that's for sure."

Bile rose in my throat when I realized that there must have been a horrible, deadly accident at the steel mill where Daddy worked. I'd heard the stories about how hot and dirty and dangerous the environment was, but Daddy never complained. He made good money to provide for our family, one that allowed him to pay for our house and car and vacations every year.

But I knew it was hard, dangerous work too. I'd seen the burns and bruises on his hands, watched as he scrubbed grit from his face and beneath his nails. Listened as he told Mom about near misses and scary moments when he thought I wasn't listening.

Slowly, I crept back to bed, my stomach roiling with fear. I didn't know how Mr. Sedlak had died, but I didn't want to. All that mattered was that it was possible, and that my Daddy, my one and only Daddy, worked at the same place, doing the same job, every day. Just so he could buy food and clothes and toys for me and my brothers.

I squeezed my eyes shut and tried to think of pleasant things—chocolate chip cookies, robin's eggs, Grandma's basement, swimming in the creek—but it was no use. All I could picture was Daddy, burned beyond recognition, being consumed by ash and slag, the byproduct of the steel they manufactured that boiled like hot lava.

Tears leaked from my eyes and I wanted so desperately to run into the kitchen to be comforted by my parents, but then they'd know that I was eavesdropping, and I'd be in terrible trouble. So I thought about what Daddy had said about praying for Mrs. Sedlak. But instead of praying for the poor mill widow, I prayed for Daddy to stay safe in the mill. I prayed for him to not get burned and not to fall and not to die. I prayed that he'd still be here to see me graduate high school and walk me down the aisle and ride me around in the wheel barrow in our yard 'til I was too big to fit.

When I woke up the next morning, I was in my bed at home. I should have felt safer, but my heart was pounding away inside my chest even before I opened my eyes.

***

Later that week, my parents went to Mr. Sedlak's funeral with Bobby and Ron. I was left behind with a neighbor and my two younger brothers; Mom said something about us being too young to witness a thing so sad as a funeral of a relatively young man.

Bobby and Ron acted like they were something special, getting all dressed up in their nicest clothes and being real somber and polite. I knew Bobby only felt full of himself because he was always making eyes at Linda Sedlak in school, and however inappropriate his timing, he wanted to be by her side at her father's funeral. Ron was just trying to act grown-up like his brother.

I hated both of them that day, hated them for being older, for getting to wear their nice clothes, for getting to mingle with adults, even on such a sad occasion. But mostly I hated them for taking Daddy with them that day. Deep down I knew he'd come home. I knew he was just going to stand there with Mom and my brothers, offering condolences and exchanging stories with his fellow mill workers, eating hors d'oeuvres and half-smiling at the people he recognized from work and church and bingo.

But the whole awful time I waited for him to come home, I had a horrible tight feeling in my stomach and my chest. My ears rang and my head pounded. I found myself so scared that I couldn't bring myself to leave the bathroom once I'd gone in there looking for something to settle my belly.

"Frances, you alright in there?" Mrs. Abbott called through the door.

"I—I don't feel well," I managed, my little voice shaking as I sat down on the avocado-green toilet.

She jiggled the door handle, but I'd been sure to lock it. I couldn't let anyone see me like this. I'd had plenty of colds and flus, even the chicken pox once, but this sickness terrified me more than any of those had. It felt like the voice of everyone I'd ever met in my life was screaming at me from inside my head, screaming horrible, frightening things about death and falling and never seeing my Daddy again. The voices were so loud they were making my head hurt, making me want to vomit. But I couldn't tell anyone about them, of course. I'd heard grown-up ladies talk plenty at church and at bingo when I wasn't supposed to be listening—people, especially women, who heard voices were done for. They got carted off to institutions for shock treatments and fed giant pills that made them babble nonsense. I couldn't decide what frightened me more—the thought of losing my daddy or the thought of being locked up in some far away hospital.

"There's some coke syrup in the medicine cabinet," Mrs. Abbott said after a few minutes. "And you're welcome to lie down in the guest room."

After I heard her walk away, I splashed some cold water on my face and wiped it dry with a fluffy orange towel that smelled of Pond's Cold Cream. Then I crept into the guest bedroom, where I lay down on top of the gold and brown comforter so I couldn't feel the plastic mattress protector beneath. I pretended to sleep each time I heard footsteps, but as soon as I knew I was alone, I stared at the oil lamp hanging from a chain in the corner—a Grecian woman in flowing robes, clutching a bouquet of flowers to her chest and casting her glance downward as if grieving the loss of something or someone. Thick bulbs of oil slid down the lines surrounding her and trapping her in her melancholy state, and I while I always assumed that the oil represented rain, I now wondered if rather they represented tears.

I could hear my younger brothers laughing and shouting outside my window, surely playing in the dirt or climbing the apple tree and jumping from its limbs while I lay inside, terrified and confused. At one point, Andrew burst into the room, smelling of dirt and sweat and sunshine and begged me to come out and play with them.

"Don't you want to play tag?" he asked, appalled at my lack of interest. "It's your favorite."

"Your sister doesn't feel well," Mrs. Abbott said gently, steering him out of the room to his twin who was waiting eagerly in the hallway. "You two go on back outside."

"Sissy," I heard Eddie hiss into the room before he turned away.

It was much of the same for the next few weeks. I refused to help Mom with dinner because I was afraid I'd get burned. I didn't go walking through the woods with my brothers and the neighbor kids because I was afraid I'd fall or get lost or get bit by a snake. When Daddy took us to the river on the last weekend before school started, I refused to put on my bathing suit and get in the water because even though everyone knew I could "swim like a fish" I was terrified of drowning. I couldn't even bare to bait a hook because I realized the worm was dying, and I flat out refused to cast a line and reel in a fish because I couldn't stand the thought of the poor, scaly animal looking up at me with its wide, frightened eyes while I watched as it struggled for oxygen and slowly died inside our cooler.

"When did you become such a sissy?" Ron sneered after snagging his third fish of the day.

"Yeah, since when are you afraid of a little fish?" Eddie asked, clutching his latest catch in his fist and waving it in my face.

"Leave me alone!" I cried, stomping over the rocks of the uneven creek bed. I hurried over to Daddy's truck, where the tailgate was still down, and an old blanket covered the scalding hot bed. I jumped up inside and curled into a ball, grateful that he had parked near a tree that afforded me a little shade from the late-August sunshine.

After a few minutes, I heard the crunch of feet on rocks, and jumped up expecting to have to defend myself against one of my brothers again. But it was Daddy, his hands in his pockets and his kind face shielded by the brim of his faded fishing hat.

"You okay?" he asked gently. "You haven't been yourself the last few weeks."

I said nothing, just concentrated on the softness of the blanket beneath my cheek and the heat radiating up from the beveled bed of his truck. As much as I loved and trusted my daddy, I couldn't trust him with this. I couldn't let anyone know I was going crazy.

He took a step closer, leaned against the truck, and sighed. "I know sometimes it's hard to talk to your old dad or tolerate your brothers, so I won't force anything out of you. But if you tell me what's wrong, maybe I can help."

I squirmed. Would saying the words protect him or hurt him? Would giving my fears a voice make them come true? Or act as a talisman against the worst? Before I could make up my mind, two fat tears leaked from my eyes.

"My brothers keep calling me a sissy!" I wailed, eventually, before I realized what I was saying. True, their teasing hurt, and I hated the way they called me names but bringing this out in the open seemed a safer choice than telling him what was really bothering me."

"I'm going to have a talk with them about that later," Daddy assured me. He momentarily removed his hat and wiped his brow with his forearm, and for the first time in my young life I noticed that his hair suddenly seemed to be disappearing. "You're not a sissy and they shouldn't be calling you one. You're just a young lady, and you don't want to play with fish and mud anymore. Is that right?

Silently I nodded.

"Ah, well. Happened a little sooner than I thought it would, you losing interest in getting dirty and going fishing, but I knew it was coming. Fifth grade this year—new school uniform, new building, home economics, the works! Next thing you know you'll be a grown up young lady."

I could only stare at him. The coming school year, new clothes, and classes were the least of my concerns. I was only terrified that he wouldn't be there to see me off on my first day or be able to greet me when I stepped off the bus.

"How about this?" he asked, turning once more to face me. "We'll turn the tide on your brothers. What if I start calling you Cissy—short for Frances? Once they hear that it's a special nickname I have for you, they'll probably stop saying it."

The stirring of a smile pulled upwards at my lips.

"Okay."

"There you go. Feel better?"

I nodded. "But Daddy?"

"Yeah?"

"Can you always call me Cissy? Like for the rest of forever?"

He paused for only a moment, as if pondering why on earth I'd ask such a question. "Well, sure, if that's what you'd like."

"Yes," I replied, enthusiastically, and roused myself from my hunched position in the bed of the truck. Finally, we had a bond, a connection that would stop the inevitable as long as I was Daddy's little Cissy, as long as we had an understanding, a secret bond, nothing would ever pull us apart. He'd stay safe as long as I was his Cissy

***

Balancing carefully in my brand-new platform heels, I made my way across the patio and onto the grass to pose in front of the towering evergreen at the edge of our yard. I stood awkwardly at first, feeling self-conscious with so much makeup on my face and wearing my flowing, royal-blue gown with the square cap and dangling gold tassel that tickled my cheek.

Mom pushed her glasses up on top of her head and fumbled with her brand-new camera that she'd bought just for the occasion. Grandma and Grandpap stood beside her reminiscing about how Ron and Bobby had posed in this same spot before their own commencement ceremonies years prior.

I squinted in the sunlight toward the backdoor, waiting for Daddy to join the rest of us. He'd rushed home from work at the mill and was hurrying to clean himself up before we jumped in the station wagon and headed to the high school. I didn't want him to miss this family tradition of his only daughter standing in front of the evergreen before receiving my diploma.

"There we go," Mom announced, pressing the camera to her eye. "Smile, Frances!"

I gave her a tiny grin, still watching the back door for Daddy. Even though I knew he was right inside the house, it felt wrong to be doing this without him. I wanted him to be present for every single moment of this night.

"Come on, a real smile," Mom coaxed, and I tried to relax.

She snapped a few more shots before the sound of tires on gravel turned our attention to the driveway. I watched as Ron's orange Pinto slowed to a stop, then chuckled when my brothers climbed out of the vehicle and made their way over to us.

Ron's hair was even larger and curlier than I'd ever seen it, and Bobby's platform shoes rivaled mine. Even though I thought they looked ridiculous trying to mock John Travolta in his latest movie, I was happy to see my brothers. Now that they were college men, our reunions were few and far between.

"There's our little sister!" Ron called, running up and wrapping me in a hug.

"You're making me feel old," Bobby added, giving my tassel a poke, which sent it swinging in my eyes.

"Boys, come on, I'm trying to take your sister's picture!" Mom cried.

They ignored her. "So, business school, huh?" Ron asked.

I nodded and felt my cheeks burn. "Yeah."

"You'll make a good secretary," Bobby said, and I knew he was thinking about his latest girlfriend, Donna, who had just secured a position in downtown Pittsburgh.

"Sure you don't want to go away to school like I did?" Ron asked. "It's a blast, I'm telling you." A knot formed in my stomach at the mere mention of living in a dorm, hours away from home—from Mom and

Daddy. "No," I replied quickly. "I can take the bus to class every day and save money staying at home."

"Being on your own is far out, though," Ron added.

Before I could think of another excuse to stay close to home, the back screen door banged open. I looked up expectantly and broke into a huge grin when I saw Daddy making his way across the lawn toward us.

"Ron! Bobby!" he called, greeting them with handshakes and claps on the back. "Staying out of trouble?"

The three of them laughed and then my brothers stepped aside so Daddy could take his place next to me in front of the tree. He placed his arm around me and kissed my cheek, then held me close enough so I could smell the Old Spice and Dial soap on his skin.

"I'm really proud of you, Cissy," he whispered as Mom snapped even more pictures. "And between you and me, I'm really glad you're staying home instead of going off to college."

"Me too," I replied happily, leaning over to peck his clean shaven skin. "Me too."

In that moment it didn't matter that I felt less than enthusiastic about business school. It didn't matter that deep down I might have wanted to explore journalism and was jealous that my best friend, Ruth, was going to live on Penn State's campus three hours away. All that mattered was that I'd be home close to Daddy. All that mattered was that I'd be there to make sure he came home safe every night.

***

I sat on the edge of my bed in my nightgown, glancing around my bedroom for the very last time. The walls were bare but I could still see patches where my posters and diplomas from high school and business school hung until recently. All of my possessions were stacked in the garage, waiting to be moved to the new house—our new house—when Marty and I returned from our honeymoon in two weeks.

My wedding gown hung on the back of my door in its garment bag, and I couldn't help but get up, unzip the plastic, and run my hand over the elaborate beading one final time. Despite the nerves that had my stomach twisting in knots, I smiled. *Tomorrow I'll finally be a bride, and after that I'll start my new life with Marty.*

I wasn't nervous about making such a commitment or standing up in front of hundreds of our family and friends or fainting in church. I wasn't worried that my hair wouldn't turn out right or that the catering staff would drop the wedding cake, nor did I feel uncertain about my wedding night, as much as I tried to fake it for Mom.

No, this bride-to-be was instead dreading the prospect of not seeing her father every day after spending nearly every spare moment with him for the last twenty-four years.

Sure, there'd been long weekends where he and Mom celebrated anniversaries and left me to my own devices, and I'd even ventured out a few times with friends overnight for short periods. But two weeks in the Bahamas was just the beginning of a lifetime away from my Daddy. Even though I was looking forward to having plenty of alone time with my husband-to-be, a bigger part of me couldn't help but shudder when I thought about the prospect of something terrible happening to him when I wasn't around. Part of me knew that the belief from my childhood was superstitious and completely illogical, yet my approach had worked so far, hadn't it?

I'd scribbled the hotel's long distance phone number on the back of an extra wedding invitation and secured it to the fridge with a magnet in case my parents needed to reach us in case of an emergency, but Mom had waved her hand and chuckled, "Don't worry about us, just enjoy your honeymoon." I didn't have the nerve to tell her that the honeymoon was only the tip of the iceberg.

Zipping the garment bag once again, I heaved a deep breath, crossed the room, and settled myself in bed. Though I doubted I'd get much sleep, I had to at least try. I certainly didn't want dark circles under my eyes in my wedding photos.

Just as I leaned over to switch off the bedside lamp, a faint knock sounded at my door.

"Come in," I called, expecting it to be Mom with another one of her speeches about becoming a wife.

But it was Daddy who pushed open the door with a bashful smile and made his way to sit on the edge of my bed like he had when I was a little girl.

"Feeling okay, Cissy?" he asked.

I nodded. "Nervous but excited."

"Good." He paused and looked around the room as I had done a few minutes ago, probably conjuring up images of how the décor had changed from the time I was little until now.

When he didn't speak again after a few moments, my heart thudded with dread. Daddy was very rarely quiet. Was he about to deliver some sort of bad news?

"Are *you* okay?" I asked cautiously, not sure if I wanted to know the answer.

He turned back to me and smiled, then reached over and patted my hand. "Just being a dad. Can't believe it's time to walk you down the aisle tomorrow."

I smiled back, and it was then that his eyes filled with tears. "Daddy!" I cried, and leapt up to wrap my arms around him. I had never, ever seen him cry. He chuckled and squeezed me back. "Ah, don't mind me." His voice was gruff with effort. "Thought I'd save this for the church but I guess it's hitting me now—my only little girl, all grown up."

"I can stay here if you like," I replied immediately. "I'm sure Marty won't mind living in my old bedroom for a few years." He pulled out of our embrace and shook his head firmly. "No, Cissy. I'll be okay. You have a life to live. Don't let me get in the way of that."

I hugged him again and closed my eyes so I could memorize the feel of his solid arms around me and the familiar scent that had remained unchanged since childhood. "Daddy, you could never get in the way of anything." Emotion choked off the next sentence I wanted to say but didn't have the strength to deliver. How could I tell him that he was the reason I'd never wandered far from home, that I'd insisted Marty and I only look for houses within ten miles of here? How could I ever admit to anybody that I still harbored those fears from childhood, that the man I loved most in the world could be ripped away from me without a second's notice? It sounded ludicrous, even inside my head—the notion that my absence would leave him vulnerable, that I'd concocted this idea that my presence kept him safe.

"I know you're going to be happy with Marty," Daddy said eventually. "And you're always welcome here."

"Thank you, Daddy, for everything."

Finally he stood up and rubbed his face, then winked and gave me the smile that I treasured. "Get some rest now. You don't want to sleep walk through your own wedding."

***

"Thanks for offering to keep an eye on them, Mom." My voice was soft in the silence of the living room.

Mom smiled from the sofa and turned her attention away from Johnny Carson. "No problem. I'm too old to stay up too far past their bedtime myself."

I chuckled and glanced toward the back door where distant laughter and music pulsed through the thick summer night.

"Did they go to sleep easily?"

"Kate fought me a little, but Allie could barely keep her eyes open." I thought about my two girls, ages three and five, hopefully fast asleep in their shared bedroom upstairs.

"Might want to tell them to turn that music down when you go back outside," Mom suggested.

I nodded and stifled a yawn myself. "I will, but both of them sleep like rocks. A volcanic eruption couldn't rouse those two."

Mom chuckled. "It's been a long day."

"Yeah, but a good one."

She waved a hand in the direction of my backyard. "Well, go back to your party. But tell your father I'm dragging him home at midnight come hell or high water."

I flashed her a sleepy smile. "Will do."

Quickly I made my way through the living room into the kitchen, then pushed open the screen door to step out onto the back patio. Only half a dozen guests from Daddy's retirement party remained, but the mood was still lively. The poker game he'd been playing with Marty and my brothers had been forgotten; spades and hearts lay scattered on the table among half-empty Iron City cans and barbecue chip crumbs.

Lightning bugs mingled with the dull glow of the honky-tonk lanterns strung across the yard, and my brothers stood in the center of the yard, arguing good-naturedly about who was the better imitator of MC Hammer's dance moves.

They looked ridiculous, of course, even if it hadn't been for their haphazard dress clothes or inebriated states. Marty and Daddy looked on from their seats on the patio, laughing hysterically and intermittently puffing on celebratory cigars.

Ron's wife Angela waved me over to where she and Bobby's wife, Janet, sat on the porch swing, and I hurried over to join them.

"Best seat in the house!" Angela cried, handing me a wine cooler and yelling encouragingly to her husband.

"I wish I had the camcorder," Janet added as I settled down between them. "We need video evidence of this."

I dissolved into laughter as I watched my brothers humiliate themselves to the sounds of MC Hammer, Vanilla Ice, and The Electric Slide. My sisters-in-law occasionally abandoned our swing to join them, but within the hour everyone was showing signs of tiring and we began to wind down.

"This was a really awesome party," Janet commented as she helped me collect abandoned beer bottles. "I think your dad had a good time."

"I hope so," I replied. "He deserves it after working his ass off at that mill for forty-some years."

"By the way Jan," Angela added. "Bobby's speech at dinner was the best. He had everyone laughing *and* crying."

Janet shot her an appreciative smile. "Thanks. He worked for hours on that thing."

"I never thought about a job that way," she continued. "His dad giving his life to the mill, but the mill giving him a life—good pay, vacations, healthcare for all the kids. It really makes sense."

The two of them chatted back and forth about Daddy working nearly half-a-century at the infamous steel mills of Pittsburgh. In my exhausted, slightly intoxicated state, I couldn't help but let my mind wander as I collected empty Styrofoam cups and discarded cocktail napkins. There had been a lot of news and talk recently about former mill workers being diagnosed with specific forms of cancer, ones caused by the dangerous materials used in their work environment. Working in a law office myself, my stomach clenched each time I saw the strange words on depositions and court filings—asbestos, Mesothelioma.

Daddy never talked about any of these things, and he didn't know anyone who'd recently been diagnosed, but the anxiety gnawed at my subconscious on a regular basis. Was cancer an inevitability?

The sound of the screen door slamming jolted me back to reality, and I turned to see my brothers, Marty, and Daddy making their way inside.

"Time to call it quits?" Janet asked, going to her husband's side.

Marty approached me with glassy eyes and an amused smile. "I would say 'see you upstairs' but I'll probably be passed out by the time you get there."

I smiled and shook my head as he pecked my cheek, then turned to Daddy.

"Thanks for putting this whole thing together, Cissy," he said affectionately, placing one arm around my shoulder and squeezing.

"No problem, Daddy," I replied. I rested my head on his shoulder momentarily and caught a whiff of mingled scents—Old Spice, cigars, and whiskey.

"I better go find your mother before she finds me." He chuckled and released me, then winked and waved. "Kiss those grandkids for me."

"I will, Daddy."

"Love you, Cissy."

"Love you too."

***

Marty emerged from the bathroom with his polo shirt hiked several inches above his waist, cinching his belt and gesturing toward the last hole on the buckle. "Frannie!" he cried, and his face lit up with joy. Even though his laugh lines were deeper and his hair was speckled with gray, he looked better than he had in years.

I raised my eyebrows, impressed, and slid my feet into my summer sandals. "Wow! I guess this Atkins guy really knows what he's talking about."

My husband waltzed over to the full-length mirror in the corner of our bedroom and tucked his shirt into the waistband of his almost-too-big khakis. "I'm telling you, this is the last diet anybody will ever have to go on."

I chuckled, and before I could reply, Kate appeared in the doorway.

"You guys ready?" she asked, her voice edgy. Normally I would have told her to check her tone, but I knew she was excited and nervous for the final performance of her senior year. She'd dreamed about being first chair of the flute section since she started playing in sixth grade, and the last nine months of her high school career was filled with highlights of her perfecting solos on stage and traveling across the tri-state area to compete in regional band competitions.

Besides, she looked so pretty, so utterly grown up, that it took my breath away for a moment and I had to gather myself before I replied. "Just about."

"You look pretty, honey," Marty called over his shoulder, and winked.

She flashed him a grateful smile and looked down at her red and white floral wrap dress and three-inch heels. She'd finally mastered the art of wearing makeup and styling her hair to highlight her natural features and gone was all the baby fat she'd carried around with her until recently.

Tears gathered in my eyes as I thought about how she'd be off to college after one short summer. Though her major was so far undeclared, she'd mentioned dabbling in everything from teaching music to graphic design and photography over the last several years. Whereas most other parents were panicked over their child's lack of decision, Marty and I had enough confidence in our daughter to know that she'd figure it out as she went along. Kate was destined to succeed no matter what she pursued.

A shout sounded from the kitchen, and the three of us hurried down the hall to find Allie, the baby of the family, reprimanding our new puppy, Maggie, for trying to steal a piece of pizza crust out of the trash.

"She's so sneaky!" she declared, and I could tell she was trying hard not to laugh. "But she's so stinking cute."

The three of us laughed as Allie ruffled Maggie's ears and proceeded to clean up from our hurried dinner. Our youngest daughter had chosen a bright orange knee-length sun dress to attend her sister's final concert, and she looked much older than her sixteen years.

When did I get old enough to have two teenage daughters? I wondered, my chest swelling with pride.

The shrill ring of the cordless phone interrupted my sentimental thoughts, and I rolled my eyes. "Ugh, I do not have time for a phone call right now."

Marty peeked at the Caller ID, something the girls had persuaded us to get only a few months ago. "It's your mom."

Knitting my brow, I snatched up the receiver with a tiny ball of anxiety creeping into my stomach. "Hello?"

"Frannie, hey," Mom said, and I heard the exhaustion in her voice right away. "I'm really sorry but I don't think we're going to make it to Kate's concert tonight."

My heart fell. "Is everything okay?"

There was just enough hesitation to make the tiny ball of nerves turn into a raging tornado of worry. "Your dad's back is still bothering him, and it's getting worse."

I let out a shaky breath. "Has he made a doctor's appointment yet?"

"Next week."

"Okay." I looked around the kitchen at my family, all dressed up, playing with the dog, anticipating Kate's upcoming performance and impending graduation celebration. Kate would be heartbroken if her grandparents weren't there.

"Everything okay?" Marty asked after I hung up.

I plastered a smile on my face and nodded. "They're just going to be a bit late."

The four of us grabbed our purses and wallets and headed towards the garage where our brand-new Isuzu waited to take us to the high school. As we buckled our seat belts and backed down the driveway, I tried to quell the guilt and worry that was now eating away at my conscience.

Kate didn't have to know anything was wrong with her grandfather was the logic I told myself. Nothing should spoil this night for her. And if Daddy's back problem was easy to fix, there was no point in causing everyone stress. I'd simply keep everything to myself until the doctor made a diagnosis.

I did my best to focus on the music that night, on how beautiful and talented my daughter was, up on that stage under those lights, playing those flowery, happy notes in front of hundreds of people. I tried to focus on the audience's applause, the praise the director gave the seniors, and the glow on Kate's face when she accepted bouquets of flowers from us, her uncles, and her boyfriend.

But one thought plagued me throughout the evening. *Will Daddy make it to Allie's senior orchestra concert two years from tonight?*

***

Cancer.

Mesothelioma to be exact—caused by the dangerous asbestos used in the steel mills where Daddy had spent decades working.

Suddenly the terms and prognoses I skimmed over blandly at work every day had a personal responsibility for upending my entire world. Suddenly my worst nightmare was about to come true—I was going to lose my daddy.

I'd known, of course, that chances were that I'd outlive him. I knew that most everyone buries their parents. But the thought of it actually happening caused my breath to shorten, my stomach to seize, and my vision to swim so I avoided thinking about it at all costs.

Now it was all I could think about.

Mom handled things with business-like precision. She only let her guard down when Daddy wasn't around. She only became emotional when she heard the prognosis, and she was only angry at him for a few hours when he decided he didn't want treatment.

Six months, the doctors told us, but in the end it was only three.

I stood clutching Mom's hand in the front pew of the church while Marty and my brothers served as pallbearers. I let her cry and ground my teeth until they hurt to keep from letting my own tears fall. Someone had to be strong, right?

It wasn't until hours later, after the reciting of prayer, after the rainy graveside vigil, after the wake with its rich food and dozens of people clad in black and dark blue that I collapsed onto my bed and bawled and screamed into the pillow.

Six months, the doctors had said. It would have been Christmas time. But Daddy would never sit down to a holiday dinner with us again. He wouldn't see Kate start college, he wouldn't see Allie graduate high school. He wouldn't attend his granddaughters' weddings or become a great grandfather. He'd never help Marty with another home improvement project, he'd never tell another stupid joke, would never push out his false teeth in attempt to make everyone blanche and laugh ever again. He was only seventy years old.

Suddenly I was that little girl again, huddled in her grandmother's back bedroom, listening to the hushed conversation of adults down the hall. I'd prayed that night that my daddy would be saved from the dangers of the mill, from the heat and the accidents and the unpredictability of the fickle material they worked with.

But the mill had taken him in the end anyway.

And he would never call me Cissy ever again.

***

Pappy had been gone for six years, and the mills had been gone since before I started kindergarten.

Mom didn't understand my fascination with the relics that

remained, and I wasn't sure I understood it myself.

But when it came time to choose a subject for my first solo project at work, my first six-page spread in The Burgh magazine, I couldn't think of anything else I'd love to photograph more than the remnants of Homestead's steel mills.

A few seemingly random structures remain, dotting the steel valley's landscape with hulking smoke stacks and massive iron edifices that defined a generation.

They stand proudly, almost eerily, relics playing witness to the swift changes of a modern world. The smokestacks, with their thousands of towering clay-colored bricks, are now surrounded by an establishment known as The Waterfront, complete with chain restaurants and hotels, casting shadows over bike paths and movie theaters, ATMs and coffee houses. Its sister structure, the squat building on the other side of the expansive shopping and business district, known unremarkably as The Pump House, now hosts weddings and fundraisers, full of cocktails and people in designer dresses posting pictures on their Pinterest boards. There are historical markers, of course, signs faded by the sun, dotting the walking trail that snakes along the Monongahela River, regaling tourists and enthusiasts about Pittsburgh's past, about the industry that built this golden triangle now famous for its sports teams and universities.

The centerpiece of my project, situated across the Monongahela, is the Carrie Blast Furnaces —the common, unassuming girl's name that tells nothing of the fierce heat they contained, say nothing of the dangerous work environment, nothing of the deadly material thousands of men breathed decade upon decade.

I am filled with a mix of trepidation and excitement as I make my way to the site on a chilly autumn evening. I've dressed sensibly, in baggy cargo pants that are easy to move in and sturdy hiking boots on my feet. The landscape is still rugged in places, spotted with bits of broken concrete, patches of uneven ground, and flecks of metal dust and other unidentifiable metallic debris.

The last tour group of the day is wrapping up as I unpack my equipment to take a few test shots. The sun will be setting soon, and I hope to capture the brilliant orange rays as a backdrop to this symbol of fallen industry.

As I peer through the lens of my camera, I can't help but think about what the site must have been like fifty years ago, crawling with men, filthy and sweating, laboring relentlessly as they worked to support their families back home in the surrounding suburbs and growing communities of the steel valley.

For a moment I am disgusted with myself. Am I glorifying my hometown's complicated past, complete with unsafe working conditions, deadly strikes, and the use of dangerous chemicals that infested my own grandfather's body with the cancer that killed him?

Or am I capturing the magnificent remnants of what put this city on the map, of a site that allowed thousands of immigrants and first-generation Americans to pursue their dreams?

The tour group breaks up after they snap a few last pictures with their smartphones and the guide answers a spattering of questions. I venture closer to the furnaces, trying to conjure up a conversation with Pappy, as if he were still on this earth, by my side.

"It was hard work, dangerous work," I remember him saying, year after year. "But I met some of my best friends working at the mill, and we made good money. I got to give my kids and my wife most of what they wanted, and we took plenty of vacations over the years."

I chuckled out loud to myself as I squatted down to capture the structures from ground-level against the rapidly changing sky. Mom and my uncles told so many stories about their many adventures every summer—from camping in state parks to exploring the beaches of the Outer Banks and venturing to places like St. Louis, Acapulco, and Florida in the seventies.

The mills had provided them with a near-idyllic lifestyle, one I knew every single one of them cherished, including my grandfather.

And if the cancer from the asbestos hadn't come for him in the end, it surely would have been something else eventually—dementia, heart failure, or simply old age.

So was I proud of my family's ties to Pittsburgh's steel mill past or was I bitter and angry that our patriarch had been one more casualty of this bygone era?

The sunset was on full display now, golden and pink rays lighting up the furnaces and the landscape with the surreal glow of an autumn evening. I snapped a series of photos in rapid succession, my heart rate increasing as adrenaline coursed through my veins. I loved taking photos of any kind, but my real passion was capturing images like these—inanimate objects with storied histories and complicated, even controversial pasts.

I paused for a moment to review the images on the tiny digital screen and felt my chest swell with pride at the results. Even before editing, I could tell that my boss back at the office would be impressed. I was young, and I'd only been working at The Burgh for a year, but I'd been told I was one of their most promising photographers. With any luck, this project would get me one step closer to a promotion. I could already see my name splashed across the glossy pages —*photographs by Kate Zielinski.*

I circled the massive furnaces one last time, racing to capture their façade before the sun sunk completely into the horizon and then disappeared into the night. When I finally surrendered to the darkening evening, I packed up my equipment and listened to the stillness around me as I made my way back to my car.

The site was mostly quiet, but in the distance I could see the glow of The Waterfront across the river where the towering smokestacks and darkened Pump House sat quietly among the bustling restaurants and shops. A barge chugged steadily through the waters of the Monongahela and a train whistle sounded in the distance.

The mills may have been gone and Pappy with them but this Pittsburgh suburb was still a bustling source of income, development, and maybe even dreams.

Since my grandfather's death, I'd seen my family's past and even my own future shadowed by the history of this steel town. But as I drove home with my windows down, letting the breeze off the river flow through my car, I realized that the remnants of that same steel mill still had more to give—in the form of art, in the form of history.

My latest photo project would be a success; I could feel it in my bones. The steel mill was still providing opportunity, pumping out life, decades after its own death.

Man Down

Robert McKean

He was a bony, itchy, uncomfortable man. If there existed a divinity of nuisance and welter, it was Hoot Sutherland, Charley decided, whom that deity had chosen to most bitterly inflict. He met Hoot the first day of summer, the morning of his transfer downriver six miles from Tin Mill to Blast Furnace. Hoot was sawing the tread from a truck tire into two kidney-shaped hunks for the soles of his boots. As Charley came abreast of him, the hacksaw leapt free of the rubber and slashed Hoot's knuckles.

You would've thought, whoever this old bird was, that he might pause to bind his hand. But no, for its stubbornness, Hoot attacked the tread with renewed venom. Shielding his thermos, unwilling to deal with someone quite this possessed quite this early, Charley edged around the old man and stepped into the soot-blackened shanty wedged beneath a jigsaw tangle of hissing pipes and looming ramps—this his third labor gang since March.

In three months he'd met a legion of ancient laborers. Represented men had to retire at *some* age, but, whatever that mandate, if their minds were not entirely fogged, their joints not entirely arthritic, it seemed as if they could—and did—go on working forever. Perhaps they had nothing to retire to or on; perhaps they simply were unable to resist the compulsion of habit that impelled them to plant one unsure foot before the other and thus, day after day, carry themselves past the armed guards through the gates. Frail old men were given light duties, like tending a single washroom or pushing a broom up and down a deserted corridor—slight, silent figures you hardly noticed, men who the seasons no longer seemed able to age but could only rarefy, beating them like gold thinner and thinner.

True, there were a few rosy cherubs for whom time's dominion had been more benign. Thomas Quinlan, for instance, a funny old hen who over his three score years appeared to have grown only shorter, stouter, and more foolish. Mornings, the symphonic gurgle in Quinlan's lungs sounded a pulmonary matins across the locker room of lost souls that comprised Skeet Dorsey's Tinplate maintenance gang. Jowls wobbling as he mauled his hot lunches, Quinlan cackled at his own stories, scooping up handfuls of horseshit to hurl at the mounted constabulary in one of the town's early labor actions and taking, in turn, a truncheon across the temple that bequeathed him an enduring scar his waxy old fingers absently traced and retraced.

"Charley, you ever have any trouble, you know, getting your motor going?"

With Quinlan, you seldom knew where he was headed. "Not usually, Tom."

"Well, if you do, sprinkle a couple drops of rye on the end of your pecker. Doesn't take much and—*presto!* Ready for action!"

"What if I don't have any rye?"

"Well, it don't exactly *have* to be rye. Bourbon'll work. Just stay away from gin."

"What's wrong with gin? I like gin."

"I'm just telling you," the old man squealed, "gin'll rot your liver six ways from Sunday!"

But that was then, and now was now. For reasons revealed only to management, with the college boys showing up for summer jobs, once again Charley had been transferred, and, by the conclusion of his first week in the Blast Furnace Department, he could see that Hoot Sutherland stepped to the beat of a different drummer altogether. No orderly retreat into old age for Hoot, no blossoming of wisdom, no respite from the follies of youth. Say what you will about Tommy Quinlan—after all he'd gone through, he was not a bitter man. Say what you will about Hoot Sutherland—he was.

Time, as customary, had delivered Hoot of mane, teeth, and probably libido. A lifetime of foolhardy speculations had delivered him of his savings. But it was the doctors, the conniving doctors who were Hoot Sutherland's all-time nemeses. Even that first morning, emerging from a lavatory stall, peevishly banging the door that had dared to snag a belt loop, he lighted on Charley, the new face.

"*Hey you!* Ain't it right the more the doctors cut, the more money they git? Ain't that right, sonny boy? Bet your sweet petunia that's right! Thievin' butchers—strapped me down, cut me like I was a slab of saltwater taffy! *Looky!*"

He wrenched up his shirt, crawled out of the top half of his union suit, and exhibited a scar that angled like a purple turnpike across his scrawny torso and dove straight ahead into his pants. Thumb at his nose, stretching his arm like a dry-goodsman measuring worsted wool, Hoot yawped out his losses. "One yard! Two yards! Three yards! *Butchers!* Hey! What's your name? Where you'd get all that hair? *Hey!* You deaf or sumpin? What's your name?"

Charley Rankin told him his name, not that Hoot remembered it, and, while he wasn't the boss, when they worked side by side Hoot ran the show. Mornings, Hoot careened his mud-spattered pickup in from Union Township near the southern border with West Virginia, accepted whatever tool handed him, and worked clumsily, compulsively, frenetically—bullying his way through jobs without stop because, Charley concluded, once Hoot got underway it hurt too much to stop. If they were sweeping, Hoot lowered his head and shoved his broom indefatigably up and down the same corridor, overlooking the same trash every time he plowed past, until Springer, the foreman, or Boles, his subforeman, the pusher, steered his breakneck course down another corridor. And because Hoot refused to moderate his personal pace to a more sensible union pace, other members of the gang disliked working with him. Since he was not a college boy nor one of the lifers, neither fish nor fowl as Quinlan succinctly put it—Charley had little choice, and Springer replaced Morey Simonian with Charley and teamed him and Hoot to operate the pig-caster.

"Stay awake," Springer cautioned. Jim Springer had played defensive tackle for Ganaego High the same Depression years that Charley's father had played tenor sax in the marching band. But the man looked older than Charley's father, his heavy body giving the illusion of inexorably crumpling in on itself. "Don't be woolgathering under the pig machine."

No doubt, staying awake was important. But it was not a job that required much beyond dumb muscle. After the furnaces were tapped and the molten iron drained into pugh cars, or, as the men called them, torpedoes—railcars that looked like pudgy submarines—yardmen trundled the cars across the department to stand over a conveyor of pig molds. The first laborer, the man on the top, controlled the angle at which the torpedoes were tipped so that the iron spilled evenly into the molds—like a spigot filling a moving ice cube tray. The metal on metal conveyor, screeching appallingly, hauled the molds up an incline under a cooling spray toward high-sided gondola cars where the conveyor tucked under and the pig-iron ingots, cherry-red but solidified, tumbled into the gondolas' hoppers. Most of the ingots, that is. Perversely, some stuck to the molds and rode the conveyor back underneath. There, the ingots would loosen of their own volition, clattering down through the conveyor's trestles like hundred-pound glowing snowflakes, or they would be pried free from the molds on the move by the second laborer below, the man on the bottom, wielding a six-foot crowbar.

Hoot coveted working the pig-caster because the job was worth an extra point, about ten cents an hour. "Count this one of your red-letter days, sonny boy," he'd announce, tramping off across the yard. "*This* you're gonna see in your poke!"

Bracketing the man on the bottom stood two colossal pots of boiling water to which he fed fifty-pound sacks of lime so that steam carrying lime dust might waft up and coat the returning, now upside down, empty molds. As the day wore on, the inside of the bottom man's mouth, like the chambers of the molds, would whiten with lime. His eyes, bloodshot from the fumes, would smolder vampirishly in his powdered face. His back, arms, and hands would undertake a journey through weariness and ache into a dizzy incandescent region beyond numbness—and all this, Charley, that man on the bottom, twenty-two this summer and at a low-water mark in his life, had frequent opportunity to ponder, for an extra eighty cents.

What was he doing here?

Or maybe the question was better phrased: How much *longer* was he going to be here? This experiment he'd intended to be of a limited duration, a month or two to gather funds and then off to Europe. A good plan, even if everyone, particularly his father, seemed to disagree. Only trouble was, he hadn't left. He'd come home in March; by now, he was supposed to have been long gone. If he found his on-again, off-again girlfriend on the boulevards of Paris and they worked through their problems, fine. If not, it'd still be fine. Some days it was Paris his plane touched down in, some days Amsterdam, some days Barcelona, one week Munich, and, as vague as he was on his geography, on his deadlines, he appeared to be ten times more so.

Next week, he promised.

Hoot, the man on the top, spent *his* afternoons poking his glossy cranium out of the pig-caster shed that he'd fashioned into a home-away-from-home and fulminating at all and sundry who regretfully chanced by. He launched ribbons of tobacco juice out over the trestles where they landed sizzling on the ingots and leaked down the trestles like a thin brown blood. Summoned by nature, he'd empty his feeble spray over the conveyor. On his evil days, the washing machine of his guts churning away inside him, he'd withdraw into his shed and study the tabloids he scarfed up from the lavatory floors. The most lurid pictures—three-headed babies and two-thousand-pound teenagers—he nailed around the room. You'd hear him up there hammering away like a pissed-off woodpecker. And on especially warm afternoons, overcome by the fumy, soporific humidity that settled across the steelworks, a chemical molasses you could hardly move your body through, Hoot had a disturbing tendency to doze off—while molten iron at two thousand degrees poured out unsupervised over Charley's head.

The gang's collective opinion was that Hoot had cancer. And the vehemence with which the first syllable of that Hippocratic oath, *Bas,* exploded and the second rancorously dragged *tuuuuurds!* coming up his throat like a grappling hook, combined with the increasing number of days his wife called him in sick, convinced Charley that he probably did have cancer.

One of Hoot's daughters and her children lived at home. The son-in-law languished in jail. One evening in July driving out to Hoot's farm after work to deliver his check to him—he was on medical leave again—Charley came up against Hoot's people: three polished little blond faces, azure eyes drawn into premature squints, rising up in his car windows.

"Whacha doin' here, mister?"

Charley, questioning whether Springer's offer to let him go an hour early for this excursion was worth it, held up an envelope. "Hoot's pay."

A shout from the porch, and they sullenly withdrew. Following the directions of Hoot's wife—seemingly as gnarled and ill-tempered as Hoot. But then the diminutive nut-brown face broke into a rather sweet, crinkled smile when he introduced himself. Charley stepped around a Billy goat with a long, distinguished countenance and into a bone-clean house. In the living room a makeshift bedroom had been established. Hoot sat propped against a tall headboard, union suit unbuttoned to the waist, looking small, mean, and querulous in the expanse of the bedcovers. Charley laid the check next to Hoot's cold pipe on the television.

Hoot snapped at his wife, "Can't you see the man's thirsty?"

A moment later Charley was handed a glass of sweetened iced tea, and Hoot, galvanized by a visitor, flew into a standard paroxysm. "They fed me a lot of fiddle-faddle about one thing and another, pulled up my shirt and poked me all over, but I'll be back, sonny boy, don't order the lilies yet. Fact is, I'd been in to pick up my paycheck myself, though I thank you for making the trip. Work with Porky on the pig machine today?"

Charley shook his head. "Dug up a broken pipe. Morey Simonian and me."

"Chews his nails. Gets my goat."

A middle-aged bachelor who lived with the widow of the man who'd taken him in as a five-year-old orphan, Simonian was a bashful, quiet fellow. Lunchtimes, while the maintenance gang lay sprawled across the locker room benches drifting in and out of stuporous fogs, Morey pored over booklets from a TV-repair correspondence course he seemed perpetually enrolled in, pages and pages of spidery schematics and tiny gray print. Hoot hated him with a passion.

"Morey's all right," Charley defended the man.

"Dip his fingers in the lime pots, that'd put an end to it."

"Well, it is a bad habit."

"They doctor in posses anymore, you know? Not just one sawbones, but one leading and five tagging along like alotta baby ducks. One of 'em was a *female* person! Can you abide that? Pulling up my shirt in front of her! I ain't goin' back. I tole Bess—my guts fall out, she can darn them up like socks. You inform Jim Springer, Monday I'll be in."

Hoot looked haggard, pipe-cleaner arms hugging the sunken wicker basket of his chest, liverish pools beneath his rheumy eyes, veins in his trembling hands standing out like blue yarn. He shivered on this warm evening even though he spurned his wife's offer of a shawl. At one point one of his grandson's little blond visages showed up bearing a grievance. Hoot heard the boy out, then picked up a cane and brought it down hard on his shoulders. "Go tell your ma your hardships!"

Whatever a fair assessment of his son-in-law's character might have been—he'd been clapped in jail for beating the living daylights out of someone with a tire iron—Hoot had weighed him in one department and found him wanting in all the rest. The young husband liked to buy old cars and customize them. "Bad enough he got hisself worked up and throwed into prison, but I got an autymobile in the barn looks like a one-car circus and four extra mouths to feed!"

Charley, struggling to make conversation, asked, "What kind of car is it?"

"How the dickens do I know?"

Maybe conversation wasn't what Hoot needed. Charley set his glass down, and Hoot beckoned him. "Ain't never tole anyone this," he said in a husky whisper. "Taped to the inside of the front leg of my locker is a key. If I don't git back, I'd appreciate it if you'd bring my stuff out here to me—without snooping through it! You willing to do that?"

"Sure, Hoot."

"I'll be back Monday so it don't matter. But it can't hurt to take precautions. The Good Lord don't always confer with me in advance, if you know what I mean."

"He doesn't check in much with me, either."

"That's between you and your Creator," Hoot said stiffly. "I thank you agin for delivering my rightful wages. You wanna look at my dogs before you leave, you're welcome. Gotta couple beauties. Do much huntin'?"

"No, sorry."

"You like dogs? You gotta like dogs!"

"I like dogs a lot."

"Well, praise the Lord for that much." Hoot sank back against his pillows. "Go look at my dogs, I'll see you Monday."

On a buffet stood a collection of family photographs. One, a black and white print in a tarnished frame, caught Charley's eye—a boy standing before an unpainted house. The boy was barefoot, his hands jammed inside the pockets of his short pants. He wore a collarless, pinstriped shirt buttoned to the chin and a cap pushed back on his blond hair. The boy's face was beautiful: pug-nosed, freckled and honest, his gaze square on the camera. Even without asking, Charley knew that boy was Hoot, and on the drive home he got to wondering about the transformations that must have occurred in Hoot's life. When had he changed from that composed and uncomplicated child into the foolish speculator who'd thrown away good money after bad on one get-rich-quick scheme after another? When had the lines appeared in his face, the deep trenches angling down from his nose alongside his mouth, the multitudinous wrinkles fanning across his withered cheeks? When had the eyes narrowed, hardened, dulled? When had the cancer, if that's what it was, begun to gnaw at his insides?

Do you ever know these things about yourself? Can you?

Union Township lay not far from where Charley's mother had grown up. Drifting down through the country hollows, he studied the tea-hued light bathing the tumbledown farms and hardscrabble communities nestled in the backwater pockets the state route wound through and thought of his mother, child of a Welsh coal-mining family whose life was largely unknown to him. The newspaper reported that thousands of trees this summer had been defoliated by gypsy moth. You could see where the larvae—released from sacks that hung in the branches like gossamer lanterns announcing where death had visited—had stripped whole trees. The remaining few leaves, whitened with summer's dust, glittered where the slanting sunlight knifed through their chewed membranes.

Since his return, however, more than the countryside, it had been the industrial landscape that had taken on for Charley a vividness it had never before possessed. Reaching the boulevard along the river, he looked across the sunset-tinted water to the steelworks. What had always been little more than scores of anonymous roofs engulfed in an everlasting collar of smoke was now a recognized territory. Buildings he could identify: the Tin Mill with its sprawling yards crowded with shiny coils of steel; the Welded Tube, where he'd spent three weeks; the Open Hearth and last remaining Bessemer; the chain-mail tent called the skull-breaker, where the huge slag beards that formed inside the slag pots were smashed; the pyramids of ore, limestone, and coal that the ore bridges rumbled over; the massive cylinders of the blast furnaces and their stubby stoves; and always, the slender stacks of the coke ovens stretching in a sentry line against the sky, the signature of the valley. Through the gates of this nine-mile-long steel mill beside the Ohio his father and both his grandfathers had walked—and now so had he. Even the mill whistle—the familiar tone set a shade higher than the whistles of the trains and the horns of the tows—had acquired a deeper significance. It could still be, when he happened to be outside and free of its summons, the brilliant shaft of sound he'd grown up hearing, the valley's official timekeeper people set their watches by, especially on rainy evenings when the shrill flute carried pure and undiminished mile after mile up and down the river. But now that he'd come home to labor in the works, he'd begun to regard the whistle the way the other men did, not pretty, not sentimental, but an auditory tyrant unyielding in its demands.

And that *was* a difference in his life, he recognized.

As the balmy June afternoons gave way to July's and August's humidity—when for weeks the burning ball of the sun seemed to have come to rest directly over the steelworks, enclosing them in a radiant opalescence that stopped consciousness in its tracks—Charley had felt his resistance to the lethargic, hypnotic rhythms of the mill weakening. *Temporary,* he kept telling himself, *temporary.* A few more days and he'd put in his notice, maybe next week after all, certainly the week after that. But with the season smoldering beneath him like the glowing scoria the men poured down the riverbank, it was beginning to feel—as lost this year as he'd ever been—a little too temporary.

You can go on fooling yourself only so long.

***

"She always wanted you"—his father is saying—"to have grandma's diamond."

Late March. Not the reception Charley has anticipated. But in the hour or so since he's come home unannounced, he and his father in an unstated truce have stuck with safe subjects. After his grandmother May's death, his father distributed everything of May's that was of value: her husband's watchmaker bench she cherished; her mahogany mantel clock and heavy Empire furniture; her china cabinet through whose shimmering glass shells Charley used to gaze at her peasant village of porcelain figures; her beloved Philco Transitone, its Art-Deco-inspired case swooping up to one side; her clothes and jewelry, everything except for the old ring.

"It's what's called a briolette, *a good-sized stone. But I can't vouch for the quality. Knowing Dr. Rankin, you'll want to have it appraised. Like everything connected with him, there's a funny—or not so funny—story behind it. He forged Grandma Ophelia's signature to withdraw the money from her account to buy it, essentially stealing her money to buy her a gift so she'd forgive him for stealing money from her on an earlier occasion. If you like, we can go down to the bank tomorrow and get it?"*

Before Charley's eyes floats a scene: into moist cemetery earth, he sees, high heels sinking; women, needing to be assisted up a steep hill, their faces remote, turned inward. That's not right, he thinks. The bus trip from Portland through Salt Lake City, across the Rockies and the Prairie, through Chicago, across Indiana and Ohio into Pittsburgh and then to Ganaego has taken 75 hours, three continuous days, bequeathing him a headachy lassitude. As fatigued as he is, he's confused a memory of his mother's death with May's. The difference is that his grandmother was prepared to die. She'd been preparing for death for a long time. In fact, that was the problem: Her preparations had gone on and on, and death would not come. Her diabetes had worsened; she'd lost weight. It was as if her flesh were slowly being consumed by the disease. She complained of angina and slipped nitroglycerin under her tongue.

Charley remembers his father's phone call, the rushed trip home from university and final visit in the hospital ("I just want to go, Charley"), and the second call, a few days before the holidays.

Once a long time ago May had pried open a little brushed velvet case to show him a ring, minuscule gold prongs supporting a prismatic teardrop gem. Wistfully, he imagines the antique diamond on his ex-girlfriend's finger. "That was nice of her," he says, wondering if anyone will paste May's obituary in the scrapbook of obituaries she saved, in a sense completing it, knowing of course no one will. "Some other time."

Since her death, his father has done over her old rooms. He shows them to Charley. "I'm not sure why I bothered. Anybody in their right mind would sell, but I'm not ready yet. I know you don't like painted woodwork—your mother was the same way—but heaven knows how many coats of varnish it had on it. Other than the woodwork, you like it?"

May's two rooms, bereft of the familiar presence one had grown to expect in them, are as anonymous as a display you might wander through in a furniture store. Charley supposes he ought to be shocked. But no, last December was when the shock came, walking into the kitchen—as he had all those years—and not seeing May turning at the stove, giving him the high sign, her singing heart, the largest of her spirit after his mother's death, her arms like wings. He senses his father waiting for his approval. "The rooms are fine, Dad," he says, an imploring note creeping into his voice. "They look real good."

There occurs the awkward pause that eventually had to come. "It's your grades," his father says. "That's what I don't understand. I don't care about the probation. You didn't hurt anybody but yourself, as I understand it. And this business in Oregon, I don't even pretend to know what that's all about. But your grades? Up until this year they were fine? It doesn't make any sense?"

For a month, after getting thrown out of his girlfriend's apartment, he's been sleeping in Portland's flophouses, sometimes the backseats of unlocked cars. Charley understands his father's frustration. Even if he withholds what he's been through, he knows he's required to say something, to acknowledge what even he agrees has been his erratic behavior. But what is there to say? That he's immature? He knows that, and he's ashamed of it, ashamed to be eternally the baby of the family, the one in trouble, the one asking for money, help, forgiveness. "It doesn't matter."

"Yes, it does. Your grades matter a lot."

"No, they don't. I'm not going back."

"Don't talk nonsense. You're almost done. Maybe you can take some courses here at the branch campus—you know, to get back in the swing of things?"

"I want a job in the mill."

"Sure." His father nods dismissively. "It'll be nice to have you back this summer.

They always make some slots available for the college boys."

"I mean now. I want to make some money and go to Europe."

"No! Absolutely not!" Always there has been this paradox: Despite his loyalty to the steel mill, Don Rankin has been adamant that his sons would only work there summers, if at all. Having never attended college himself, getting a college education has assumed to him a kind of grandeur, an unquestioned requirement that his sons must fulfill.

"All right, I'll apply at Federated then."

"Charley, I'm worried about you. You've got us all worried."

"I'll deal with everything, I just need some time."

"As far as I can see," his father scowls, "you haven't dealt with anything. But all right, here's what I'll do. I'll try to get you in, but only if you enroll at the branch campus. I'll see if I can have you placed on one of the maintenance gangs—Skeet's Tin Mill crew is all daylight. You can take night classes. One of the fellows in the office has a boy doing that. Why you always insist on making it twice as hard on yourself is beyond me, but if that's what you want, so be it."

Walking up Roosevelt Avenue earlier, Charley had stopped to look at the reflections from the fires in the steelworks feathering the clouds. He smelled the sulfur and limestone fumes curling between the small grimy buildings. Why had he come back? He could've gotten a job in Portland. But staying there after his girlfriend left—impulsively quitting her job and taking off for Europe, as they had planned to do together—seemed pointless. "I'm sorry, I don't mean to be worrying everybody."

"I'm just happy to have you home in one piece." His father closes the door to May's rooms. "Look, tomorrow, sleep in, okay? Take it easy. And eat something—for heaven's sake, you're as skinny as a flagpole."

Upstairs in his old attic bedroom Charley tries to accommodate himself to the once-familiar mattress, but can't sleep. That's been the problem all along. And it started before his girlfriend broke up with him. Either he couldn't get to sleep or couldn't stay asleep. He'd wake in the middle of the night, his mind a tumult, and he'd be compelled to get up, dress, and leave the building. He wandered the streets, gesticulating, talking to himself. Was he having a nervous breakdown?

Below, he hears a window rumbling down, the latch thrown, then it grows quiet, and the old house, timbers shifting and murmuring, settles into its own sleep. From the sheets an odor of must stirs. He composes himself, attempts to sleep. But it's no use. He feels the Greyhound pulling beneath him, bearing him, a hostage, across the Prairie, over the mountains, back to Portland and that locked door. He climbs out of the bedcovers and sits at his desk. In his absence his father has hung up his great-grandfather's ancient diplomas. Time has darkened the glass and browned the parchment, but the oversized certificates, either fraudulent or meaningless, obtained *with a single purpose in mind, to impress illiterate laborers, are, in themselves, wonderful objects. Charley, recalling the stories of the family's black sheep, Dr. Rankin—or the title he liked even better, the Esteemed Leading Knight—studies the one over his desk. Issued by a school of optometry in Philadelphia, the diploma is gargantuan, with an official embossed seal and enormous, spidery calligraphy.*

With that on your wall, who wouldn't trust you?

Before long his father will be up, white shirt and tie, steel-toed wingtips already on, whistling as he fries a single egg and two slices of Canadian bacon, butters his toast and boils just sufficient water for a cup of instant Maxwell House. The family's accustomed to thinking of his father as a solitary, self-contained, indestructible sort of person. Donald Rankin carries that aura. Sometimes talks about himself in the third person. Yet his father, Charley knows, before May's death has never lived alone in his life, has certainly never slept a night in the backseat of a stranger's car.

Crawling into bed, shivering beneath Dr. Rankin's fanciful diplomas, Charley wonders, his anxieties rising beyond their banks, if he will ever come to peace with himself. For a moment he panics: How much money do you need for a year in Europe? Where do you stay? And then, as he drifts into a half-sleep, he's seized by the notion that he should get dressed and go outside. In fact, it seems as though he is outside. Through the branches of the old maples he sees the glittering constellations, then takes the path down through the ravine, past the pine boughs he loves to brush against, until he's out of sight of the house and all he hears on the dry pine needles are his soft footfalls, and, when he pauses, nothing, nothing but a crystalline silence so profound you could gather it up in your arms.

***

Come Monday a month later, Hoot was back.

How he managed to persuade the company physician to approve his return was anybody's guess; nonetheless, there he was, first one in, blaspheming the sack of lime he was dragging over to the pig-caster. Jim Springer, sighing, motioned to Charley, and, as if they were taking over for the third shift in a wartime munitions plant, he and Hoot got off to a roaring start. That afternoon he caught glimpses of Hoot above, hovering over the pugh car, two mis-focused eyes glued to the silver lake of iron sliding toward the lip. Once, after winding up with the crowbar and giving a particularly recalcitrant ingot a resounding *whack!*, he was startled by Hoot hollering down, "Key-rist Almighty, sonny boy, felt that booger all the way up here!"

No one else working the top position would take such an active interest in the affairs of the bottom man. By the same token, however, when he hauled off and missed banging down an ingot, no one else but Hoot would have whined, "*Hail Columbia,* that's three in a row! You need one of my dogs down there to help you?"

"It's the angle you're tipping the torpedo!" A member of the union in good standing now, Charley felt he could assert his rights. "Damn things are hardening up way too soon today!"

"Don't fuss at me, boy." Hoot clamped his discolored dentures around his tobacco-less pipe. "You do your job, I'll do mine."

Hoot wore a stiff new pair of Sears, Roebuck dungarees, already ripped at a knee, and beneath that and his ever-present union suit was, Charley ruminated, all that interceded between him and a thousand gallons of liquid metal. And just what *was* that? What by now remained of Hoot Sutherland? A few whiskers, some flakes of itchy skin, a gold tooth or two, a little unpleasant gas, a head full of recriminations. There were safety catches to prevent the ladle from tipping too precipitously. There *had* to be safety catches—still, a moment of forgetfulness brought on by an especially rosy delusion, a stab of bilious rage directed at a particular *nurse educator*, and Charley was never too positive that at any stray moment he might not be drenched in molten metal, given an honest-to-goodness suit of iron, white hot.

End of shift, Hoot grudgingly shut them down. According to him—and he was the only one counting—they had set a new record and earned the same additional eighty cents they would've earned had they worked at half the speed. Charley heaved the crowbar into the lime-syrupy girders and wormed his way around the furnaces to Springer's shanty. There, he peeled off his clothes, which were as white as a shroud, and plunged into the showers. The tiles undulated with quivering silverfish, and the steam billowed with the stench of the greenish-yellow germicide the washroom attendants sloshed around that never seemed to do any good. But if the silverfish didn't object, neither did he, and he stood under the scalding spray for a long time loosening his sore, upstretched neck and knotted muscles. When he stepped out, he noticed Hoot hammering a piece of twisted metal with a brick.

What purpose he had in mind only he and his Creator knew.

But it was destined to be a short return. Wednesday afternoon that same week, while extracting a sack of lime from under the legs of a fellow dozing in the lime shed—late afternoon, members of Springer's gang were apt to be randomly deployed among the lime sacks like snoozing tent caterpillars—Charley heard a peculiar moan. He dropped the lime and clambered up the rung ladder to the control platform, where Hoot knelt beside a fresh torpedo, his face screwed by pain back to the bone, a pool spreading beneath him of vile-colored liquid.

"Take it easy, old-timer," Charley told him and ran for Springer. The medics carried Hoot off the pig machine in a litter, eyes sunk in his head.

Man down, the men in the mill said.

***

Mornings, before the gangs commenced work, their foremen were required to deliver short safety lectures. Whether it was also required that each day the lectures be identical, Charley didn't know, but for the three gangs he'd worked on the foreman had delivered his same word-for-word speech day after day in the same soulless monotone. Jim Springer—who was only marking time until he could retire and raise the exotic sheep he'd pry open his wallet to show you snapshots of—seemed, even more than his crew, to dread these daily talks. The men slumped forward on the benches, staring vacantly into the empty bowls of their hard hats. Springer had to at least pretend to show some enthusiasm.

But this morning in September, two weeks after Hoot's collapse, Springer set aside his lecture to tell them that he'd spoken yesterday with Hoot's wife and that Hoot had died. Springer went on to say something to the effect that on these occasions it was customary for the gang to take up a collection. He threw a ten-dollar bill in his foreman's white hardhat and started circulating it. Since Charley volunteered to buy the flowers, he knew how much the gang contributed to Hoot's funeral. Seventeen dollars.

After work he talked to Springer and cleaned out Hoot's locker. He found the key taped to the leg, and, as promised, scooped Hoot's belongings into a grocery bag without rifling through them. Then reconsidered. Surely, Hoot's family had no need for his library of gruesome tabloids and pornographic picture books. Charley discarded what was unsavory and consolidated what remained—two faded plaid shirts, a pair of baggy-knee overalls, and Hoot's cracked-leather boots with the ruined soles he'd never succeeded in repairing. He added another three dollars to the kitty to bring it to an even twenty and agreed to a modest vase of flowers that the florist described as having *masculine* colors. That evening he drove the sixty-five miles south to a country town just this side of the West Virginia border.

The funeral home shared a small building with a Lennox furnace contractor. The carpet in the lobby was thin and colorless, worn to threads in patches. Charley checked Hoot's grocery bag with the funeral director and carried his flowers down the hall. When he turned into the parlor where the family was gathered, the little blond faces that had confronted him when he delivered Hoot's paycheck confronted him again, scrubbed scrupulously clean tonight, string tie knotted beneath each defiant chin. On a sofa sat Hoot's wife in black.

"I'm…"

"I recall you very clearly, Mr. Rankin," she said, rising. Her hands, lying in his palms, were dry and weightless as two autumn leaves, but the sweet, forthright smile he'd noticed before broke through the nest of wrinkles that comprised her face. "Let me present you to my family. Walter would be honored you came all this way to pay your respects."

Other than family—Hoot's two grown sons and hopelessly ostracized daughter, their spouses and children, and a spinster sister of Hoot's, all, it appeared, as gloomy as Hoot—only a few people visited while Charley was there. Conspicuously, no one from the mill. He remembered a story of his mother's: she, as a child, meeting with her father on their way to church four men whose faces were seamed with coal dust bringing home the body of a workmate to lie in his bed one last time. Coal mining and steelmaking these days was immeasurably safer, and that certainly was to be desired. But as Charley looked around the quiet, sparsely populated room, he couldn't help but think that perhaps along the way some things had been lost.

Still early, he thought. *Maybe more people will come.*

Hoot's small body, nearly lost amid the plush cushions, had been crudely made up and dandified. Whoever prepared him had been generous with his pigments. Hoot looked like he might leap from his casket and break into a vaudeville routine. He wore a plaid suit with five-inch lapels, a floral tie and handkerchief, a large gold wristwatch. But neither the cosmetics nor the suit could disguise how emaciated he'd become. His wedding band, standing up from the flesh, cast a faint shadow on the bony fourth finger beneath, and the skin at the tips of his fingers splayed flatly, insect-like.

As Charley was about to leave, Morey Simonian walked in. It took

Charley a second to recognize him. Morey was wearing a voluminous black suit, which, as ample as it was, barely spanned his girth. His shoes, also black, gleamed; his unruly hair, slicked down with lotion, lay close to his skull. He'd shaved after work, and his pale, pillowy cheeks, usually shadowed with a dense mat of whiskers, shone like his shoe caps with a high gloss. As arresting as his appearance, however, it was what Simonian carried before him that drew everyone's attention.

He held, cupped his hands, a small model airplane.

They were all a little stupefied. It was Hoot's wife who took the initiative. She walked toward Morey, her diminutive, solemn face betraying her perplexity. For a moment Charley feared that beneath the good-natured smile Hoot's wife would turn out to be every bit as irascible as Hoot. Likewise, Hoot's two lean-faced sons, having gotten their dander righteously roused, closed in behind her, hooded eyes narrowing to suspicious glints.

Simonian, bashful even on his most courageous days, must have screwed his nerve to the hilt to come here. But what courage had gotten him this far was swiftly deserting him. His face and neck flushed an alarming purplish-red. "We—I, I mean, me and Hoot—used to talk, you know… while we was working? One day we talked about… *airplanes.*" Here, Morey glanced down at the model plane couched in his hands: A bomber of some sort, gaily decorated with numbers, emblems, military insignia.

"That's nice," Hoot's wife volunteered.

"He said he'd never been up in an airplane! He told me that!" Simonian, looking wildly from side to side, lifted the model as if to show us or prove something to us. "When I was in the service, I cleaned this plane! I *flew* in it! They took me on a mission! We got hit, and I was so scared I puked, but it was *exciting!* It was the most exciting day of my whole life! And I meant to tell him that, but I didn't, I never told him that."

There occurred a period of stunned silence as everyone, each in his or her own way, pondered Morey's declaration. Simonian himself turned aside, passion spent, his shoulders drooping. Fingers to his mouth, he looked like a child waiting for a dressing down. Hoot's wife, barely two-thirds of Morey's height, a fraction of his black expanse, stepped forward, and brought her tiny arm up under his. Laying her other hand on his arm, she turned Morey toward Hoot lying in repose.

"This is a remarkable day," the old woman said distinctly enough for everyone in the funeral parlor to hear. "Walter is exalted in the Kingdom of Heaven, and we are thankful for the blessings of his friends who loved him so much to bring him gifts."

She lay the model plane in the casket beside her husband.

***

Recent deaths have a way of recalling ancient deaths. After Hoot's funeral, drawn by an internal summons, Charley wended his way down through the Ganaego valley. He followed a state route that he usually made a point of avoiding, passing a church whose stones were blackened from mill soot, then a state hospital whose floor after floor of identical windows stared blankly across a deserted common. He parked along the road, down from the chained gates of a cemetery, and climbed the brick wall.

Because it was one of those cemeteries that do not permit raised markers, you had to know where you were going if you had any hope of locating a particular site. He'd not been here in many years, and, in the dark, he worried that he might wander aimlessly. He remembered that the March evening he came back to Ganaego he'd recalled a fleeting reminiscence of women, faces darkened in sorrow, teetering on high heels on a steep hill. He recollected a turn-around, where the car had been abandoned, and a walk through a valley and up a grassy hill to where lay before them a sweep of rumpled hills stretching into what seemed a hazy, blue infinity.

Indeed, for forty-five minutes he searched fruitlessly. Without a flashlight he was forced to go down on his hands and knees to sight across the brass plaques in the moonlight, and he began to question his purpose. He sat on a bench smoking a cigarette. That he retained so few memories of his mother had always bothered him. He was seven when she died. Old enough for him to have thousands of memories, but he didn't. The scenes he preserved he reviewed so often that they had become pressed flowers, real memories probably but without scent or life. Peculiarly, however, his mother's voice he *could* recall perfectly. And it was not as if he consciously summoned her voice. No, her voice was an aural presence independent of him that had come to be at home in his mind. Like a river alternately running in view and then underground, his mother's voice would of its own volition unexpectedly surface and, just as unexpectedly, fall away.

No one said *Charley* like she had.

And then his bearings clarified. It was as though the plans of the cemetery were on a large roll of photographic film in his imagination. As the chemistry of memory worked on it, gradually the topography of the park developed and revealed itself. Charley stubbed out his cigarette, crossed through a shallow depression and climbed a small rise. Of course, he thought, *How stupid: When I was little, the depression and rise would've seemed much bigger, like a real valley and hill.* It took him only a short time to locate the marker and brush the overgrown grass from the tarnished raised letters: *Catherine Anne Thomas Rankin.*

But though he had few memories, this much he knew. Before he returned to the university last fall, he'd asked May directly. She, uncomfortable with his questions, gravely ill, but unwilling to lie to him, confirmed what he'd long thought: His mother, that youngest child of a coal-hewer, died in the state hospital he passed on the way here, and she died at her own hands.

Charley smoked another cigarette, then lay down alongside the grave and, for the first time in months, slept soundly.

The Next Big Thing

Phyllis Woods

"I wish he'd stop saying that," Felicia grumbled, removing her guitar strap as she walked backstage.

"Saying what?" her sister Iris asked, coming behind her. She removed her guitar, placing it on a stand.

Felicia didn't answer but walked to where they had come and pointed to their brother and their friend still occupying the small stage. They weren't performing. Brother Roy was with friend and drummer, Calvin, taking final bows for the performance.

Their habit gave the females in the audience a final chance to gaze and swoon over the guys in the band. Roy was quiet about adulation, while Calvin was more vocal, cheerleading for admiration, which always included the phrase Felicia most hated.

"Y'all know the Jackson Five, right?" Calvin shouted.

The crowd let out a roaring cheer.

"Well, we're gonna be the next big thing outta Gary! We are Chariot!"

Another roar from the audience.

Felicia winced. "That's what I'm talking about, the next one outta Gary stuff."

"What's wrong with that?" Iris asked. "We could be."

Felicia only sighed, and the two continued to watch them from backstage. Calvin was definitely the hype master, always ready to grab attention with his gift of brag.

"And now, about the band!" Calvin continued, "I am the expression of true rhythm, the power of the music that keeps you all on beat to move your body and your feet! My name is Calvin 'Veritas,' The Truth Streeter, and the brother by my side is the bringer of the fire for your souls with every touch on that flaming guitar. He is LeRoy, The Wizard of Sound Wayne, master of miraculous melodies!" Calvin slowed down slightly, continuing in a less dramatic tone. "Now I know you gentlemen would like another look at the sisters, right? Am I right?"

"Better strap that guitar back on, sister," Iris said.

"I know, I know," Felicia answered. She was well familiar with the encore signal and strapped on her bass guitar, awaiting the cue.

"C'mon out, my beautiful sisters," Calvin announced as he retook his position behind the drum set and began pounding out a rhythmic downbeat. "Even 'The Jackson Five' ain't got sisters as fine as these!" He added.

The men in the audience agreed with boisterous yells as the sisters came on stage; younger sister loved the attention, smiling wide as she plugged into the amplifier. Switching on, she hit her chords in rhythm with the others. Felicia tried not to look at the audience as she plugged in and switched on. The wide-eyed, whooping males in the audience did nothing to thrill her. The one who thrilled her wasn't there tonight. Felicia let a small smile cross her lips as she thought of her boyfriend, Michael. Thinking of him inspired her to punch out a rhythm with the bass strings, aggressively adding a percussion-style melody to the music of the others.

Roy began his lead guitar solo with a howling beast of a chord before firing off a flurry of notes, leading the melody of the musical improv, then dropping back into a more familiar melody of a previously performed piece. After a raucous rhythmic beginning, the rendition turned softer as Calvin began his final hype speech, "And now I will properly introduce the Ladies of Chariot…".

The crowd roared as they swayed and clapped to the beat.

"Chariot," he continued, "has a princess of icy cool rhythm on rhythm guitar, one of my favorite ladies of music, and I'm sure yours, Princess Iris Wayne!"

Iris took her cue as her brother took over the rhythm, sliding into a flowing solo riff playing by weaving a jazzy thread of melody through the music. Once her solo was complete, she and her brother switched back again.

"And now the lady that brings the thunder with the storm," Calvin continued. "She's laying down the heavy, steady, low blows of power keeping us all in that circle of sweet, soulful rhythm, our own Storm Queen Felicia Wayne!"

Felicia took over and drove the rhythm by slapping and popping the bass strings as she played, then plucking out chords as the drums followed her lead. Her sister and brother filled out the melody, bringing all the parts together into a high-energy crescendo, then falling into a sudden stop.

"That's our show for tonight!" Calvin shouted as he stood up from the drums. "Thanks to you all!" He took a bow and his band members bowed as the crowd continued to cheer. One by one, they left the stage. Calvin took extra bows in front of Roy causing him to gently but firmly pull Calvin backstage.

"Whew, listen to that!" Calvin started. "They love us, man. What a glorious end!"

Calvin held out his hand for a high five and Roy returned it. "Ok," Roy announced, "It's time to go see Mr. J.R. and finish up."

A big grin came over Calvin's face as he looked at Roy, and added, "Yeah, time to get paid!"

Roy joined him in another high five as Calvin added, "Who knows, maybe this ain't the finish."

He led the way through the backstage door to J.R.'s office.

Felicia watched them leave while packing her equipment. "Hope they won't take long," she sighed, "Mike's coming back tonight." She turned when her sister didn't respond. "Iris?" She went to the stage and found her sister talking to a man. She smirked as she thought of her flirty younger sister. "Another admirer, huh?" she muttered.

Felicia realized Iris wasn't just flirting. She was gathering their accessory equipment while the man with her was simply helping.

Felicia joined them and overheard the man saying to her, "I hate to see J.R. wasting your time."

He quieted as Felicia approached. "So he's gonna cheat us, huh?" she surmised.

The man cautiously continued. "No, he'll pay you what he said. But staying with him, that's when you'll get cheated." He handed Iris a wound microphone cord. "It's just words of advice. You're good, don't sell yourselves short." Turning, he walked away from the stage and out of the club's main floor.

"Who's he?" Felicia asked.

"Said his name is Martin LaSalle," Iris answered. "He caught our show and was just hanging around. Asked me if I needed help and he seemed friendly, so I let him. I told him our brothers were coming back, but he still wrapped cords and then started telling me about not staying with J.R."

"I agree," Felicia said. "I'm glad this gig is over."

"I guess I'm glad too," Iris sighed, "but I'll miss the money."

"You're going back to school next month. What do you need money for?"

Iris gave her a glare, "I'll be a senior, remember!"

"Ok, miss senior," Felicia replied, laughing. Looking around at equipment yet to be packed, she added, "well, they need to come on, I want to get back, cause…."

"Yeah. I know," Iris interjected, "Gotta get that call from Mike."

Felicia only smirked. "I'm going to bring the van around," she added.

Iris nodded.

Taking equipment, Felicia headed backstage. Grabbing her instrument and keys, she exited the hall which led to the outside door. The hall was quiet; she had hoped to see the guys headed back, but there was no sign of them. Outside, she backed the van close to the door, then returned to the building. This time, the hall wasn't empty. She could make out Calvin at the end of it hugged up with a woman. He was kissing her, pressing her against the wall. Felicia could hear them whispering. They didn't notice her until she let the heavy door slam. They parted, with Calvin looking annoyed.

Felicia glared at him. "I assume you've finished with J.R.?"

"Yeah, almost," he said quickly as the woman kissed his ear. He stopped her for a moment, to add. "J.R. wanted to talk to Roy about doing more gigs."

Felicia grew angry. She stood, hands on hips. "He's supposed to be paying us what he owes!"

Calvin hurriedly raised both his hands. "He paid us," he said quickly. "Brother's got your money."

Felicia huffed, heading back to the room. "Better c'mon and get the drums broke down," she said over her shoulder. "Get your little girlfriend's number."

Returning to the room, she could see the drums were being packed. This meant her brother was back. She went through the stage door meeting Roy as he headed out, the bass drum in hand. Looking at her he said, "We got paid, Sis," he panted, making his way past her with the heavy drum.

"I heard," Felicia answered, "What's this about more gigs?"

Roy snorted. "Nothing," he mumbled, as he struggled to put the bass drum in its bag. Felicia took the bag from him, helping him place it before zipping it up.

Iris came in with some cymbals and upon hearing her sister's question, she said, "More gigs?"

Roy only shook her head and said, "No more gigs, he's paid us, we're done here." He then reached and took the cymbals from Iris, placing them inside their covers as Felicia stood by.

"So what's Calvin talking about?" Felicia asked.

"Like I said, nothing," Roy added without looking at her. "I'm going to put these in the van. You brought it around, right?"

Felicia nodded before adding, "Calvin is out there; you shouldn't have to do that, too."

He didn't respond, only stretched his free hand once out of the door, and Felicia, remembering she had the keys, tossed them to him.

Felicia sighed. Turning to her sister, she added, "that J.R. must have been up to something talking about more gigs."

"I wouldn't have minded a few more," Iris said. "They were fun!"

"Yeah, for you, princess of flirting," Felicia laughed.

They were laughing together when the door swung open and Calvin entered. "What's so funny in here?"

"You," Felicia replied quickly.

Iris giggled, "It's always you."

Calvin looked from sister to sister without smiling. He straightened the bill of his worn cap as he spoke dryly, "Roy was wondering what was the holdup, so I came to see."

"Would've been out of here sooner if you had been here to help pack up stuff instead of entertaining one of your groupies," Felicia said. "And why'd you say J.R. was talkin' about more gigs?"

Calvin snorted. "The man was just talking about some plans he had for us, but your brother…"

"What plans?" Iris asked.

"Plans your brother wouldn't hear out," Calvin continued. "He just shut J.R. down." He looked at the two sisters and sighed, "But, I don't have no say, only Roy does." Calvin took some of the bags and left.

Felicia and Iris looked at each other, then quickly gathered the rest of their things and followed.

"Calvin is pissed," Iris whispered.

"So is Roy," Felicia whispered back.

Roy saw the three coming and started the van. He had the windows rolled down, finding the breeze a remedy for his weariness. Music playing through the speakers was a partial composition of a new song. Recorded by Roy on cassette, it was drum and guitar only. He was penciling in the song's accompanying parts in a booklet of sheet music. He had the ability to compose music almost anywhere and used it as a way to relax. Tonight, it wasn't working, as he felt frustrated and angry. Things weren't going according to plan. When the others boarded the van, he closed his book and popped the cassette out of the player. The FM radio came on, already tuned to a local station. A Motown song filled the vehicle with the soulful sounds of Gladys Knight and the Pips singing *Midnight Train to Georgia*. As the others piled in, Roy found himself wishing he were on that midnight train.

With a quiet sigh, he shifted the van into drive and took off. Calvin had gotten in beside him as he was dropped off first. Iris was directly behind him in the back seat, with Felicia beside her. They rode for a time in silence until Iris spoke. "So, is everyone glad to be done with J.R.?" There was more silence.

"Some are, some aren't," Calvin muttered.

Iris noticed Roy gave Calvin an angry glare before returning his eyes to the road. "We completed our agreement with him," Roy said in steely tones, "It was time to leave."

"Maybe for you, but not for me!" Calvin started, his voice elevated.

"You wanted to sell us out to stay with J.R.!" Roy yelled back, "You told him about the demo tape for Glen Park Recording."

"Why not? J.R. could help us get a record deal easier than with them. Plus, we'd be getting paid, 'cause we'd still be doing shows!"

"But he would own us, Calvin! Everything we would do would belong to him!" Roy laid his cards of disapproval on the table.

Felicia broke in, "What, J.R. was going to get us a record deal?"

"I didn't know he could do that," Iris added.

"He can't," her brother answered,

"He knows nothing but how to scam!"

"You don't know that," Calvin snapped.

"I talked to one of the Silky Times members," Roy continued, "J.R. was cheating them bad. That's why we had to replace them so often. He had promised them big things, too. All lies!"

"He wouldn't do that to us," Calvin said. "He liked us."

"That's not what this man said," Iris began. "He said we shouldn't let J.R. be our main gig."

"What man?" Roy and Calvin asked almost in unison.

Felicia answered, "He said his name was Martin LaSalle, and that we were too good to stay with J.R. He was warning us."

"Screw it," Calvin said suddenly. "You've made up your minds."

He turned and looked at Roy before he repositioned his cap, pulling its wide bib to sit lower on the left side of his forehead. He then smacked his lips in approval of his appearance in the side-view mirror. Slumping back into his usual 'gangsta lean' riding posture, he muttered, "Coulda been our big chance."

It was quiet now, except for the radio. The 'Ragman' was concluding his Saturday night program. As he said goodnight to his listeners, he played a familiar closing song and one liked by the four. It was Jesus is Love sung by the Commodores.

Roy glanced at Felicia through the rear-view mirror as she looked up at him. They began to sing along with the radio. As the other two joined in, immersing into the harmony, it could have been the perfect call for peace. They sang until the 'Ragman's radio show signed off but the peace didn't last.

It dissipated when Calvin spoke again, "Roy, stop at Grant Street Liquors over there on 26th, ok?"

"Why?" Roy asked, dryly, glancing over at him.

"Cause, I want me a 'forty' and we could get that check cashed. Since it's all over, I wanna get my money tonight."

Roy returned his eyes to the road and simply said, "No."

Calvin immediately began to grumble, "It ain't outta your way. Why you gonna make me wait till Monday?"

"Calvin," he said angrily, "I'm not stopping at no liquor store this time of night for no drink and especially not to cash a check! You just looking to get jumped!"

"Aw man," Calvin said, his voice slightly rising. "We'd be alright!"

"What world you livin' in, fool! Cause in this one, gettin' jumped is all you'll get this time of night!"

"I'm gettin jumped now, so what's the difference?" Calvin replied wryly. "Have it your way, man."

"I'll get the check cashed Monday and bring you your cut," Roy said.

Calvin gave Roy a look of indifference, then nodded in response.

The sisters in the back seat glanced at each other but said nothing. The continued conflict between them was unusual.

Calvin arrived home and as he got out, he turned and said, "See you

Monday, Roy, and catch you ladies whenever, good luck." He walked up the short path to his back door, disappearing inside.

"Wow," Iris began, as she climbed into the front seat beside Roy. "He's quitting on us. I almost feel sorry for him."

As Roy turned the van around to leave, he muttered, "I don't, cause he's thinking more of J.R. than about us." Spinning off the gravel of the driveway, he headed back to the road.

"I don't understand," Felicia began, "He's siding with J.R. against us? He's not even going to help with recording the demo now?"

"Doesn't matter," Roy said as he looked up into the rear-view mirror at his sister, "I finished that demo alone almost a month ago."

"What, really?" Iris asked, her eyes wide.

Roy took a long sigh. "Yeah, I remastered some tracks of our songs played live, then did the rest myself. They wanted just a sample, five to eight tunes. I did seven." They were at a red light, and Roy took the moment to look at his sisters. "You two upset with me?"

Iris shook her head, while Felicia said, "No, I'm just surprised."

"I had to do it," Roy continued, as he pulled off when the light changed. "J.R. had us take that other band's place, promising us extra money, which he never paid. He was trying to talk me into continuing that way, and it wasn't going to leave us time for anything else. After Calvin talked so much at the studio, I thought I needed to get a tape to them quick or they would write us off as crazy."

"You did the right thing," Iris added.

Roy nodded. "Some good it did. They said I'd hear something in a couple of weeks; it's been a month."

They reached home and pulled into the driveway behind their father's Chevy Impala. The three grew silent for a time lost in their own thoughts.

Calvin and Roy had been friends since grade school, united by a love for music and performing. They were just drums and guitar at first, practicing in garages. They quickly found other musicians their age and moved on to entertain at house parties and became popular around town. The only thing slowing them down was keeping dependable band members. Illegal drug use among their peers was sometimes the reason.

Roy then looked to involve his sisters in the band. Calvin laughed at the idea, but what he didn't know was how Roy had shown his sisters to play bass and rhythm guitar as a way to have practice partners. It took some convincing to get his sisters to consider performing but once done, they were hooked, and Chariot was born. They always had a vision of where they wanted to go but without Calvin, the vision grew hazy.

They unloaded what they thought necessary, bringing in only their guitars and some electrical equipment. Their mother greeted them at the door. "Long night, huh?"

"Yeah," Iris said as she entered the side door first.

Her mother watched as all her children entered. They put the equipment they brought in with them on the landing leading to the basement. As their mother was still up, they knew she must've had something she needed to tell them. They watched as she poured hot tea into her cup.

"Anybody hungry? Want me to reheat dinner?" she asked.

"Sure Mom," Roy began, "but we could do that, so what's up?"

The quiet smile on her face grew wider. "It's good news."

"What Mom? Daddy's ok, right?" Felicia started.

"Sure, Daddy's fine," Iris quipped, hunching her sister.

Their mother finally verified, "Yes, he is fine, he had a good day today, and…" she continued, "he's hoping to have another good day tomorrow, in church, and wants you all to attend service in the morning." She paused, giving them a steady look.

Daddy's girls had no objections to going to morning service. Roy, on the other hand, was not feeling the same. He looked off, worn out from a night of frustration. Despite this, he would comply.

Their mother, glad for their agreement, reheated dinner for them. "I love you all," she whispered from the hall leading to the bedroom. Her children whispered their love to her as she left.

Roy was first to finish and cleared away his plate leaving it in the sink. He departed for his basement bedroom without saying a word.

"He's upset," Iris said when she was certain he was out of earshot.

"Yup," Felicia said in agreement, "but it ain't because of going to church in the morning."

"Yeah, I know," Iris said, "it's just everything else."

There was silence for a time as they finished their meal.

Felicia got up suddenly. "I wonder, did Michael call? I'll see if I can reach him."

"For real? You forget he lives with his mama too?" Iris said.

Felicia only sighed as she went over to the sink to wash off her plate. She washed out her brother's plate as well.

As Iris brought over her plate, Felicia took it and washed it. "His mom already seems like she doesn't like me," she muttered.

"Well, coming home to find her son and you in her bed didn't make her fall in love with you," Iris smirked.

"Oh, shut up girl," she said as she hunched her sister. "Never should have told you that!" They laughed together softly.

Soon after, Iris parted, heading for her bedroom at the back of the house. She was the only sibling that had a bedroom on the main floor near her parents. Her older brother and sister had their bedrooms in the finished basement of the home. Roy's bedroom also served as a recording and rehearsal studio. Between their bedrooms was a small kitchenette and sitting area, all constructed by their father when they moved in. Felicia was five years old when they moved, LeRoy J.R. was three and Iris was two. Soon after Felicia's birth, the Waynes dreamed of a home with a big backyard and plenty of lawn. They hoped for a driveway, as well, to park their car away from busy streets.

These dreams became reality, not only for the Wayne family but for many families during the 1960s especially if the head of the household worked for the U.S. Steel Works in Gary. In that city, there was a saying: You can go beg, or you can go borrow, but if you want to live, you better go Steel... U.S. Steel. Many men took that saying to heart and surrendered their life and breath to the steel mill for a chance at a comfortable middle-class existence.

***

Times changed as life went on and the steel mill went through changes due to recession and cutbacks. Using cheaper foreign labor reduced the number of steel jobs in Gary. Other businesses built on the prosperity of the steel mill dwindled away leaving the town unable to regain the economic stability it once knew.

The Waynes, like many from the time of prosperity, did well. Their home was paid off and even when Mr. Wayne retired from the steel mill on disability, his monthly check was sufficient for him and his stay-at-home wife. Their children, however, didn't have as many opportunities. Felicia graduated from high school three years before her siblings. She hoped to go away to college and with the school grants it was feasible, but not comfortable. Her parents would have to spend money they couldn't afford. Realizing this, Felicia canceled her college plans in favor of using the money for her father's health care. Attending a beauty college instead, she took up the former profession of her mother and her grandmother and found work in a local beauty shop.

Roy never sought a college education. He had no particular plans other than creating his music in his makeshift recording studio. New opportunities came for him and Chariot when they were hired for weekend gigs at local clubs. Another opportunity came from his former high school music teacher. She offered him a job teaching a music course Monday through Friday as her assistant. They taught children how to read and perform music. It was only a summer job but that didn't matter. The opportunity to work with his mentor Besse Tatum was too irresistible. Roy had been her star pupil in her progressive music theory program during his senior year. The class taught music students new ways of composing and constructing music with the aid of electronics. The program was ahead of its time as was the demure musical genius creator of the educational program. Now, as an assistant instructor, he had this inspiring teacher back in his life again.

Iris was the only sibling still in high school. A year behind her brother, she was going to be a senior in the fall. She made no real plans except to enjoy the summer and enjoy the fall, her last year in high school. When she became involved in the weekend gigs, she was thrilled. She loved the performing and the attention. The money was a plus as well.

The two older ones remained home with the youngest. Their positions didn't give them the ability to financially support themselves. So, they pooled their money to help with the expenses of the house and their band. For this, their parents weren't too dismayed as they understood the world their children found themselves in was no longer the world in which they had prospered. The parents' present dream was to see their children self-sufficient and someday reach their dreams as well.

***

Felicia finished clearing the kitchen. Clean dishes were in the rack with countertops wiped down. All was quiet as she listened for sounds from the bedroom of her parents. Her Dad was having a peaceful night which meant her mother was as well. There were no spasmodic coughing or whirring sounds of the breathing treatment machine.

This made her smile as she turned off the kitchen light.

A night light on the kitchen stove was sufficient to guide her down the basement steps she knew so well. Her bedroom was to the right of the stairs. She looked across the open area to the door of her brother's room. There was light coming from under his door. He obviously was still up. Despite some unsettling events of the night, she felt peaceful. Hoping to share the feeling with her probably troubled brother, she crossed the dark open area and knocked gently at his door.

"Roy?" She heard the creak of his bed, then the door opened.

"Hey, what are you still doing up?" he said.

"Could ask you the same thing," she snickered.

He opened the door wider. "I know what you're looking for." He grinned mischievously. It's over there on the nightstand. She followed his pointing finger viewing the long-corded phone. "Gotta make that call to Mike, right?" he smirked. "It's cool, I'm done with it."

"No smarty," his sister replied, "I don't need the phone, I was coming over to check on you."

"Why?"

Felicia shrugged, "To offer encouragement?"

He smiled as he sat back down on the side of his bed. "I'm fine, Sis. Besides you're not the only one who had somebody special coming home."

Felicia suddenly remembered, "Oh yeah, Miss Lisa," she said with an upturned nose.

"You just ain't trying to like her, are you?" Her brother remarked.

"And I don't see why you like her; she's so snooty."

"But that's what makes her so hot!" he snickered.

"Ugh!" his sister groaned.

Roy mostly ignored her as he continued about their plans for meeting up. "Was hoping to meet her in the morning but with us going to church, I just invited her and told her I'd pick her up."

"Oh God," Felicia exclaimed as she dramatically sank in a chair across from her brother's bed. "What's gonna happen when she crosses over to holy ground? Surely she'll be consumed!"

Roy wanted to be insulted but found himself laughing. "Ok, that's enough," he chuckled, as he tossed one of his bed pillows at her.

Felicia caught and held it, studying her brother for a moment. "So you really aren't upset about going to church in the morning?"

"Nah," he answered, "I'm glad Dad is feeling up to it." Then, sitting up and growing closer to her added, "Calling Lisa isn't the only call I made tonight."

When his sister gave him a curious look, he answered, "I called Calvin. I apologized to him and told him I'd talk more on Monday."

"Really?"

Roy nodded and shrugged. "I thought about it. I kinda see what he was trying to do."

"Yeah, trying to get us messed up."

"He said he was sorry, too, and I told him about the demo tape."

Felicia sat back in her chair. "What did he say?"

"What could he say?" Roy muttered. "It's done. But I told him I want nothing to do with J.R. Don't care what he's offering. He agreed."

"Well, that's good," Felicia said, "I'd kinda miss him."

"Well, I also told him he's still part of us."

"What did Calvin say to that?"

"He said he knew we couldn't do without him."

"That's Calvin," Felicia smirked. "So we're alright now."

"If the studio had called," Roy continued, "we would really be alright." He laid back on his bed.

Felicia sighed, "Don't give up, brother. It could still happen."

Roy was staring at the ceiling, lost in thought. "You remember when we were little," he began, "and we would watch 'Hard Day's Night' every time it came on TV?"

Felicia smiled, "Oh yeah, and don't forget 'Help'. Didn't matter when those movies came on, we were hooked. We were really into the Beatles."

"That's all I wanted to do," Roy went on, "I wanted to be part of a band, to make music and play guitar."

"And you have that," his sister reminded him. "We all wanted to make music, not to sing anybody else's songs, but our own and we're doing that, too. Because we're not the Beatles, and we're not the Jacksons; we're Chariot." Felicia stood up then, taking a long stretch. Looking down at her brother's smiling face, she felt her mission accomplished. "We better get some sleep, now." She said, smiling back at him.

"Yeah," Roy said, "Goodnight Sis."

Felicia laughed softly as she left his room, "You mean, good morning, right?" she added as she left his room, closing his door behind her.

***

The morning hit the basement residents like a hailstorm as the sounds of their mother's Sunday breakfast preparations filled the house. There was the clatter of pots with the running of water and the sounds of oil frying in skillets. There were also constant sounds of walking and though their mother's footsteps were light, the creaky tiles and floorboards multiplied the sound of her every move as though a battalion of soldiers marched above.

Roy awoke to the sounds first, with his mind in a fog and his body feeling no better. He decided the best remedy was a hot shower. His sister awoke when the sounds from above combined with those coming from her brother in the shower. Roy managed to get in the bathroom before her. Shrugging it off, she gathered her clothes and headed for the bathroom upstairs.

"Hey Mama, hey Daddy," she said softly as she stepped from the basement stairs into the kitchen. Her mother turned, headed back to the stove. Felicia gave her a quick kiss, then in one step she was near her father, giving him a kiss on the forehead.

"Hey baby," her father said between munches of toast. "You're up huh?"

She nodded, smiling, "And so are you," she added as she snagged a slice of toast from the stacked plate of it on the table.

"How about my son?"

"He's up too," she began, chomping down a few bites as she spoke. "That's why I'm up here. He beat me to the bathroom."

"That's why we have two," her mother said quickly from the kitchen. "Iris is out, so go on in there, and hurry up. I'm about to cook these eggs."

Felicia didn't hesitate but headed for the bathroom nearly colliding with a fully dressed Iris.

"What time did you get up?" she asked her.

"Obviously earlier than you," Iris grinned, as she headed towards the breakfast table.

Felicia gave her a smirk before bounding into the bathroom.

Half an hour later, the family was seated around the table for breakfast though in varied phases of readiness for attending church service. Once breakfast was over, there was a flurry of putting final touches on their individual Sunday looks. Once men's ties were tied, suit coats donned, ladies dresses zipped and accessorized, they were on their way. The father drove his beloved Chevy Impala with his wife by his side and his two daughters in the back seat. Roy drove the van as he was picking up his girlfriend for church.

Associate Minister Wayne hadn't been in the pulpit for over six months because of his illness. Neither had any of the family attended during that time. Mrs. Wayne watched her husband as he filed in behind the pastor and his three other associate ministers. She smiled, thankful in her heart for this moment. There had been weeks of hospital stays, tests, and then rehab, along with learning care regimes, dosing medicines, and giving breathing treatments. All were part of living with a loved one diagnosed with Chronic Lung Disease. Looking at him now, however, in his present state of recovery, was like a miracle.

Barbara Wayne and her husband LeRoy had always been smokers but had only recently come to understand the dangers of this habit. She knew smoking contributed to her husband's condition but she didn't see it as the sole factor. She remembered a time, as she washed her husband's work clothes, seeing collections of pin-sized holes dotting the material of his shirts and pants. Even his tee shirts worn under the work shirts showed the same damage. She can still recall how her husband blew off her inquiry about the strange holes in fairly new clothing. He said it must have been the 'blow off' from the acid tanks. "It's in the air," he told her. "If you can't patch them, throw them away."

His wife had gently chided him for thinking that patching them was her only concern. She didn't voice her real concern as she felt he would blow it off as well but her question would have been: If the steel cleaning acid from the vats blowing around in the air was chemically burning holes in clothing, what was it doing to those breathing that air? His continued exposure to the 'Pickling Vats,' as they were called, was troubling to the concerned wife, as his primary job was to monitor the chemical effect on the processed steel to ensure it was free from undesirable impurities. She suggested masks should be used. Her husband said they were available but no one ever used them and so ended her suggestions. LeRoy Wayne was not going to be told how to work at his living—not by young new buck supervisors who were all educated and not experienced or by new young blood employees whose only interest was how much the job paid, not doing the job well—or especially by a wife, whose well-being fully depended on his making a living. So his wife patched and what couldn't be patched was thrown away.

The morning church service began with Associate Minister Wayne giving the call to service and opening prayer. His wife hadn't heard him pray out loud for a long time and relished hearing his firm voice as he poured out his gratefulness before God and before the congregation. When his prayer ended, he made a request of Pastor Johnson and congregation,

"My brothers and sisters," he began, "and to my pastor; if you would indulge me for just a little longer."

The Pastor and the people murmured an 'amen' consent before he continued.

"You see my brothers and sisters, in addition to my dear wife being here with me, my three children are also here and they got up early," he continued his voice rising, "and got ready, despite working late last night, to be with me here today."

More congregational 'amens.'

"And I don't know who among us can be sure, but... this could be the last Sunday we are all together, and I would just love to hear my children sing 'Precious Lord' for me."

All three of them, sitting apart from each other simultaneously and silently released a gasp. Nevertheless, Roy, sitting in the second row with his lady Lisa, was the first to stand and walk to the front.

Iris, seated on the opposite side of the church in the back row, quickly released the hand of her latest crush, the son of one of the church deacons.

"Daddy's doin' this on purpose," she whispered to him before standing up. "He saw us sitting together."

Iris' companion smiled, giving her a knowing wink before she left and headed to the front of the church to join her brother.

Felicia was the last to rise. She had been sitting with her childhood friend, Valerie, in a middle aisle. "I love my daddy," she whispered to her friend with clenched teeth.

"Let the Lord use ya," Valerie replied, snickering.

Felicia gave her an eye roll before heading out into the aisle then down to the front with the others.

The church rumbled with choruses of 'amen' as the three gathered. The pianist moved aside, letting Roy take over, and the three of them looked at their father still standing at the podium. Roy hit the intro chords and the three of them began singing. They hadn't sung it for a long time but they sang as though no time had passed. When finished, there was applause, plus they were inundated with members, suggesting they rejoin the choir. The three took their seats, still hearing from those around them with that request.

Their mother also wasn't exempt from the membership's pressure. "Sister Barbara," said Bessie Hogan, the wife of one of the associate ministers, "those children of yours know they need to come back and serve the Lord and stop serving the devil by singing in those nightclubs." She was seated behind their mother speaking loud enough for most of the members to hear.

As another chorus of 'amens' arose, their mother grew angry and stood up suddenly. Her children watched from their seats, knowing a sharp rebuke was coming. She was not one to sit in silence when it came to the defense of her family. She would not allow them to pass judgment on her children.

Their father had sat down to the right of the podium knowing his wife was prepared to set them straight.

"I thank God for your gracious welcome for the return of my husband, of me, and our family," she began. "I also thank you for letting my husband hear the voices of our children singing, and I've heard how you've enjoyed it. So, as you have enjoyed the song, I urge you to remember that my children continue in the service of the Lord in this place and wherever they are ,and I am very proud of them!"

There was applause, punctuated with 'amens' and 'hallelujahs.'

Their father rose from his seat and added, "And I am very proud of them too!" before sitting back down.

Then, the pastor rose and stood at the podium and the congregation grew still. Hoping to quiet any dissension among the members, he began, "I am also proud of Minister and Sister Wayne's children. I agree with their mother, and I have no doubt that they bring the light of the Lord wherever they go, and we will continue to pray for their strength." Following this statement, the Pastor began his intended sermon, and the remainder of the morning service continued as usual.

When it was over, the Wayne family left in their two vehicles; parents and the daughters in the car, while Roy had Lisa with him in the van

Once home, their mother immediately immersed herself in the boiling water, the hot popping oil, and the fired-up oven as part of the Sunday meal preparations. While her husband, in more comfortable attire and in his recliner, immersed himself in the television with a baseball doubleheader.

Both daughters were on board helping with the peeling, chopping, and grating of side dishes while their mother prepared the main event, the fried chicken. "I'm almost done here," their mother announced. "That boy better get on back here."

"He ain't bringing her here, is he?" Felicia asked.

Her mother sighed, "That's not the plan; it's family day."

"Does Roy usually stick with the plan?" Felicia continued as she pounded away at mashing the potatoes.

"He better today; he's bringing dessert."

"Mama," Iris called, "look at the table. What do you think?"

She looked across the kitchen to the attached dining area, and smiled, "Oh it's perfect."

Felicia smiled and nodded in agreement.

"Forget the table," their father said from the living room, "where's the food?"

The women laughed. "It's coming, honey," his wife answered.

"What dessert is he bringing?" Felicia asked.

"A chocolate layer cake from Lula's Bakery. Your Daddy loves cakes from there."

"Roy better come on. Daddy's not the only one ready to eat," Iris said as she watched her mother turn the last batch of chicken.

"It's done," Turning to Iris, their mother said, "Call your Daddy to the table." She was about to direct Felicia to put the food on the table when they heard the van pulling into the driveway.

Felicia rushed to the kitchen window that gave a view of the driveway. "Looks like Roy missed the part about family-only dinner," she began. "Guess who's sitting beside him."

"No," Iris said.

Their mother only groaned softly.

"Wait," Felicia continued, "Only Roy is getting out. He's bringing a box."

Their mother responded by rushing to the door and opening it before Roy did. With a startled look, he handed his mother the cake box. "Oh hey, Mama. Here's the cake and, uh, I'm going to take Lisa home and I'll be home later, save me a plate, ok?" He leaned in, kissing his mother on the cheek before bounding away to the van and leaving.

Their mother stood in the open doorway until her husband asked, "Was that Roy?"

"Yeah, it was," she answered as she closed the door. When she turned, her husband was standing at the kitchen entrance.

"Where'd he go?"

His wife wouldn't look up. "He's going off with Lisa," she muttered. She sat the cake on a counter near the dining table.

"Well, he'll be back later," her husband said casually. "Lisa is leaving for Howard University tomorrow. He just wanted to see her off." He walked over to the kitchen and looked into the deep dish his wife was loading up with fried chicken.

"That smells good!" he said as he took a deep whiff of the scents of the kitchen. Turning, he exclaimed. "I'm hungry, let's eat!" His daughters standing nearby laughed in agreement.

Their father sat at the table with his daughters and their mother. They had brought all the meal items to the table. Now, they blessed the food and began eating, still laughing and talking, enjoying their meal.

***

Father heard the van in the driveway. He whispered, "Not too late, I guess." He had been waiting as he ate another piece of cake, glad he would see his son, too.

Roy saw the light on in the kitchen and came to see who was still up. "Dad?" he said.

"Hey son," he said, greeting Roy from his seat at the table.

"I know I'm too late for dinner," he began sheepishly. "But I…"

"Not too late for dessert," his father said. "C'mon sit and have a piece of cake with me."

Roy got a plate and fork, then joined his father at the table. His father cut the cake and placed a generous slice on the plate.

"Ah, boy," Roy said, "this looks good!"

His father watched him, smiling.

"So," Roy began as he took a big bite of cake, "Mom know you up gobbling down cake this time of night?"

His father gave him a sly smile and answered, "It's my cake and It's my time. Besides, I'm doing more than that. I'm having cake with my son."

Roy smiled, but he knew there was more to this than eating cake.

"I heard from the girls that you're not doing shows for that J.R. anymore."

"That's true," Roy said.

His father took a slow, deep breath before speaking. "I can't say I'm sorry about that. We had disagreements about you and your sisters working there."

Roy started looking off. His father didn't want any negative feelings to arise, so he spoke fervently. "Son," he began, "I am very proud of you."

Roy looked at his father as he continued.

"You kept your sisters safe. You weren't so caught up in your music that you couldn't keep your mind on business and when you saw there was nothing better coming, you packed up. As I see it, that's the way a good man handles himself."

There was silence for a few moments. "Your sisters also said you're trying to get a recording contract, someplace?"

"Yeah Dad, Glen Park Studios."

His father nodded. "You know," he began reminiscing, "When I bought you that guitar, how old were you?"

"Twelve," his son answered, unable to keep from smiling as he remembered.

"Boy, were you happy," his father recalled.

"I remember you weren't." Roy snickered.

His father laughed, "I was thinking you wanted a toy guitar, but no, you wanted not only a real one, but you wanted it electric with an amplifier!"

At this, they both laughed out loud, then quieted, not wanting to wake the others.

"I thought you would discard it like a toy after Christmas," his father said, softly laughing. Growing more serious, he added, "But you didn't. There were times I didn't want to hear it, but there was no denying I heard your music and your gift."

Looking at his father's expression as he spoke prompted Roy to talk about his recent setback. "I gave a recording studio a demo, a sample of our music, and… nothing happened. They won't even answer my calls." He looked up at his father's comforting smile.

"I know, waiting is hell, ain't it?"

Roy was surprised at his statement, but it was the truth. He only nodded.

"That's how I felt when I was waiting to find out if I had cancer," his father continued. "But I learned you can't get discouraged. If what you seek is worth it, then you'll wait. If you pray about it, then you'll find out if it's worth waiting for. The news doctors gave me was worth that wait." His father glanced over at the clock on the kitchen stove.

"Oh, look at the time." Looking back at his son, he asked, "You gotta go to work in the morning?"

"Yeah Dad, and you need to go to bed," Roy added as he stood, then bending down gave his father a hug.

"Thank you, Dad," he whispered as he held him. "Thank you for everything."

"Goodnight, son."

Roy went on to the stairs. He paused a moment, listening as his father got up and turned off the light.

Roy continued down the stairs. There was no light under Felicia' bedroom door, which was unusual since she would wait up if he was out late. He figured she and Iris, plus their mom, were all disappointed with him for missing dinner. Special time with his dad, however, took away the stings of those thoughts and he went on to bed.

***

Calvin got up early. He tiptoed around in the dim living room to find the phone. Theo, his mother's boyfriend, had it beside the sofa on the floor. He crept over and got it. Calvin looked down at the passed-out man with disgust. He had come back a few days ago, which meant Theo and his mother had been using drugs since then. He pulled the long phone cord across the living room to his room. Briefly glancing into his mother's room, he noted her similar state, then went on to his room. The phone's cord reached the foot of his bed and he placed it there.

When Roy's call came, all that was needed was for him to await his arrival. Calvin rushed through the home's side door when Roy arrived and jumped into the van. Roy was surprised by Calvin's sudden appearance, but even more surprised by the two people yelling at him from the open door.

"Just drive, man, ignore their asses. Just drive!"

Roy obeyed, pulling off as the man flung back the screen door and headed for the van.

There was silence as Roy sped down the street. He glanced over at Calvin, who was sitting, head down, saying nothing.

"That was Theo, wasn't it?" Roy began.

Calvin nodded. "I was trying to get out before they woke up, but…" There was silence again.

"You want me to take you somewhere?" Roy asked, I got time. "Work doesn't start till ten for me."

Calvin looked over and flashed a weak smile. "Want breakfast? I'll pay."

Roy chuckled, "I'll take you. I've had mine."

"Moms got up early, huh?"

"No smart ass," Roy laughed, "I heated leftovers."

"And who cooked them leftovers?"

Roy laughed, "Alright, you got me!" He turned into the restaurant. "Drive through or going in?" He added.

"Nice Day, drive-in's cool."

As they waited in line to place their order, Roy pulled out an envelope and handed it to Calvin.

"Thanks, brother" He opened the envelope and pulled out a twenty, then put the envelope in his pants pocket. Calvin ordered his breakfast and a coffee for Roy.

"So," Calvin began between munches, "You turned in this tape a month ago and ain't heard nothing?"

"Nothing."

"You called?"

"Yeah, I left messages."

"Unbelievable," Calvin said.

He took a deep, slow breath. "Roy, have you gone there?"

He sighed, looking down before mumbling, "No."

Calvin looked at him, shaking his head. After a pause, he said, "Then you need to get your tape back."

Roy felt foolish now. Checking his watch he said, "Well, I can't go now, gotta head to work soon."

Calvin nodded. He was lost in thought. Roy could only wonder what about.

"I guess I better get you back so we can take in your drums."

Only then did Calvin snap out of his meditation. "How long you think those drums will last in the crack house?"

Roy hadn't thought of that. He felt ashamed again. "Ok, they'll stay with me."

He dropped off Calvin. Before they parted, Calvin said, "I thank you, brother, 'cause I know you got me and you best believe I got you."

Roy understood and smiled as they shook hands.

Finding his mother and her companion gone, Calvin quickly hid his money under the floorboard in the corner of his bedroom. He would attend to his real mission now, to find out about Chariot's demo. Glen Park Recording was on Broadway and Calvin reached it by bus. Arriving, he found it appeared vacant. Even the large business name sign had been removed.

"Damn," He grumbled. "They're nothin' but jive time phoneys!"

Calvin peeped through a dark front window and saw a light in a back room. Seeing a man and a woman there, he banged on the glass. The two looked but didn't come to the front. He banged harder. Finally, the man slowly came closer. When he asked what Calvin wanted, Calvin yelled his demand for the return of the demo tape. The man, Calvin noticed, was a security guard. He beckoned to the woman, dressed in business attire. She came closer and unlocked the door. "Are you the one that's been leaving messages?" She asked as he stepped in.

Calvin, for a moment, was distracted by her brown skin beauty and her curvy figure before answering, "Uh, yeah, I mean no. It was Roy Wayne that called, but I'm here for him."

Calvin was about to voice his complaints when the woman said, "Would you wait just one moment?" She then walked back towards the lighted office.

Calvin watched as the man also moved closer to the office, but continued watching him. "What the hell is this?" He said to the man. "You helping guard this fake place, pretending to be a recording studio?"

He was about to rage on when the man held up his hands. "Look, I'm just here to assist the lady with moving, ok?"

The woman appeared at the door. "Sir," the woman began, "Mr. LaSalle would like to speak to you."

"And just who is Mr. LaSalle?" Calvin quipped.

Calvin walked over as the woman walked ahead. As they entered the office, the woman handed him the phone. "Hello, this is Martin

LaSalle. Who am I speaking to?"

"Calvin…. Streeter," he answered.

"Oh! Mr. Veritas, 'the truth' Streeter!" Martin exclaimed, "You're the drummer, right?"

"Yeeaaah," Calvin answered cautiously.

"First, I apologize for this," Martin explained. "We're in the process of moving and…"

"You know what? I don't care what you're doing, I just want my brother's tape back." Calvin interjected.

There was silence on the other end before Martin replied, "Ok, I understand. The tape is with me and I will be there personally to hand it back to you because I would like the chance to explain. Can you give me that?"

Calvin sighed, "Fine man, just bring me my brother's tape."

"I will," He responded. "I'll meet you there tomorrow, say 10 a.m.? And one more thing, could you keep this meeting just between us?"

"Sure man." Calvin handed the receiver back to the woman. As he left, the woman said, "Please come back tomorrow," she said pleadingly, "It is not what you think."

He turned, smacked his lips at her before slinging open the door and leaving.

He returned and spoke with Mr. LaSalle. The woman was right; It turned out to be nothing like he expected. As explanations were given, he ended up spending most of the day talking with Mr. LaSalle.

When the time came for Calvin to leave, he not only had the tape but some important documents and was driven by Mr. LaSalle's driver. He was headed to see Roy, to give the tape and to follow some very specific instructions.

"What's this about, man?" Roy began when he opened the door to him.

"You'll find out. The family's all here, right?"

Roy only nodded.

As they came downstairs, Calvin greeted the family, "Hey Moms, Hey Pop." Turning, He waved at Iris and Felicia as they came downstairs.

"Ok," Roy said as he stood in front of him, "What's happening?"

"This" Calvin answered as he handed Roy his cassette tape. "Play it," he added.

As Roy did, familiar music began to play, it was their music. They all looked at Calvin for an explanation.

"Don't it sound good," he laughed.

"Calvin, what is this?" Roy demanded.

"Just wait, it gets better."

The song faded, and a voice came over the tape. "Hello Chariot, my name is Martin LaSalle. Your sisters may remember me. Knowing how determined Calvin is, I'm sure you're together listening to this. Glen Park Studio is no more. Our recording company is Steel City Recording. We acquired your demo and after hearing it, my partners and I would like to offer you a contract to record with us and become Steel City recording artists. Calvin has the contract. If you have questions, he knows the number, call us."

The sisters began to cheer and their parents laughed as they all hugged each other.

Calvin calmly pulled out the contract and handed it to Roy, "Well my brother, ready to go steel?"

"Yeah, my brother," Roy answered, "Let's be that next big thing."

Homebodies

Bianca Roman

Twin City

After leaving the old Twin City, I tried to erase its impact on me. I forgot that a place like that cements you there. It reeks of sulfur, gasoline, and rotten eggs. The city of lead contamination and home of Inland Steel. The city is horrible, disgusting, and riddled with violence. And yet, the city was the only place I could consistently call home.

It isn't the warmest and it isn't the easiest place to live. The soil is poisoned with its roots in racism and the forgotten histories of the people before us. If you grew up there, you would dream of leaving every chance that you get. Someone will tell you, "Compared to South Chicago, living in East Chicago is manageable." That's exactly what it was and still is. Just—manageable.

If you want to get groceries for the family, you are better off driving to the neighboring cities. You'll drive past the crumbling abandoned houses until you reach the main streets with signs that say, "I love my city" and feel the city's false sense of pride sink into the veins of your eyes. Maybe it isn't a false sense of pride. Maybe the pride of the city is where the heart of the city lies. Despite all the city's flaws, you never let anyone who did not grow up there judge it. It is an unwritten rule. Do not speak badly of the old city, unless you grew up with it. Then, you are allowed.

A part of me is frustrated with the idea that part of my identity is shaped by that place. I never felt like myself there and yet it defines parts of me. I am sure that if someone dissected me, they would find the tie to why I am grounded there. My relationship with Twin City is magnetic. I can try to stay away, but as long as someone puts me close enough, I am stuck there. I will be stuck there until someone pulls me away again.

CHILDREN OF STEEL

***

 I could not tell you if I love my home. Ava tells me it is because I will always have complex feelings about what home means since I never had one. She's strangely philosophical for someone who hasn't lived through much. She asked if she could take a ride with me to my Sunshine's new apartment, we both haven't seen it since she moved two months ago. Sunshine doesn't want anyone to see it until she has furniture. It's strange. I don't know where she gets that mentality from when we have visitors stand while eating Christmas dinner. I get it, though. We all want better than we had in the past.

 I set the GPS in the car for the address to Sunshine's apartment and think to myself about how grateful I am for this technology. Ava is rambling on about something she read online and I give her a quick "mhm" to show that I am listening.

 Seeing this part of the city is like a blow to the stomach. Old memories start filling my mind and before, I could let them pass, ignore them like the other useless thoughts that flare up, but I can't. I just passed the Clemente Center I used to go to every day after school. That's where my siblings and I would roughhouse with the other neighborhood kids and be lucky to eat a meal. My mom was by herself, always working.

 "You want clothes on your back or what?" she would snarkily say if we dared question where she was.

 A part of me still has some bitterness about how absent she was when I was a child but another part of me shoves it away. Who am I to talk? I am a hypocrite. When I was kicked out of her house, I never intended on coming back. She was notorious for making me Mommy Jr., insisting that I had to take care of the kids she had from another marriage.

 The GPS is telling me to head onto Fir and Broadway. Why the hell did she move here? This must be the universe testing me. I drive through the city often, but I never go down these streets. This was territory I never planned on visiting again.

 Everything is brought full circle the moment I see the apartment complex that Flo got beat up at when she was fifteen. It was over some drugs. I thought I would never see the Harbor again. The park that I didn't know had a name until now looks exactly the same, Edward Valve Park. All the boys would play basketball, do dance battles and act like they were going to be famous rappers one day there. All of us girls would wait around for one of the boys to call us out and entertain us until the sun would set across the pollution-cloud-filled sky. I told my kids many stories of the trouble I used to get into at that park. There is a strangeness about coming back here. It makes me more uncomfortable to think about how many people may still know of me here.

Of all places, why did she move a couple of blocks away from where I grew up? She will never understand it but there's a strange sensation in my stomach as I'm seeing one of the churches my mom would force me to go to at a distance. It looks almost the same as it was when I was a kid. It is weathered down with overgrown grass but the sign in front has been updated to say *"Que Diós les traiga amor y luz. Estás un paso más cerca del perdón."* I don't want to be superstitious here, but I think that was meant for me to see.

Sunshine's car got broken into the first night she moved into her apartment. I warned her to not move to East Chicago, but most importantly the Harbor. I notice now that I grew up never saying the Harbor was East Chicago… It was always differentiated. We were all tribal here in that way, you stay with your people.

Sunshine is my stubborn one, I don't think she ever took my advice until it was too late. Now she is nearly thirty and in the same neighborhood. I moved out before I had her.

God, I remember this place when it was bustling. People would bring their living room couches and chairs out in the front to chill. Kids were screaming at each other from the windows. The houses were closer together back then, you could talk from the window and gossip like you were in a high school chick flick. Things were simpler and they weren't.

Families were struggling and extremely poor, trying to recover from the Inland Steel layoffs. Everyone knew everything about everyone. The moment someone heard you were struggling, they would offer you a horrible-paying job and curse at you for turning it away. "Go on and work at the corner store then, tell your children why Papi can't put *frijoles* on the table!" Angel, our neighbor who sold drugs for a living, would yell at men he was trying to recruit. I always knew to walk fast with my eyes on the sidewalk in front of me whenever I had to walk past him. He smelled of cheap cologne and piss.

"Mom! Shoes off!" Sunshine yells at me the moment I walk in.

The apartment is nice, newly renovated, but cold. Nothing like what I was used to seeing in the Harbor growing up, my apartment was dark and cramped. The coldness is the same though. This city seemed to always lack warmth. In the spring and summer, the air has a sticky moist consistency. Nothing like the weather in other places I have been. The air made it hard to breathe. Maybe it was because I never exhale.

"You know I used to live a couple of blocks away from here?" I say looking out the window. Of course she knows. I ranted about this place most of her life.

"Yeah, it was all I could afford though. Hammond is riding up all the prices!" She exclaims with annoyance on her face. She looks just like her dad right now.

"Oh, I know! We are gonna be stuck renting until we die over there," I chuckled.

There is a strange silence. We sit with the thought that we may never leave here. I wish I were joking. I could see in my daughters' faces that they know there is some truth to that statement too. There's a deep love-hate relationship with this place that I can't shake. My entire life is here. Or was here. I brought children into this world here. I hate how much of myself has been defined by my experiences in this damn city. Then I moved to a city nearby as if it could be different, like I could escape the magnetic pull this place has and yet here I am. In East Chicago again.

Maybe if I moved away from here. If we could get out of this liminal space built for a time we are no longer in, we could find a home that's ours.

A Wake

I stare out onto the vacant road in the middle of nowhere as the sky quickly shifts from cotton candy pinks and purples, angry red hues that resemble fire, to black nothingness. Tonight is the night of my father's wake. A night that I am both thankful for and dreading. It is difficult to explain why I care about what will happen to him. It must also be difficult to gather everyone around to say nice things about him without lying to themselves, to each other, and to his decaying body that will lie in the front of the reception room.

My daughter's life is currently packed up in the car after spending three months away at college. She decided to transfer after one conversation with me on the phone. It felt nice that she listened to me even if her mind was made up before she called.

I know she has had a long day. Hell, I had a long day. But it is too late to just drive straight home now. I am fully in this.

"Do you want to go to this wake with me?" It comes out of my mouth sounding more desperate than it did in my head.

"Sure, I don't really want you going in alone. You have a habit of letting them get to you."

If she was younger, I would have forced her to come with me anyway. She hasn't seen her aunts and uncle in years either; this is her state of return too. We are both in this.

She is right about me, though. I have let my siblings get away with so much. I know that I shouldn't but I am my mother's daughter. I have let everyone take advantage of me. I don't even know how else to interact with my siblings if I am not doing everything that I can for them. More than half of my life has been devoted to living for others and doing things to please other people. Finally, I can't take it anymore.

I am so, so tired. Tired of being used by my family, tired of facing death alone, tired of being used by my family, tired of being the only one that didn't completely let myself go, tired of letting my family use me. Just tired.

I have reached East Chicago and my breaking point. My siblings have been calling and texting me since our dad died, which was about three weeks ago. The man has been rotting, hopelessly waiting to be put in the dirt while his children scramble for money. I remember the first call so clearly now. The details were cut short, my sister sobbing about how we don't speak, he was sick, they can't afford to bury him.

"Please Monica!" She says my name with the accent of our older cousins. *Moan-ee-ka*. I hated hearing my name like that.

"I don't know what to do! I'm the only one doing anything. His other kids haven't said anything. I don't know what the hell to do about the services. Someone has to do something."

"Listen, I did everything by myself when it was mom. I told you I wasn't doing this again. I never associated myself with him, why would I organize his funeral? Why are you contacting me about this at all?" I spoke as calmly as I could have. I knew what she wanted to ask me. She wanted me to take over. Big sister does all the dirty work.

"Monica, please! I know we aren't close, I know! But Flo and our piece of shit brother won't do anything and these people keep calling me!"

***

I don't know what my family expects from me. I promised myself then that I would only attend the wake. I can't do funerals, I especially could not do this one. It's like everyone forgets what happened to me. What happened to Flo and me.

I take a deep breath and turn the car off. I want to sit in this warmth of the heat but I am already late. I don't want to make this more uncomfortable than it needs to be. The funeral home is dated and gaudy. Everything is white and gold. The lights are so bright and are not doing anything or anyone any favors. I mumble a quick *Oh God* and turn to my daughter who is also in awe of the tackiness that has been bestowed upon us. We are redirected to the chapel where everyone is sitting in white and gold seats.

The room is stale and nearly empty. My dad's brother, who also happens to be a pastor, is speaking at the podium about God and nothing to do with why we are gathered here. I look around to see who is here and who's not here. There are so few people here that it is starting to concern me. Did they call our dad's entire family in Puerto Rico? Any of his friends? His kids from his other marriage? Why does this all feel so rushed when they waited three weeks to do this?

I want to leave to clear my head and I am starting to regret coming at all. The amount of fake gold in this building is starting to make me feel sick or maybe I just wasn't ready for this.

"You look so familiar!" my uncle stops his speech.

I look around to see who he's talking to.

"You! You look so familiar," he tilts his head like a confused dog, "What's your name?"

Shit, he's talking to me.

"Monica, Ana's daughter."

"Oh! Ana! You look just like her. Wow!" He waits for me to respond. Does he want me to say thank you?

"And that's your daughter?" I nod.

"You are both beautiful women. Thank you for coming."

My sister, Lucia, looks back at me with a slight smile. The kind of smile you give a stranger that holds the door open for you. Fake.

This man has been rambling about how much of a good man his

brother was and how he is with God now and I can't help but shift in my seat at the uneasiness. My brother walks in and spots me. He puts his hands on the back of my shoulders and squeezes. He smells of cheap beer and cigarette smoke. This is going to be a nightmare.

Abuela

"People used to call her Loquita," he told me. Crazy girl. "She came to the states, but my grandpa stayed on the island. I never met him but I heard he was a douchebag." He flicks the cigarette ashes on his plate. It must be nice to know where you came from. It's always been my mom, my siblings, me, and whoever she was dating at the time.

"Funny, isn't it?" He's on about his mom and her escapades.

"What?"

"That our grandparents tried so hard to get out of PR for jobs and opportunities. We just want to go back there to party." I'm not even sure my grandparents are from Puerto Rico, but his mom liked that I was Puerto Rican so here I am.

"We all want what we can't have," I sighed. I feel like I'm being tested. It's like he's looking for confirmation from me, a "yes! I agree, let's run away to Puerto Rico!" He must know I'm bored of this conversation. He steps out of the metal chair and walks to his car. "Un Rayo de Sol" plays on the car radio and he shifts his weight side to side to the beat of the song. I smile.

The only time I heard Spanish music was with him or my mom's friends. My mom only spoke Spanish around her Spanish-speaking boyfriends. I wonder if my mom would tell me anything about my grandma. I wonder if she's like Luis's Abuela. Did she leave her husband behind on the island, too? Does she make pastelillos like mom? I could imagine mom and an older version of her arguing over when it was ready to turn the rice around in the big, black rice pot.

"Sha la la la la, whoa-oh!" Luis sings offbeat, trying to get my attention. "Come on, my Loquita!"

He comes back to me, grabs my arms to lift me off of the cold chair, and we sway with the music. I should remember this moment. This one happy moment between Luis and me. This is a moment I hope my children will tell their kids.

The Breakfast Club

"Have you ever thought about separating from Dad?" Sunshine abruptly asked.

I was driving her to work, as I usually do since she got into that car accident and swore to never drive. I remember getting into a pretty bad argument with Luis earlier that day, it was a back-and-forth thing. Not something you think much about until the next bad argument. Now, I am realizing it may seem to her that all our relationship has been a pattern of bad arguments, but she has also never been in a romantic relationship so, what does she know really?

It was bad though. I should have made sure she wasn't there. No, she should see that relationships aren't perfect. People argue.

"No, I've been with him for over twenty years. An argument doesn't change everything."

"I feel like you have been telling yourself that but you don't really think it," she pauses to look at her phone when a Snapchat notification appears, "I don't know. It's none of my business but it is, you know?"

"I get it. But, it isn't your business."

I looked forward to the red light before the turn I needed to take to drop her off. The sight of it annoys me. It is a reminder of all the times I am a chauffeur to someone. If it wasn't Luis, it was Sunshine. Or it was my sister or my other daughters. I have always been driving other people. I have always been doing things for other people. It is so odd, I don't remember my own mom being in this position. She had people like me around.

I turned into the parking lot of the grocery store Sunshine works at and said our usual goodbyes. I sulked in the silence of the car before driving back onto the road. Being alone in the car felt almost euphoric. The only person to attend to then was me. I turned on my throwbacks playlist, the one I play only when I am alone.

When "Don't You (Forget About Me)" by Simple Minds came on, though, I immediately turned off the music. I start to think of *The Breakfast Club* and can imagine almost every scene in my mind as though it was being played in front of me. This has been happening to me often when I am listening to music in the car, I get too distracted and my mind wanders. One thing leads to another and I forget that I'm supposed to be driving home.

Going home means facing the heaviness of the argument with

Luis. He was mad about some altercation with one of his co-workers. Something about some guy not taking orders from him even though he is the supervisor. He came home in a fit, breathing like a child who just got yelled at and told to clean their room. He huffed and puffed around the house ranting about whatever. I remember being dismissive, his behavior was immature and I didn't want to entertain his act.

"Did you cook? I'm fucking hungry." He knew I hated it when he asked that question. He never asks *How was your day?* or *How are you feeling?* It was always "Did you cook?" and "Did you wash my work clothes?"

"Nope, I figured you could find something to eat when you are hungry."

He smacked his lips together with a *mmcht* and slammed the bedroom door. I wish I remembered what I said to him after because I was so angry and annoyed at him for storming off like a child. It wasn't the first time, I thought, and it wouldn't be the last. There was yelling back and forth, mentions of threats to leave, a slam of the bedroom door, and then heavy silence.

Going inside the house after everything meant that I had to face what happened before. Things must be worse than I am imagining if my daughter was asking me about leaving her father. Surely, that should be enough to make me realize the severity of the situation, right?

I kept telling myself that I wouldn't be like my mom, I will provide a two-parent household for my children. I did what was needed for my family, right? Sacrifices sometimes need to be made to avoid repeating the faults of your own parents. This is a cycle I am supposed to break as the firstborn. My kids are alright.

I'm doing alright.

An Indiana Harbor Christmas

Jane Ammeson

It would be my father's last Christmas and though no one, not the doctors, my brother, my mother or anyone else in our family, had acknowledged that quite yet, at some level we realized he'd grown weary of fighting his illness. He was moving away from us and into whatever comes next.

And so we met at my parents' house in Indiana Harbor, the home where I had grown up and my brother had spent his last years in high school. It had been their home for forty years and my mother was determined that if my father had to go, he would do so in his own bed, and she would be there with him. We had tried hiring a nurse, after all she was 86 at the time and losing weight from all the care she gave him. But when I returned home for a visit (I had moved to Southwest Michigan after college) and I found the nurse sitting at the dining room.

"Where's my mother?" I asked.

"She's in the bedroom with your father bathing him," she replied.

"Can't you help?" I asked.

"She won't let me," the nurse replied. "She won't let me do anything. I told her she could take a nap and I would take care of things, but she won't let me. I really don't think you should be paying me to just sit here."

And so we let her go.

***

What I think of now as my dad's last Christmas Day started with an edge to it, a strain as we all tried not to think of what future holidays would be like without my father. My mother and I cooked a large turkey and my mother made her special gravy and also carved the turkey, a job she always did anyway. My father just ate a few pieces and then returned to his bed. The rest of us played cards, as always there was a sports event on in the background, but we were more quiet than usual—no invectives about politics, no gossip about the neighbors, just the sense life was changing, and we couldn't stop that from happening.

As usual, when Christmas Day eased into night, I began compiling a list of who wanted what type of Mexican food. In my family, Mexican food late on Christmas night was as much a part of our holiday ritual as the turkey, stuffing and mashed potatoes during the day.

The night was very cold and the wind strong and so my daughter Nia, who was eight at the time, and I put on our heavy coats along with gloves, hats and scarves to drive the few blocks east to Main Street towards El Patio. The stores along Main were darkened and empty but as we approached the last block before the street dead ends at Guthrie Avenue I could see the weak light from the large windows highlight the swirling snow before their rays disappeared into the deep black night.

I was young when El Patio first opened on the 137th block of Main, one among many vibrant stores and eateries. But over the decades, one by one, they had all closed until finally El Patio, with its elaborately patterned tiled walls and lovely aromas of freshly fried tortillas and stews of beef and pork, was the only business left.

My Michigan friends were often anxious when we drove past the empty storefronts and remains of the once glorious theaters but as a true Indiana Harbor girl, I knew once I stepped into the warmth and the light of El Patio I would be safe and in some ways home. After all, there is no other restaurant in my life where I had eaten for so many decades.

My daughter, who is Korean, held my hand as we walked in. The waitress recognized me and said, "Hey Chica," like she always did. And as usual, a group of men, mostly older and weathered by age and life, sat along the Formica covered counter, sipping coffee and talking in soft tones.

It is not a place where English is spoken frequently. And I know little Spanish. But one of the men, looking up at us, didn't speak in either language. Instead his words were in Korean and he was addressing my daughter. Nia, no matter where she was born, is an American girl by choice, looked at him in bewilderment, hearing a language she didn't understand. And I too was surprised to hear Korean being spoken by a Hispanic man in a Mexican restaurant in the only business left on an empty block in Indiana Harbor on a cold Christmas night.

We chatted in English and he told us he'd fought in Korea, talking about a war that had taken place more than 50 years ago and had learned to speak the language there. When my bags filled with tacos, sopas and enchiladas arrived, I said goodnight and Merry Christmas, and ventured back out into the cold.

My dad perked up a little at the smell of the food and he smiled, just slightly, when I told him about our encounter at El Patio. But it was the biggest smile we'd seen in a month as his strength ebbed away. He would be dead within the month, but I believe he loved hearing the story about El Patio. It was, to all of us, what Indiana Harbor was all about. A place where an American woman with a Korean child could walk into a Mexican restaurant and meet a Hispanic man who greeted them in Korean on a Christmas night. It was what his town—and country—meant to him: a welcoming place for all, including his parents who had arrived here as teens from Romania. America and Indiana Harbor as a shining beacon was what he had believed in all his life and so it was a fitting tale for him at the end of his life.

Sprightly Aphrodite
Gloria Ptacek McMillan

Aphrodite Magaris went by Affie to most of her friends. She had a good, solid job in the accounting office of the Midwest Steel Corporation headquartered on Michigan Boulevard just kitty corner from the Art Institute. She lived in Harbor City, Indiana, a steel mill suburb about 35 minutes by the expressways and city streets, though, not in the expensive apartments in the Loop.

When the management bumped Affie up from the local Harbor City operations building to the PR palace in the Loop she recalled how thrilled she had felt. However, being a child of practical immigrant parents, Affie made some decisions. *No way in hell* was Affie going to pay a huge parking fee and get her car all ding-marked trying to fly down Lakeshore Drive or the Dan Ryan to work each day. As long as Harbor City's bus system ran a bus on the hour all day, she decided to commute by bus.

Each work day she hopped on the bus across from the Art Institute.

"Hello, Mr. Ortiz! Aren't we lucky it's not as cold as yesterday? I had to wear two layers under this cape. But it is better today, huh?" Affie had seen the driver's name on the plate next to him. She always spoke to her bus drivers because too often people just dropped coins in the pay slot and never made a connection. Besides, she liked having company she knew on her trip home. Mr. Ortiz looked a bit like Ramon Navarro from the old movies she used to see at The Indiana Theatre in her childhood. But—no, she had no room for men in her life anymore.

"Hi, Ma'am," the driver would reply. "You look nice today." Yes, Mr. Ortiz would smile and compliment in a warm voice, but she had made her peace with being a single woman living with her little nephew and that was it. She liked being admired, even so. Who doesn't? thought Affie, patting her luxurious black hair drawn back in a bun. Affie always took extra care with her wardrobe and she smiled that Mr. Ortiz noticed. That pleased Affie. Always a gent, though, her favorite bus driver. She could count on Mr. Ortiz to never take liberties.

Yet… life can become flat, she thought, as she settled into a favored seat,. Funny how she felt a slight bit elated when that row and that particular seat was available, even now that she had company on her trip, a few regulars who knew her name and that driver who was always so friendly. Affie had never married. She had a small nephew whom she was raising at home. Little Theo. She rummaged in her large tote bag. *There! Can't forget it. Not when I've promised. One jumbo deluxe pomegranate from Stop 'n Shop.*

Stop 'n Shop was legendary in the whole Chicagoland area. Their produce was the best. *Theo—he loves his pomegranates,* Affie mused, turning the giant fruit over in her hand. *This was what Persephone took with her to Pluto's realm, wasn't it?* Returning to the scenery, such as it was, Affie couldn't say she felt oppressed on *this* ride home on the bus. But seeing that same industrial landscape roll by day after day emotionally flattened-out the end of her workdays. A few weeks into being a bus rider, the reality of these daily bus trips was beginning to settle like a pall upon Affie. Rain beat on the window in a staccato rhythm, then ran in a staccato trail down her window in the commuter bus from Chicago's Loop crossing the state line to Northwest Indiana. The view followed some routine changes as mind-numbing minutes rolled by.

"Land of romance and adventure…" Affie mumbled as they drove past the sign saying "WELCOME TO INDIANA" from the current governor. The governor's name had just been changed.

She often wondered, *What are these others thinking?* Affie tried to guess their thoughts as a kind of game, as they sat slumped in their seats looking bored, dejected, or studious and reading. Daydreaming once again, Affie was counting the days to her next cruise to Corfu and then on to the Peloponnese with its great ruins of classical theaters like the Orchomenos of Arcadia. *How sublime it was that day on my last trip home to watch the sun rise across the theatron's rows of seats from west to east as the sun stepped higher and higher above Kandila's hills!* Affie sighed as her mind took her to those craggy ridges. With those sites in her childhood, who can blame her for being theatrical? Affie felt theater down to her bones! Since childhood when her cousin Spiro told her the bad news that *women* weren't allowed to act on stage in ancient Greece, Affie decided—*Okay! So be it and who cares?* Affie knew, in this unfair situation, *I would have been a Thalia, a muse of the theater.*

"Shut up, the two of you!" Ivanka Blesich gave five-year-old Drago and three-year-old Milica the famed "Mommy stare" as they reached crystal-goblet-shattering pitch over a bag of caramel corn. She added a couple comments in Serbian about being as wild as pigs in the parlor and took the corn. Ivanka thought, *They should have been good at least on the way home after this fun trip to the Field Museum. What's wrong with these kids?*

"Mommy, he had his turn!" Milica shrieked. The bag of corn went into Ivanka's purse. Ivanka's ripping the corn bag away stopped this spat. Her life was made up of kids and cleaning. She knew everything that was going to happen to her. Her life was all too predictable. Why didn't I on to college? She wondered. *Why did I marry right out of high school to a good-natured steel worker like Dushan? It was his eyes. That's why. He had those great, dark Lassie collie eyes.* Yes, before he died, her Tata told her he wished she would go for an education, maybe in music, since she had been first violin in the Harbor City High orchestra.

These and other second thoughts about her life alternated in Ivanka's mind, as she went on hushing the two kids. "If you behave, you can go to your Kuma Elena's for 'potica' nut roll..." The two children squirmed around in their seats with joy at this promise. They could taste honey and ground walnuts in a buttery, flaky crust. In their mind's eye, they could envision each slice with its perfectly spiral interior. Milica had often watched Kuma Elena and Mommy make potica: the grown-up women's hands deftly swinging a long dowel rod around the big sheet of thin pastry dough in fast passes as the dough thinned out, then came the filling, and finally they quickly rolled the sheet up into a big, fat log of dough. And how that oven smelled—yum! The smell rose into and lingered in their little nostrils as it filled the kitchen.

Sometimes, Milica remembered, her Mommy and Kuma let her practice with a short piece of dowel rod and a small square of dough on a little card table in the kitchen corner, well out of the way of their production line for making a hundred Potica rolls. The grown-ups had a check list and Milica was told to stay out of their way and practice. This was a big business for grown-ups only. Kuma Elena packed the plastic bags with name labels: one or more roll for each relative and some bags piling up with no names to sell at church. These visions and scents dancing in Milica's and Dushan's heads made it worth while to *simmer down*, at least for a while.

CHILDREN OF STEEL

***

Melba Rollins had climbed on board the bus at Van Buren Street after a late day shopping for petit fours (each petit four with its Field's-style pastel icing flower), velvety cream puffs, and decorated Napoleons at Marshall Field's Loop department store for Mrs. Richardson. Melba's three shopping bags said, "mission accomplished." These signature desserts were some of patisserie chef Pierre's finest work, covered in filigreed scrollwork of icing curlicues that Mrs. Richardson craved.

Everybody who came to the Richardson's house recognized these unique pastries and the *Frangomints* carefully placed on each coffee table as that haute cuisine Marshall Field touch. Not that Melba couldn't make petit fours, too, but she never quite got that Parisian scrollwork in the icing on top... no time to practice, with ironing and all.

Melba breathed an audible sigh of relief that the lady with the two yelping kids had taken some decisive action. Now settling back into her seat Melba thought ahead to the weeks coming; she hoped that she wouldn't have to iron all those damask curtains again, since her back was only now recovering from all the tablecloths and linens she had *just ironed* for Mr. Richardson's 75th birthday. *My feet hurt*, thought Melba, *Lordy, I am so glad summer's gone and all those yard parties Mrs. Richardson gave one after another with her charity friends.* Then Melba realized that Christmas was just around the corner. More or less. And more ironed table linen. Big women like Melba always had some problems with knees and feet.

"Comes with being "statuesque," as her husband Clyde put it. *Oh, well, steady work, anyway.*

Melba looked at the rain streaking down her window and gave her tired feet a rest by kicking off her shoes. *Wonder if they'll let me... just close... my eyes a bit...* Melba got off 'way at the far end of Harbor City some time away yet, *if* those two little children across the aisle let her.

***

Jim Howard had been drinking a bit when he got on the bus at Stateline in front of Voglen's Restaurant. He wished the driver a "howdy" as he shifted from side to side and loped down the aisle on long spindly legs to the back of the bus. He needed a rest from his day. Republic Forge had just laid Jim off, so his response was to, as the saying goes, self-medicate. Jim began to feel the blues come over him and he wished he could be back in Arkansas.

"Ain't no way I got money to go home to Ash Flat for Christmas," he shook his pale blonde head. "Nor any time soon to Possum Grape, Avoca, Locust Bayou, or Goobertown..." Jim went on lamenting the many towns along rivers in Arkansas he had rafted down in his youth. *Man, I miss those ol' hoot 'n holler towns on highways. I used to cruise the main roads after I got my license to drive. Ha! Even before I got any ol' license. Country boys... every man son of us can hide on back roads from deputies...* He yawned. Jim's voice droned on wistfully listing towns, sounding like a conductor of the Atchison, Topeka, and Santa Fe Railroad.

As Jim continued his lament in a loud and drawling voice, Melba thought, *Lord, I don't need this right now. Truly, if it isn't asking too much, could you please put this poor child in the back to sleep and stop him recitin' names?*

To Affie, this cacophonous backdrop was a sign. She knew that the Greek chorus signified the opening of the play. Her ear was attuned to Euripides and Sophocles. Yes. Every hair on her arms stood on end because she felt the power of drama at this moment! *Evtáxei All right!* While stylish in her ensemble, Affie was also a monumental woman. Large but not too large, theatrically imposing in a navy blue, paisley tunic with aqua beads around her neck and matching giant earrings. So when she rose to speak on the swaying bus, people looked up.

"Listen—I mean, hello, my dear Ladies and Gentlemen!" Affie opened, loving the musical sound of her voice, just as powerful and enchanting as it had been at last year's AHEPA Marathon performance of *Lysistrata*.

"We have just crossed into a place of magic, a land of much mystery and adventure: Lake County, Indiana!" Jim snorted as if waking up in the back seat—but he didn't quite manage the waking up part.

"If you will but look to your left, you can see the plumed clouds of the Standard Oil burn-off towers! And to the right is a labyrinth of petroleum retaining tanks!" Aphrodite swept her arms open to embrace her muse. "Is this how Odysseus felt when he forded the narrows to his home port between the two monsters Scylla and Charybdis?"

Melba nodded and replied, "Uh, huh! You got that right, honey!" *This is almost getting as good as hearing Pastor Williams at the AME church on Guthrie Street,* thought Melba, as she looked at the oil burn-off flames keeping going despite the rain. That, for some reason, reminded her of the teeny tiny spider who went up the waterspout that she taught the children. "Down came the rain and washed the spider out." But Melba smiled at the upbeat ending, "Out came the sun and dried up all the rain, so tiny, little spider went up the spout again!" Maybe she wouldn't have such a bad week next week.

"*Look*! Is that Pegasus I see?" Affie noticed a winged horse on an oil company sign. "Children, the winged horse, he flies over us—now! Listen… " Just then a jet screamed over and Affie swept her hands over her head as Drago and Milica followed her every move with wide eyes. Milica wasn't quite sure about this big lady and hugged her mother's jacket tightly.

"Ah, now we approach our own Harbor City!" Affie announced, as if she were Odysseus pulling into the harbor of Ithaca. The huge smoke stacks of Midwest Steel hovered over the entrance to Harbor City like the Colossus of Rhodes. As the bus turned onto Michigan Avenue in Harbor City, Affie announced, "Before you stands our noble institution the Auditorium Bar with its famed backrooms!" Affie leaned across to Melba, beaming ecstatically. "Was it here that Hades, Poseidon, and Zeus threw dice in order to split the Universe between them?"

Melba shrugged. News to her. She chuckled and called to Affie, "I don't know about you, but the Lord and I don't hold with no gambling by ancient Greek gods or otherwise."

Ivanka grinned and nodded.

Smiling, Affie went on to list the wonders to be found in Mrs. Borowski's drug store, leeches and potions to ward off all manner of ills, just as in Athens Hermes with his caduceus cured the leper and the rich man suffering his bile.

Jim woke up in the back and said, "I put three bucks on Caduceus in the fourth race at Arlington Park on Wednesday! Damn nag came in last."

Affie looked at Jim with Elysian sympathy. "The gods can be fickle," she sighed.

Nelson's furniture store was next to be transformed into something strange. "How is it that we never hear of the powers to turn one tree into another except at Nelson's store?" Affie smiled darkly. "Pine comes in the door and—hah!—teak goes out the door. Amazing." Milica and Drago were truly impressed even if they didn't understand some of the words. Affie's stage presence was irresistible to young and old alike.

"Oh! This is my stop!" Affie almost went through her stop, due to being on stage. "My dears, I bid you now adieu!" Affie smiled warmly and blew a kiss to the two children, bowed to one and all, and walked to the door. "Parting is such sweet sorrow," with a sweep of her voluminous navy-blue cape, she flowed out the door into the swirling fog and drizzle. Raindrops shimmered, outlining Affie's figure in a corolla of light as the little street lamps began to blink on one-by-one on down the street. Jim Howard waved good-bye and Melba began to hum "The Teeny, Tiny Spider" softly to herself.

Drago pulled Ivanka's sleeve. "Mommy, will that big magic lady be here the next time we ride the bus?" Dazed, Ivanka could not speak and just shrugged. She silently handed Drago the bag of caramel corn… and smiled.

Contributing Writer Biographies

Jeff Manes ("Monarchs") was born and raised in northern Newton County, Indiana. He has worked in the steel mills, fished on the Kankakee, and he developed his writing skills by talking to and learning about his friends and neighbors. His syndicated column "Salt" is 10 years of interviews in the *Post-Tribune, Lowell Tribune, Cedar Lake Journal, Crown Point Star*, and the *Southtown Star* (Illinois). Manes was the screenwriter of the award-winning documentary "Everglades of the North: the Story of the Grand Kankakee Marsh." Emmy-nominated. He was awarded the Union Label Award from the Northwest Indiana Federation of Labor for being supportive of all labor unions.

Joan Paylo ("BlueCollarLand") thrived on the polluted air, water and soil of Whiting Indiana, a close-knit company town on Lake Michigan, home to the mammoth Standard Oil refinery. Even her National Merit Scholarship to Northwestern University's Medill School of Journalism was awarded by Standard Oil. Summers, she was a reporter for the Hammond (now NWI) Times. She earned an MS in Television from Syracuse University's Newhouse School and has spent most of her award-winning career in broadcast producing/writing, non-profit public affairs. and government and politics in New York City. Now studying at the Writing Institute at Sarah Lawrence College, she is ever grateful for the company pensions that saw her blue-collar relatives through their last years.

Kathy Bashaar ("The Girl from Bethel Park") is a lifelong, fourth-generation Pittsburgher and a University of Pittsburgh graduate. Pittsburgh is part of her soul—and probably literally in her DNA, after several generations of ancestors drinking its water and breathing its air. Her desire to write was sparked when she was a little girl and read the Betsy-Tacy children's novels. The character Betsy aspired to be a writer and Kathryn wanted to do everything Betsy did! Kathryn's short stories and essays have been published newspapers, magazines and literary journals. Her first novel, *The Saint's Mistress* is published by CamCat. She blogs on books and Pittsburgh history at www.kathrynbashaar.com.

Karen Banks Pearson ("Granny's Traveling Trunk") spent her formative years among the sights and sounds of a bustling steel town, East Chicago, Indiana, along Lake Michigan's shore. The industrial, multi-ethnic make-up community and the times—the fifties and sixties—influenced her storytelling and writing skills; later honed formally at retreats and UW-Milwaukee, Johns Hopkins (Baltimore) and Oxford (UK) universities, and the Paris American Academy. A student of culture, particularly how words and language portray unique human qualities, Granny's Trunk glimpses a matriarch's life and the key role she played in her family's migration to opportunities. Rosemary C. Smith and Sophia Szilagyi, two dedicated public-school teachers, are recognized for their imprint on this work and others—a historical non-fiction, an international adventure, and a grandchild's world view, they could not see forthcoming.

Patrick Michael Finn ("Smokestack Polka") was born and raised in Joliet, Illinois, one of the westernmost steel towns of the Rust Belt. He is the author of *A Martyr for Suzy Kosasovich*, *A Place for Snakes to Breed*, and *From the Darkness Right Under Our Feet*, named a best book of the year by *GQ* magazine. His fiction has appeared in *Ploughshares*, *Quarterly West*, *TriQuarterly*, and *Best American Mystery Stories*, among many others. He lives in Mesa, Arizona, with his wife, poet Valerie Bandura, and their son. He is at work on a new novel and collection of stories.

Sharon Hale Hotko ("Toe Picks and Hoar Frost") was born and raised in East Chicago, Indiana, a steel mill town, into high school. She has always written stories and has had an article published in Scanner Magazine. Sharon has been a friend to many pets over her life, especially, pug dogs. She lives shuttling between Monticello, Indiana, and -a home in Florida, viewing her favorite films, doing traveling and activities with her husband John, and writing.

Curtis Mazzaferri ("The Other Side of the Fence") was born in and raised around Middletown, Ohio, where he spent the first twenty-five years of his life. Shortly after graduating high school, he took a job as an electrician's apprentice in Middletown's AK steel plant. He would spend roughly four years as a maintenance electrician in the AK steel plant before a work-related injury would end his career. Since leaving behind the electrical trade, he has written about his time in the steel industry as a way of understanding and expressing the Rust Belt steel culture that he spent the majority of his early life immersed in.

Barbara Dubos ("Consumed") is a freelance writer, raised in the small steel mill town of Campbell, Ohio. She had a blue-collar childhood, which influenced her writing. After following the traditional path at the time of graduating high school, getting a job, and raising a family, her passion and longing for attending college gained her a mid-life college degree. She completed her BA in English, minor in Sociology, became a Grad Assistant and gained an MA in English with TESOL concentration. As a college lecturer, she taught various levels of college composition courses and ESL for 18 years, presented at academic writing conferences, and contributed to academic publications. After attending fiction writing workshops, she began writing short fiction stories. When she is not writing she resides in Boardman, Ohio and enjoys spending time with her husband, children, and grandchildren.

Joseph S. Pete ("Lo, the Steel They forged on That Boundless Lake") was born in Hammond, Indiana and raised in Highland, Indiana, in the heart of Calumet Region steel country, Joseph S. Pete is an award-winning Times of Northwest Indiana reporter, an Iraq War veteran, and a frequent guest on Lakeshore Public Radio. Pete is the author of Lost Hammond, Indiana, Secret Northwest Indiana and 100 Things to Do in Gary and Northwest Indiana Before You Die. His work has appeared in more than 100 literary journals, including Stoneboat, Proximity Magazine, and McSweeney's Internet Tendency. His writing has been in several books, including Indiana at 200 and Poets to Come: Walt Whitman's Bicentennial.

Kurt Samano ("Clockwork") was born in Chicago in 1967. His father and mother worked for US Steel. He moved six miles from his neighborhood to Whiting IN. Though trained in construction trades, his SAT allowed him acceptance to Indiana University in 1985. He trained in Secondary Special Education, obtaining certification. and co-founded an at-risk youth program CBHS in Chicago. After 20 years in teaching and administration, he retired. He has a son and spouse. He has written curriculum, editorials and short-stories.

John Szostek ("Time Hangs a Louie") was born in Gary, Indiana. He, his grandfathers, father, and uncle worked at Gary Works, forging his early life in the culture of the mills. His experiences inspired him to pursue a fifty-year career in theatre. The Institute for Career Development of the United Steelworkers asked him to direct, Steel & Roses, a set of one-act plays written by steelworkers, He holds an Emmy Award as an ensemble member of Beyond the Magic Door. The City of Evanston honored him with the 2009 Artist of the Year Award. He is currently working on a sci-fi novella, *The Watcher*.

Hardarshan Singh Valia ("Volcanoes of NW Indiana") is an Earth Scientist from Northwest Indiana, who has spent his professional life in the steel industry. Besides contributing mostly to scientific publications, he has published poems, stories, and essays in various journals. However, in his spare time, he visits local area schools. Armed with his earth-wares and wealth of stories, he sings to them Songs of Earth and tell stories of Life's Evolution. The poem, without photo of Blast Furnace and Coke Plant, was first published in Indiana Bicentennial Commission Newsletter, page 2, Volume 28, August 2016, <www.indiana2016.org>.

Connie Wachala ("Holy Cross") is a lifelong Northwest Indiana resident whose grandparents came from Poland to work in the steel mills of the Calumet Region. She has taught creative writing classes at area colleges, has written for local newspapers, and has had stories published in various local and regional publications. She is the leader of Highland Neighbors for Sustainability, a grassroots group of activists trying to coax their town officials into the future. She was named a 2023 Hoosier Resilience Hero by Indiana University's Environmental Resilience Institute.

Alice Whittenburg ("What the Dogs Knew") grew up in the Mahoning Valley when it was the Steel Valley, and her father worked at Republic Steel. She now lives in Tucson, Arizona, and co-edits the online magazine *The Cafe Irreal*. Her fiction has appeared in *Atlas & Alice*, *Riddled with Arrows*, and *Eclectica Magazine*, among others. Her essays have appeared in *The Journal of Working-Class Studies*, *3:AM*

Magazine; and *The Ekphrastic Review*. She is a member of the National Writers Union Tucson Chapter.

Stacy Alderman ("Steel Valley") has contributed several articles to her local newspaper and won the Children of Steel Fiction Award in 2021. Her writing has been featured by Robert Morris University's *Rune Magazine*, *Macro Magazine*, *Capsule Stories*, and several others. She lives near Pittsburgh, PA with her husband and two rescue dogs. If she's not writing or reading, she's probably watching hockey or (dreaming about) traveling.

Robert McKean ("Man Down") was raised in Hopewell Township, a Pennsylvania community adjacent to the steel town of Aliquippa. Populating his novels and stories are five hundred residents of Ganaego, a mill town in Western Pennsylvania. His latest novel is *Mending What is Broken* (2023) Livingston Press. His short story collection *I'll Be Here for You: Diary of a Town* was awarded first-prize in the Tartts First Fiction competition (Livingston Press). His novel *The Catalog of Crooked Thoughts* was awarded first-prize in the Methodist University Longleaf Press Novel Contest. Recipient of a Massachusetts Artist's Grant for his fiction, McKean has had six stories nominated for Pushcart Prizes. He has published extensively in journals such as *The Kenyon Review*, *The Chicago Review*, and *Armchair/Shotgun*. See also: www.robmckean.com.

Phyllis Woods ("The Next Big Thing") was born in Gary, Indiana, 1955 and is a retired Health Care Worker (Respiratory Therapist), 40+ yrs. She studied Organizational Communications Indiana University NW Campus. She is a lover of writing, mostly short stories, inspirational pamphlets and some poetry favorite authors include Ursula LeGuin and Isaac Asimov.

Bianca Roman ("Homebodies") is a student at Indiana University Northwest. Her writing is deeply rooted in her family's upbringing in East Chicago. Her fascination with people's attachment to their hometowns led her to create "Homebodies" for a fiction writing course, exploring themes of family, hometown nostalgia, and coming of age. Her future goal is to write a screenplay based on her parents' upbringing, using her collection of stories as source material. With a blend of academic knowledge and personal insight, she hopes to make a meaningful mark in storytelling, celebrating the power of home and self-discovery in her work.

Jane Simon Ammeson ("An Indiana Harbor Christmas") is the author of eighteen books including a bronze winner of the Lowell Thomas Journalism Competition for best travel book for *Lincoln Road Trips: The Back-Road Guide To America's Favorite President*, *Hauntings of the Underground Railroad: Ghosts of the Midwest*, and *A Jazz Age Murder in Northwest Indiana*. She writes about travel, food, murders, and history for many publications, including weekly columns in *The Herald Palladium* and *The Times of Northwest Indiana*. A James Beard Foundation judge as well as a member of the Society of American Travel Writers and Midwest Travel Journalists Association, Jane's home base is on the shores of Lake Michigan in Southwest Michigan.

Gloria Ptacek McMillan ("Sprightly Aphrodite") was born and raised in East Chicago, Indiana, she received her MA in English from Indiana University and Ph.D. at University of Arizona. She has published three books; *The Blue Maroon Murder, Orbiting Ray Bradbury's Mars,* and *The Routledge Companion to Literature and Class*. Her play *Universe Symphony* (about modernist composer Charles Ives) was performed at the Flandrau Planetarium in Tucson, Arizona. She leads a Zoom *Tucson Hard-Science Science Fiction Group* and writes articles to bring science into better communication with the arts and humanities. She has lived in Tucson since 1973 with her patient family (husband Bob and now Los Angeles-based son Chris.) She visits Chicago and Northwest Indiana, sites of her steel mill town childhood.

BRRAM

20-Volume Series

Proves with computational linguistics, handwriting and biographical analysis:

6 GHOSTWRITERS

Created All British Renaissance Texts

First translations of inaccessible books, with annotations, introductions

https://AnaphoraLiterary.com/Attribution

Printed in the USA
CPSIA information can be obtained
at www.ICGtesting.com
LVHW091238010524
779003LV00002B/147

9 781681 146058